An Amish Quilting Bee

ALSO BY THE AUTHORS

AMY CLIPSTON

The Amish Legacy Series
Foundation of Love

Contemporary Romance
The Heart of Splendid Lake
The View from Coral Cove (available May 2022)

The Amish Marketplace Series
The Bake Shop
The Farm Stand
The Coffee Corner
The Jam and Jelly Nook

The Amish Homestead Series
A Place at Our Table
Room on the Porch Swing
A Seat by the Hearth
A Welcome at Our Door

The Amish Heirloom Series
The Forgotten Recipe
The Courtship Basket
The Cherished Quilt
The Beloved Hope Chest

The Hearts of the Lancaster Grand Hotel Series
A Hopeful Heart
A Mother's Secret

A Dream of Home
A Simple Prayer

The Kauffman Amish Bakery Series
A Gift of Grace
A Promise of Hope
A Place of Peace
A Life of Joy
A Season of Love

Story Collections
Amish Sweethearts
Seasons of an Amish Garden
An Amish Singing

Stories
A Plain and Simple Christmas
Naomi's Gift included in *An Amish Christmas Gift*
A Spoonful of Love included in *An Amish Kitchen*
Love Birds included in *An Amish Market*
Love and Buggy Rides included in *An Amish Harvest*
Summer Storms included in *An Amish Summer*
The Christmas Cat included in *An Amish Christmas Love*
Home Sweet Home included in *An Amish Winter*
A Son for Always included in *An Amish Spring*
A Legacy of Love included in *An Amish Heirloom*
No Place Like Home included in *An Amish Homecoming*
Their True Home included in *An Amish Reunion*
Cookies and Cheer included in *An Amish Christmas Bakery*
Baskets of Sunshine included in *An Amish Picnic*
Evergreen Love included in *An Amish Christmas Wedding*
Bundles of Blessings included in *Amish Midwives*

Building a Dream included in *An Amish Barn Raising*
A Class for Laurel included in *An Amish Schoolroom*

Nonfiction

The Gift of Love

KATHLEEN FULLER
The Maple Falls Romance Novels
Hooked on You
Much Ado About a Latte (available January 2022)

The Amish Mail-Order Brides Novels
A Double Dose of Love
Matched and Married
Love in Plain Sight (available May 2022)

The Amish Brides of Birch Creek Novels
The Teacher's Bride
The Farmer's Bride
The Innkeeper's Bride

The Amish Letters Novels
Written in Love
The Promise of a Letter
Words from the Heart

The Amish of Birch Creek Novels
A Reluctant Bride
An Unbroken Heart
A Love Made New

The Middlefield Amish Novels

A Faith of Her Own

The Middlefield Family Novels
Treasuring Emma
Faithful to Laura
Letters to Katie

The Hearts of Middlefield Novels
A Man of His Word
An Honest Love
A Hand to Hold

Story Collections
An Amish Family
Amish Generations

Stories
A Miracle for Miriam included in *An Amish Christmas*
A Place of His Own included in *An Amish Gathering*
What the Heart Sees included in *An Amish Love*
A Perfect Match included in *An Amish Wedding*
Flowers for Rachael included in *An Amish Garden*
A Gift for Anne Marie included in *An Amish Second Christmas*
A Heart Full of Love included in *An Amish Cradle*
A Bid for Love included in *An Amish Market*
A Quiet Love included in *An Amish Harvest*
Building Faith included in *An Amish Home*
Lakeside Love included in *An Amish Summer*
The Treasured Book included in *An Amish Heirloom*

What Love Built included in *An Amish Homecoming*
A Chance to Remember included in *An Amish Reunion*
Melting Hearts included in *An Amish Christmas Bakery*
Reeling in Love included in *An Amish Picnic*
Wreathed in Joy included in *An Amish Christmas Wedding*
Love's Solid Foundation included in *An Amish Barn Raising*
A Lesson on Love included in *An Amish Schoolroom*

SHELLEY SHEPARD GRAY
Lone Star Hero Love Stories
The Loyal Heart
An Uncommon Protector
Love Held Captive

Chicago World's Fair Mystery Series
Secrets of Sloane House
Deception on Sable Hill
Whispers in the Reading Room

Stories
A Reunion in Pinecraft included in *An Amish Summer*
The Courage to Love included in *An Amish Homecoming*
A Midwife for Susie included in *Amish Midwives*
Wendy's Twenty Reasons included in *An Amish Schoolroom*

An Amish QUILTING BEE

THREE STORIES

AMY CLIPSTON
KATHLEEN FULLER
SHELLEY SHEPARD GRAY

ZONDERVAN

An Amish Quilting Bee

Patchwork Promises Copyright © 2021 by Amy Clipston

A Common Thread Copyright © 2021 by Kathleen Fuller

Stitched Together Copyright © 2021 by Shelley Shepard Gray

Requests for information should be addressed to:
Zondervan, *3900 Sparks Dr. SE, Grand Rapids, Michigan 49546*

Printed in the United States of America

ISBN 978-1-63910-159-7

CONTENTS

PATCHWORK PROMISES
by Amy Clipston

1

A COMMON THREAD
by Kathleen Fuller

113

STITCHED TOGETHER
by Shelley Shepard Gray

215

GLOSSARY

ach/ack: oh
ab im kopp: crazy, off in the head
appeditlich: delicious
bedauerlich: sad
bobbli/boppli: baby
bruder: brother
Budget, The: newspaper
daadi/dawdi: grandfather
danke/danki: thank you
daed/dat: dad
dochder: daughter
doktah: doctor
dummkopf: dummy
Englisher/Englisch: non-Amish person
familye: family
fraa/frau: wife
Frehlicher Grischtdaag!: Merry Christmas!
freind: friend
freinden: friends

froh: happy

geh: go

gern gschehne: you're welcome

Got: God

Gude mariye: Good morning

gut: good

Gut nacht: Good night

hallo: hello

haus: house

Ich liebe dich: I love you

jah: yes

kaffi: coffee

kapp: prayer covering or cap

kichli: cookie

kichlin: cookies

kinner: children

kocha: cook

krank: sick

liewe: love, a term of endearment

maed: young women, girls

maed/maedel: young woman

mamm: mom

mammi: grandmother

mann: man/husband

matin: morning

mei: my

mutter: mother

naut: night

nee: no

nix: nothing

nohma: name

onkel: uncle

Ordnung: the written and unwritten rules of the Amish; the understood behavior by which the Amish are expected to live, passed down from generation to generation. Most Amish know the rules by heart.

Plain: Amish way of life

rumspringa: "running around" period for teenagers

schee: pretty

schtupp: family room

schwester/schweschder/shveshtah: sister

schwesters/schweschdere: sisters

seltsam: weird

sohn: son

vatter: father

Was iss letz?: What's wrong?

Wie geht's: How do you do? or Good day!

wunderbaar: wonderful

ya: yes

Yankee: non-Amish (Middlefield only)

yer: your

PATCHWORK PROMISES

———◆———

AMY CLIPSTON

With love and appreciation for Pam.
Your friendship is a blessing!
Thank you for being my sister.

FEATURED CHARACTERS

Suetta m. Ezra Lapp

Joanne   Becky

Marianna (deceased) m. Elvin (deceased) Zook

Colin Zook

Hettie Zook (Colin's grandmother)

ONE

Colin Zook woke, startled. He sat up, glanced around his bedroom, and peered into the darkness before scrubbing a hand down his face. The green lights on his battery-operated digital clock read twelve thirty.

With a sigh, he laid back down, rolled onto his side, and closed his eyes. He had fewer than seven hours before his alarm would announce it was time for him to rise and get ready for church. Just as he felt his body relax, a sob tore through the air.

"My quilt! My quilt!" his grandmother's voice hollered from the room next door. "I've lost it!"

Colin groaned, and dread pooled in his gut as he sat back up. "Not tonight," he mumbled to himself.

He pushed himself out of the bed, and his feet hit the cool linoleum as he grabbed his flashlight from the nightstand and rushed out to the hallway. He entered his grandmother's bedroom next door, where *Mammi* sobbed, curled up in the fetal position in her bed.

He kept the flashlight pointed toward the new tan

linoleum as he stood beside her bed and touched her arm. "*Mammi*, it's okay. I'm here now."

"No!" She rolled over and peered up at him, shadows falling on her wrinkled face as tears poured from her hazel eyes. "I lost my quilt. You have to find it, Elvin! I need it. I can't sleep without it, Elvin. I need it. I can't sleep without it." Her voice warbled like water over a creek bed.

Colin's chest seized as *Mammi* hiccupped and continued to cry.

"I'll look for it," he said, even though he was certain she couldn't hear him over her sobs.

The flashlight beam bounced off the new floor as he padded back to his bedroom. He stood in the doorway as *Mammi*'s wailing echoed through the small house. He took a deep breath, hoping to calm his frayed nerves.

Give me strength, Lord. Grant me patience too.

Then he moved the flashlight beam around his bedroom, racking his brain for a solution to this persistent problem. Ever since the house fire they had endured more than a month ago, *Mammi* had suffered from fits almost every night. She would cry for her family heirloom quilt that had been lost in the fire.

He'd become accustomed to her occasionally calling him by his father's name when her dementia began sneaking into her mind two years ago after his father had passed away. Although, it didn't make much sense to him since he and his father had shared few similarities. While they were both tall, standing at an even six feet, his father had light-brown hair, while Colin's hair was sandy blond, but they both had blue eyes.

Still, he could handle his grandmother forgetting his name, but the nighttime breakdowns for the quilt, which had become more and more frequent during the past couple of weeks, had become unbearable.

When he couldn't locate anything in his room that might help her, the muscles in his shoulders began to coil. He moved to the linen closet in the hallway and opened the door—pulling blankets off the shelf, sifting through the ones he'd tried previous nights, and praying for one that resembled her beloved quilt. He settled for a blue and green quilt his mother had made for him before she'd succumbed to pneumonia twenty-three years ago, when Colin was only three years old.

"Please, Lord, let this quilt soothe *Mammi* as it once soothed me," he whispered as he headed back into his grandmother's bedroom. "I found it, *Mammi*." He raised his voice over her wails.

Her crying ceased, and she looked over at him, her expression incredulous. "You did?"

He swallowed. *Lord, forgive me for lying to my precious grandmother.*

He held it up. "Here you go."

Her wrinkled temples puckered even more as she examined the quilt, and he held his breath, awaiting her reaction. When she remained calm, he handed her the quilt, hope igniting in his soul.

Mammi ran her fingers over it, and then her eyes narrowed. When she met his gaze with a frown, his hope dissolved.

"This isn't my quilt!" Her lower lip trembled. "Where is it, Elvin?"

His irritation melted away, and his posture wilted. "I don't know, but I will sit beside you. Will that help?" His grandmother had cared for him in his time of need; at the very least, he could stay with her as she grieved.

While *Mammi* began to cry again, Colin pulled his father's favorite wing chair over beside her bed, switched off his flashlight, and retrieved the pillow and blanket he'd used the previous night.

Then he sat down on the chair, covered his lap with the blanket, took his grandmother's hand in his, and stared out toward the dark doorway. It would be another long and sleepless night, but he would do his best to calm her. Perhaps they would both get some sleep before it was time to get ready for church.

———◆———

"Gude mariye!" Joanne Lapp waved to her group of friends as she and her younger sister, Becky, approached them standing by the Glick family's back porch the following morning.

The early-September sun kissed her cheeks, and a warm breeze brought with it the aroma of flowers, moist earth, and animals. It was another beautiful late summer day in Bird-in-Hand, Pennsylvania. The buzz of conversations swept through the air, while members of her district visited before the church service began in the barn.

"There the Lapp *maed* are!" Annie Smoker, Joanne's best friend since first grade, pulled her in for a quick hug. Her sunshine-colored hair peeked out from her prayer *kapp*, and her powder-blue dress matched her bright eyes. Joanne had always considered Annie, with her small nose, pink lips, and ever-present smile, one of the prettiest young women in their district. Annie was also a few inches taller than she was, but everyone was taller than Joanne, even her younger sister.

Joanne looked around the circle at her other friends. "What's the latest quilt news?"

"Mary Ellen was just talking about the projects we need to complete before the Christmas Bazaar." Barbara Ann Fisher smiled. She looked pretty today in a pink dress that complemented her blonde hair and hazel eyes. She gestured at Mary Ellen Beiler. "Plus, we have our Christmas orders. We need to get working on those. I wonder if we should meet twice a week until we're caught up."

Mary Ellen shook her head, and the ties on her prayer covering fanned her face. "Oh, I don't know. You know I have so many chores to do, and *mei mamm* expects me to help with the younger *kinner*." With her brown hair and green eyes, Mary Ellen was twenty-two, which was the same age as Joanne's sister, and she was one of seven siblings.

Joanne always wondered what it would be like to have more siblings. She hoped to one day have a large family of her own, but she was grateful for Becky, who was not only her sister but also her confidante.

"I understand." Joanne nodded. "I'm not sure Becky and I could meet more than once every week either. We also have a lot of chores at the farm."

"That's true." Becky came to stand beside Mary Ellen. Like Joanne and Annie, Becky and Mary Ellen had been close since first grade.

Lena Esh, who was twenty-five like Joanne and Annie,

shrugged. "So that means we need to make the most of our quilting bees and then also put in extra time at home when we can. We made the deadline for the Christmas Bazaar last year, so why wouldn't we this year?" She was the practical member of their group, and she was attractive with her light-brown hair and blue eyes.

"That will have to work," Joanne agreed.

"We'll have to make the Christmas Bazaar quilts the priority since the bazaar is in November. We'll still have time to finish the quilt orders we have too." Annie smiled at Joanne.

"Right. I think as long as we focus, we can make it," Becky chimed in.

They continued to discuss the Christmas quilt deadlines until nine o'clock, when it was time for the service to start.

Joanne stood between Becky and Annie as the young, unmarried men in the congregation filed toward the barn. She turned to say something to Annie just as someone bumped into her, causing her to stumble. Then a large, heavy foot landed on her black shoe, crushing her toes. She yelped in pain as she spun and found Colin Zook looking down at her.

"I'm sorry, Joanne," he grumbled. "I didn't see you there."

She blinked up at him as he stood nearly a foot taller than she was. Her chest clenched as she took in the dark circles under his blue eyes, which were bloodshot. "It's all right. Are you okay, Colin?"

But he had already moved past her, ambling beside another man, Marcus Swarey, as they followed the line of men into the barn for the service.

"Jo." Annie grabbed her arm. "Is your foot okay?"

"*Ya.*" She'd already forgotten about the discomfort. Instead, concern for Colin had overtaken her heart.

Becky touched Joanne's arm. "That looked painful."

"Oh, I'll be all right. But did you see his eyes? The look on his face?" Joanne asked.

Annie steered Joanne toward the barn as the other young, unmarried women started toward it. "What do you mean?"

"He looked as if he hasn't slept in a week." Joanne kept her voice low while they padded inside and toward the unmarried women's section of the congregation.

"I didn't notice."

Joanne sat down on a bench between Becky and Annie. She picked up her hymnal and then gazed across the barn to where Colin sat next to Marcus. He stared down at his lap while Marcus spoke.

"That family has been through so much," Joanne said. "First he lost his *mamm* when he was a toddler. Then his father passed away from a massive heart attack two years ago. *Then* his grandmother started showing signs of dementia. He's all alone on that dairy farm caring for his *mammi* and everything else. And do you remember how their *haus* was hit by lightning a couple months ago?"

"It's a lot to bear."

Joanne kept her eyes focused on Colin. Although he was a year ahead of her at school, and he had attended her youth group for some time, he wasn't much more than an acquaintance. Still, she couldn't help but worry about him and his grandmother. She glanced toward the back of the barn, where his grandmother sat with the other elderly women in their congregation. Hettie smiled as she glanced around.

When Joanne's gaze moved back to Colin, he looked up at her and then quickly looked away. She opened her hymnal and turned to the opening song.

The song leader began the first part of the verse, and Joanne and the congregation joined him. While she sang, she turned her attention to the service, leaving thoughts of Colin behind her.

———◆———

Marcus peered across the table at Colin and picked up a pretzel. "I'm sorry your *mammi* kept you up last night. You look terrible."

"I feel terrible too." Colin cupped his hand over his mouth to cover his yawn as lunchtime conversations buzzed around them in the barn. "But it's not her fault. I just wish I could do a better job of comforting her. After all, she comforted me when I lost *mei mamm* and then *mei dat*. She's always been there for me. I'm just so exhausted all the time."

"How often is she waking you up?"

Colin looked up toward the ceiling and tried to remember the long week. "I think she slept through the night Tuesday. Other than that, I spent every night this week in her room."

"You slept in her room?" Marcus leaned forward.

"I started out on *mei dat*'s wing chair, but I wound up on the floor."

"Why did you sleep on the floor?"

Colin snorted as he smothered a piece of bread with peanut butter spread. "Because the wing chair hurts my back and neck."

Marcus gave him a palms-up. "Have you tried giving her another quilt?"

Colin put the piece of bread on his plate and set his jaw. "I've given her every quilt I could find that survived the fire. I even went to that Log Cabin Quilt Shop up on Old Philadelphia Pike in Bird-in-Hand but couldn't find one with similar colors. I considered buying one anyway, but what's the use if she's just going to say it's the wrong one? Then I'll be stuck with a quilt that she won't accept. I don't know what else to do to help her. It's heartbreaking when she cries."

When another yawn took him by surprise, Colin covered his mouth with his hand. He couldn't wait to get home so he could sleep while *Mammi* took her usual afternoon nap.

Marcus ate another pretzel and then began piling lunch meat on a piece of bread. "*Mei mamm* used to quilt. I could ask her if she'd make a copycat quilt for you."

"It probably won't work."

"Why not?"

Colin shook his head. "Nothing else has worked, and I'm starting to lose hope."

Marcus smiled at something behind Colin, and when Colin turned, he found Joanne holding a coffee carafe.

Her face also lit up with a smile. "*Kaffi?*"

"*Ya, danki.*" Colin handed her his cup, and as she filled it, guilt suddenly swamped him as he recalled accidentally walking into her earlier and stepping on her foot. What a klutz! "How's your foot, Joanne?"

"Huh?" Her dark-brown eyes met his. "Oh, right! My foot." She laughed a little. "It's fine."

13

"I'm sorry for stepping on it."

"No problem. Accidents happen." She reached over and took Marcus's cup. "How are you doing?" she asked as she filled the cup.

Colin sipped his coffee, assuming she was addressing Marcus.

Joanne pivoted toward him. "Colin? How are you?"

"Me?" He pointed to his chest.

Her eyes seemed to assess him, and he felt itchy under her stare. "*Ya*," she said. "You look exhausted or maybe *krank*."

"I'm okay." He shrugged and took another sip of coffee.

She nodded and lifted the carafe. "Duty calls."

Colin watched as she moved on to offer coffee to others. Curiosity nipped at him. Why would Joanne Lapp be concerned for his well-being? If he hadn't stepped on her foot, she probably wouldn't have even noticed him.

Shaking off his curiosity, Colin turned back toward Marcus, picked up a pretzel, and popped it into his mouth.

"She's *schee*." Marcus grinned.

"Who?"

Marcus gave him an incredulous expression. "Joanne, of course."

Colin shrugged, even though he did think she was pretty. Her eyes and hair reminded him of a dark-roast coffee, and he had always liked the smattering of freckles marching across her small nose.

But it didn't matter. He didn't have time for a relationship.

After all, his hands were full with running a dairy farm alone and also caring for his sweet grandmother, who seemed to get more and more confused as the months wore on. And while the women in the congregation tended to *Mammi* on church Sundays during the service, no one ever stopped by to check on him or to ask if he needed anything during the week or on off-Sundays without a service.

Of course, the community had come out in droves when his house burned down two months ago. Colin and *Mammi* had stayed with neighbors while the men helped to clean up the rubble and rebuild the house. When they returned to their rebuilt home, the women delivered more casseroles than Colin and *Mammi* could eat in a year. But after a few weeks, the aid and concern stopped, leaving him to pick up the pieces and try to balance life as a caregiver and a farmer alone.

Colin frowned as irritation, exhaustion, and resentment coiled in his gut like a snake.

"You should come to youth group and talk to her." Marcus's words crashed through Colin's thoughts.

Colin shook his head. "I'm too tired, and I need to get *Mammi* home and settled for her afternoon nap."

"You need an afternoon off. I could ask *mei mamm* to care for your *mammi*."

"I don't think so."

Marcus held his hands up. "Just listen. *Mei mamm* could tell your *mammi* that she wants her to come visit. Then we can go to youth group, and you can pick up Hettie on the way home."

"We're twenty-six." Colin set a pile of lunch meat on a piece of bread. "Don't you think we're a little too old for youth group?"

"We need to spend time with people our age."

"I appreciate the thought, but *mei mammi* is my responsibility. She and *mei daadi* moved in after *mei mamm* died, and she raised me. I still remember how she would read to me and play with me when I was too little to help *mei dat* on the farm. She was always there to dry my tears when I fell or comfort me when I had a bad dream. She's my only family left, which is why I want to take *gut* care of her. Besides, *mei dat* would expect me to."

"Would your *dat* also expect you to be alone the rest of your life?"

Colin sighed. He was too tired to argue. "Maybe I'll go next time," he said, hoping to appease his best friend.

Marcus seemed satisfied with that. "Today we're going to play volleyball at Marvin Blank's *haus*."

Colin stifled a yawn as Marcus talked on about the youth gathering. He couldn't wait to get home and take a nap, but until then, he'd do his best to enjoy his time with his best friend.

TWO

The following afternoon, Joanne picked up a pair of her father's trousers from the laundry basket, pulled clothespins from her apron pocket, and hung the trousers on the clothesline before pushing it forward, humming as she worked.

The sky was bright blue and dotted with puffy white clouds, while birds sang in nearby trees. The air smelled fresh, and the humidity was nearly half of what it had been last week. Oh, how she loved this time of year when fall began to make its way to Lancaster County!

The storm door clicked open, and *Mamm* joined her on the back porch of the large, white farmhouse where Joanne and her sister had been born. "Need some help?"

"*Ya. Danki.*"

Mamm picked up another pair of *Dat*'s trousers and handed them to Joanne. Soon they had an assembly line going as Joanne hung the clothes on the line and then moved the line to make room for more.

"How was your trip to the grocery store?" Joanne asked as they moved on to *Dat*'s shirts.

"*Gut.*" *Mamm* handed her another shirt. "I saw Laverne Swarey there."

Joanne added the shirt to the line and then turned to her mother. "How's she doing?"

"She's doing well, but she told me something about Colin Zook."

"What?"

"Apparently Marcus spoke to Colin at lunch yesterday, and he said that his *mammi* is having a difficult time."

Worry settled over Joanne. "What's wrong with Hettie?"

"She lost her heirloom quilt in the *haus* fire they had in July and now has trouble sleeping without it. Some nights she's awake crying for hours, and poor Colin can't console her."

"So that's why he looked so exhausted yesterday."

"He did?"

"*Ya*, his eyes were bloodshot, and he looked like he might nod off during the service."

Mamm frowned. "He sleeps on the floor of her room. It's a terrible situation."

"*Ach*, no." Joanne fingered the shirt in her hands and then hung it on the line before pushing the line out farther. She hadn't been able to get Colin's sad face out of her mind since she'd seen him before the service. She'd looked for Colin during the youth gathering in hopes of getting more time to talk to him, but she'd seen only Marcus.

Joanne pivoted toward her mother. "Do you know what the quilt looked like?"

"No." *Mamm* handed Joanne another shirt from the basket.

Joanne considered how many quilts she was committed to finishing before the Christmas Bazaar. Adding another quilt to her list would be difficult, but she felt moved to help Colin. "What pattern was it?"

"I have no idea, Joanne. Laverne only told me that Hettie lost her beloved quilt in the fire. You would have to ask Hettie or Colin for details if you want them."

The screen door opened and clicked shut as Becky appeared.

Joanne turned toward her mother once again. "I can't shake the feeling that God wants me to help them."

"I think that would be lovely." *Mamm*'s smile was wide. "You're an expert quilter, and the Lord calls us to use our gifts to help others."

Becky joined them by the clothesline. "What are you two chatting about?"

Joanne shared what *Mamm* had learned about Hettie's quilt and Colin's hardship. "If I can find out what the quilt looked like, I can try to re-create it. Maybe we can stop by his farm this week and ask him to describe it."

"Oh, I love that idea!" Becky clapped her hands. "Let's go Wednesday when we're out for supplies."

Joanne nodded as the plan came together in her mind. "That's perfect. We can make them a casserole and a dessert too."

"I'm sure Colin would appreciate the help," *Mamm* said.

Excitement flashed through Joanne as she hung a clean

apron on the line and began planning what she would cook for Colin and Hettie.

But first, she needed Colin's help. Since she and Colin rarely spoke, she hoped he wouldn't find it strange or forward when she came to visit him. After all, she'd visited his farm only for church services.

Still, she couldn't deny the feeling that she was called to help him and his grandmother. She prayed she could be a blessing to them.

———•—•———

Colin stepped out of the barn Wednesday afternoon and stilled when he spotted Joanne and Becky Lapp standing on his back porch holding disposable serving dishes. A horse and buggy sat in the driveway, the horse tied to the fence.

He swiped the back of his hand over his sweaty brow and quickened his steps on his way to the porch, curiosity nipping at him.

Joanne turned, and when her gaze tangled with his, she waved. Then she handed her dish to her sister, who walked into the house. Joanne scrambled down the porch steps to meet him on the worn path that led from the house to the barn.

She tented her hand above her eyes as she smiled up at him. "Hi, Colin."

"What are you doing here?" His voice sounded slightly gruffer than he'd intended, but he didn't have time for visitors.

Her smile faded as she took a step away from him.

"Laverne Swarey told *mei mamm* that your *mammi* lost her quilt in the fire, and I want to help."

He frowned as irritation clung to him like a second skin. "Now I know for sure that Marcus can't keep his mouth shut."

Joanne swallowed, and her lips turned up a shaky smile. "I'm glad Laverne told *mei mamm* because I really think I can help you."

"You want to help me?" He gave a sarcastic snort. "Where has everyone been since *mei haus* burned down? After the construction ended, they all disappeared."

"I-I wasn't aware that you needed help." Her voice faltered and then rebounded. "Do you have any pieces of the quilt left?"

"No. It was completely destroyed."

She retrieved a notepad and pencil from her apron pocket and turned to a clean page. "Do you know the pattern? The colors?"

"I have no idea what pattern it was." He rubbed his chin and imagined the old quilt. "As for colors, maybe yellow, pink, blue, and green."

She wrote on the notepad. "What shades of yellow, pink, blue, and green?"

"I'm sorry, I don't remember and—I just don't have time to think about this today." He turned and started back toward the barn.

"You'll make time if you want to sleep," she called after him.

Colin spun and faced her, and her pretty roast-coffee-colored eyes narrowed to slits that were focused on him.

21

Then her expression softened. "Please, let me help you, Colin. I want to make the quilt for her—for you both."

Colin studied Joanne. Although they'd grown up together, he didn't know her well. Any conversations he'd had with her had been in passing and forgettable.

And now she stood in front of him, offering to help him and his grandmother. Confusion and appreciation shoved away the resentment and irritation he felt toward the community who had left him out in the cold.

Colin was aware of the quilting bees Joanne and her friends held. He'd heard her quilts supplied the stores not only in Bird-in-Hand but also in surrounding towns in Lancaster County, charity auctions, and mud sales. She obviously was a proficient quilter, and perhaps she would use her skills to help *Mammi*. Assuming she would follow through, of course.

Joanne took a step toward him. "If you describe the quilt, I can try to re-create it, but I can't do that without your help." Then she pointed toward the house. "Or would you prefer I talk to Hettie? Maybe she can tell me—"

He held his hands up. "No. Please don't ask *mei mammi* about the quilt. If you mention it, she'll start to cry."

"I see." She cringed before holding up her notepad and pencil. "How about you tell me what you remember about the quilt. Then I'll draw it, and you can tell me if I'm close. Or maybe it resembles a pattern I've already drawn."

"I'll try." He rubbed his chin.

"What did it look like?"

"I think it had blocks around it."

She flipped through her notepad and held up a sketch of a quilt. "Did it look like this with a star in the middle?"

"No."

"Were the blocks like this?" She held up another drawing. "This is a Lone Star."

He shook his head. "No."

"Hmm." Her temples puckered as she flipped through more drawings.

He took a step toward her and peered down at her notebook, perusing the intricate illustrations of quilt patterns. "You drew those?"

"*Ya.*" Pink crept into her cheeks as she kept looking through the pages.

"You're very talented."

"Not really." She kept her eyes focused on the notepad and then stopped. "What about this pattern?" She held up a drawing of a quilt with colored blocks arranged in a circular pattern.

"That's it."

"That pattern is called 'A Trip around the World.' It's an old pattern you don't see too much anymore." She turned back to the page where she'd begun making notes. "Tell me more about the colors."

"Well, they were faded." He described what he could remember, and she took notes.

"That will get me started." She looked up at him, and her eyes seemed to assess him. "I hope you like cheesy chicken casserole and brownies."

"Why?"

"Because Becky and I brought them for your *mammi* and you." Then she spun on her heel and marched toward the house, leaving him standing by the barn alone.

———— •◆• ————

Joanne's body trembled with anger and disappointment as she stalked toward Colin's house. While she'd known Colin to be quiet, she'd never expected him to be surly to her—especially when she had come to offer her help. No wonder he was still a bachelor!

When he told her he didn't have time for her and turned his back on her, she'd considered leaving and forgetting her plans to help him. But then she'd thought of sweet Hettie sobbing at night for her beloved quilt, and she was certain God had prompted her to carry on. It was their duty to care for one another in their community, no matter what. She had decided to give Colin another chance.

Still, she didn't appreciate his remark about how people hadn't helped him. After all, her father was one of the men who had helped clean up the charred remains of his house and then helped rebuild it while Joanne, her mother, and Becky had cooked meals for them. She couldn't imagine what the community had failed to do.

Joanne slipped her notepad and pencil into her apron pocket and climbed the porch steps before pushing open the storm door and walking through the small mudroom to the kitchen. There Becky sat at the table across from Hettie, talking on and on about cooking.

"*Mei mamm* suggested I try to make the cheesy chicken casserole since most people like chicken and cheese. They really go together well. Don't you agree?" Becky asked.

Hettie nodded, but her puckered brow seemed to convey

confusion. With the wrinkles around her bright eyes, her mouth, and her cheeks, she looked to be in her early eighties, but Joanne recalled how much younger she had looked before Colin's father had passed away. It seemed she had aged a decade in only two years.

Joanne's heart clenched as she imagined Hettie crying for her quilt. She would do her best to help her, no matter how disrespectful Colin was.

Hettie looked over at Joanne.

"*Wie geht's*, Hettie?" Joanne waved as she took a few steps toward the table.

The skin between the elderly woman's eyes crinkled as she turned back to Becky. "Who's she?"

Becky gave a nervous laugh. "That's *mei schweschder*, Joanne. She attends church with us."

"Your *schweschder*," Hettie said slowly, and Becky nodded. "I had a *schweschder*, but she died many years ago. Her name was Gertrude. She was so beautiful that I was envious of the suitors she had. I was certain I was invisible beside her and would spend my life alone." She smiled. "But then I met my Herman, and everything changed. He looked at me like I was the prettiest *maedel* in the community."

Joanne smiled as Hettie continued to talk about her late husband and sister. When she felt someone watching her, she peered over her shoulder to where Colin stood in the doorway. She took in his frown and found exhaustion instead of arrogance painted in the dark-purple circles under his normally bright-blue eyes. Perhaps she had misjudged him, and his frustrations weren't meant to be directed at her.

He looked past her toward his grandmother.

Hettie stopped talking and frowned as she looked at Becky. "What was your name again?"

Becky smiled. "I'm Becky Lapp, and this is *mei schweschder*, Joanne." She gestured toward Joanne.

"We should go." Joanne smiled at Hettie. "I hope you enjoy the food we brought." Then she turned toward Colin. "I wrote down the instructions for heating the casserole and taped them to the top of the disposable dish." She pointed toward the counter. "Enjoy."

"*Danki*," he said.

"*Gern gschehne.*" She gave Hettie's hand a pat before she and Becky headed out the door to their waiting horse and buggy.

THREE

L ater that evening, Colin dried the plates and set them in a cabinet before scrubbing the drinking glasses. The delicious aroma of cheesy chicken casserole and brownies lingered in the air while he worked, and his muscles ached after another day of chores on the dairy farm.

He glanced over toward the remaining brownies and casserole left in the portable dishes, and his thoughts turned to Joanne. Embarrassment weighed heavily on his chest as he recalled how rude he'd been to her when she'd first arrived at the farm.

His shame ran deep as he considered how disappointed his father would have been if he'd seen how Colin had treated her. *Dat* had taught him better than to treat a woman so poorly. Still, Colin was frustrated with the community and how they'd all forgotten him and his grandmother shortly after the fire. He felt as if he was drowning between caring for his grandmother and running the farm, and no one seemed to care.

When Joanne mentioned his grandmother's quilt, he'd

expected her to offer empty platitudes and advice, not offer to recreate it. She'd seemed so genuine, so eager to help him, but it also felt too good to be true.

He found himself worrying that she'd offer to make the quilt and then change her mind. Still, his worse fear was that she'd make it and then demand a large sum of money as payment. He'd seen the prices of the quilts at the stores, and they cost much more than he could ever afford while struggling to run his small farm on his own. He wouldn't be able to pay Joanne for her time either. Perhaps he should find her number and tell her to forget the quilt. He'd make do somehow—with the Lord's help, of course.

Colin turned his attention to cleaning up the remaining utensils and stowing the leftovers before wiping down the table and sweeping the kitchen floor.

He'd just finished cleaning the kitchen when a wail sounded from down the hallway.

"My quilt! My quilt!" his grandmother's voice hollered from the room next door. "I've lost it! Elvin, help me!"

Colin set the dustpan and broom in the utility closet. Then he leaned against the wall, closed his eyes, and sighed. He would face another sleepless night of trying to console his grandmother and then have to find a way to drag his weary body through his daily chores tomorrow. The serpent of burden wrapped tighter around him and hissed at him.

As he padded toward the hallway to *Mammi*'s room, he sent up a silent prayer:

Please, Lord, help me. Give me patience and strength. Let me be the comfort my dear grandmother needs.

When he reached *Mammi*'s doorway, he hoped Joanne

would make the quilt for *Mammi*. At the moment, it was the only thing promising some relief.

———•◆•———

Joanne sat between Annie and Becky in Lena's large sewing room Thursday afternoon.

"Have any of you made progress on your Christmas quilts since last week?" Mary Ellen asked as she spread her beautiful red and green Lone Star quilt on her lap.

Barbara Ann shook her head and frowned. "I've been so busy with chores that I haven't had a moment to quilt."

"Joanne is taking on another project," Becky announced.

Oh no! Joanne swallowed a groan as she shot her sister a look. "I haven't started on it, and I'm not sure I can even do it since I need a lot more information."

"What are you talking about?" Annie's brow furrowed.

Becky elbowed Joanne in the side. "Tell them about Colin and Hettie."

"Zook?" Lena asked, and Joanne nodded. "What project are you doing for them?"

Joanne explained how Hettie lost her beloved quilt. "I thought maybe I could recreate it for her, which would give Hettie some emotional relief and help Colin to get some rest."

Barbara Ann grinned. "Colin is handsome, and I don't think he's dated much since his *dat* passed away."

"He's also rude," Joanne quipped as she pulled her notepad from her tote bag and flipped to the sketch of the quilt she'd drawn last night.

"Rude?" Lena asked. "What do you mean?"

Annie touched Joanne's arm. "When was he rude to you?"

"What did he say?" Mary Ellen asked.

Joanne felt her cheeks heat as her circle of friends watched her with a mixture of concern and curiosity. She squirmed under their stares. "When Becky and I went to visit him, he was very short with me, saying he didn't have time to talk to me about the quilt." As she recalled how he'd spoken to her, her heart began to sink. She cast her eyes down toward the floor.

"I convinced him to talk to me about it by telling him he might get some rest if he let me try to help," Joanne continued. "After I said that, he finally gave me some information." She showed them the sketch she'd made of the quilt. "But I'm not sure if I can do it. I need to know what kind of material it was and what shades the colors were. And what order the colors were included in the quilt."

"And the size it was too," Barbara Ann said.

Joanne sighed. He'd gotten her so frazzled that she'd forgotten to ask that. "*Ya*, you're right."

Annie leaned over and studied the sketch. "You have a *gut* start."

"But if the quilt isn't exactly how Hettie remembers it, I'll have wasted my effort." Joanne shook her head.

Becky gave her an encouraging smile. "Don't give up. If the Lord is leading you to help him, then it will all work out."

Joanne fastened a bright smile on her face. "I hope so."

"Becky is right," Lena said.

"*Ya*," Annie agreed while Barbara Ann and Mary Ellen nodded.

Becky touched Joanne's arm. "And no effort is wasted if God is calling us toward it. You're doing this for Hettie."

"I just hope it works," Joanne said.

———◆———

Saturday afternoon, Colin set a dish on the drainboard and then began scrubbing the utensils. He yawned as he glanced out the window to where a bright-red bird ate from the bird-feeder hanging outside the kitchen window. He watched the bird, wondering what it must be like to not have a care in the world and to just fly free without anyone to depend on it.

He glowered. He would never know what it was like to do as he pleased or to sleep without worry. But this was the path the Lord had laid out for him, and he would make the best of it. After all, his grandmother was his only family. It was his privilege to care for her the way she had cared for him.

Colin finished cleaning up the lunch dishes before wiping down the table. The crunch of tires sounded over the rock driveway, along with the hum of a car engine. His curiosity nipped at him since he wasn't expecting company.

He peeked into the family room and found *Mammi* snoring in her favorite recliner. Then he hurried through the kitchen, tossing the dishrag into the soapy water in the sink before moving out the back door.

Colin strode out onto the back porch as Joanne hiked up the driveway and a black Chevrolet pickup truck backed down it. She carried a large tote bag and wore a red dress that complemented her dark hair and eyes.

"Joanne." He met her at the top of the driveway. "What brings you here today?"

She held up the bag. "I have fabric samples, and I want to see if I matched the colors correctly."

"Oh." He was so surprised that he was speechless for a moment. Perhaps Joanne was going to follow through on her offer after all—and the idea of a full night's sleep thrilled him more than words could express.

"*Mei dat* ran an errand, and he had his driver drop me off. They'll pick me up on the way back."

He made a sweeping gesture toward the back door. "Come in. *Mei mammi* is taking a nap in the *schtupp*, so we can talk in the kitchen."

He hurried up the steps and opened the back door for her. Then he followed her into the kitchen, where she stood by the table and gave him an awkward look.

It was then that he realized she wasn't comfortable with him. For some strange reason, that bothered him. Perhaps he needed to be a better friend to her.

"Please have a seat," he said, and she sat in the nearest chair at the table. "Would you like some iced tea?"

"Sure. *Danki.*" She began pulling pieces of fabric out of her bag.

He moved to the counter and retrieved two drinking glasses from the cabinet before pulling the pitcher of tea from the refrigerator. "Have you had lunch? If not, I can make you a sandwich."

"I appreciate the offer, but I ate before I left the *haus*." She kept her eyes on the fabric, organizing the samples in piles by color.

He carried the glasses to the table and set one down in front of her before sitting across from her.

"*Danki.*" She took a sip of iced tea and then gestured toward the piles of fabric. "I searched my fabric for the colors you mentioned. Are any of these shades close to those in your *mammi*'s quilt?"

Colin rubbed his chin and examined the fabric, trying his best to recall the quilt. Then he picked out the ones that resembled the shades he could remember. "These are close."

She opened her notebook and began writing. She looked up and pushed her paper toward him while pointing to an intricate diagram of the quilt pattern. "Do you remember what order the colors were in?"

He gazed at the diagram and silently marveled at her artistry. He glanced over at her and found her watching him, a serious expression flickering across her face. He took in her bright and intelligent brown eyes, freckles, and her pink lips. She was pretty and she was talented too.

She leaned forward, her brow wrinkling. "Did you hear my question?"

"*Ya,* I did." He cleared his throat as heat crawled up his neck. "I'm trying hard to remember."

"Could you just guess?"

He pursed his lips and then the answer came to him. "I remember a corner was tattered, and that block was yellow."

"That's a start." Her expression brightened as she pulled a pack of colored pencils from her bag. She colored the four corner blocks yellow. "What about the next blocks?"

Please, Lord, help me recall correctly! "Maybe pink?"

She colored them pink and then added other colors as he

guessed the order. He continued to silently marvel at her skill while she concentrated. "I think this will work."

"Who taught you how to quilt?" he asked when she was done filling in the colors.

"*Mei mamm* and *mei mammi*."

"You're really talented."

She kept her gaze focused on the notebook. "*Mei mammi* was much more skilled." When she looked up at him, he noticed a blush on her cheeks. "What size was the quilt?"

"Average size." He shrugged.

She sighed as if he'd gotten on her last nerve. "That doesn't help me."

"It was pretty big."

"Was it a lap quilt? Did it hang over the edge of her bed? If so, does she have a single bed, double bed, or larger?"

Colin sat back in the chair as he imagined the quilt tossed across her bed. "It was the size of her single bed. It didn't hang down too far past the edge of the mattress. Maybe a couple of inches?"

"Perfect." She wrote the size down on the notepad, picked up the pieces of fabric he had chosen, studied them, and then wrote some more.

As he watched her, he sipped his iced tea and wondered if she had a boyfriend. He'd never heard that she did, but it was none of his business.

Joanne looked over at him. "Was the quilting done in white thread or colors?"

"Uh." He stammered. "I don't remember. But I can get you a quilt that *mei mammi* made. Maybe you can see what thread she used on it. It could be an example for you." He stood and tiptoed through the small family room to his bedroom.

He rooted around in his dresser until he located a quilt that *Mammi* had made for him when he was little. Then he padded back to the kitchen.

Colin stilled in the doorway when he found Joanne standing at the counter and stowing the dishes and utensils he'd left in the drainboard for later. "What are you doing?"

"Putting the dishes away for you." She dropped the last knife into the drawer and then pivoted to face him.

He crossed the kitchen to her. "Why would you do that?"

"Because I want to help you."

Confused, he studied her.

She reached down and touched his quilt, examining it. "May I borrow this?"

"Sure. I don't use it much. I even tried giving it to *mei mammi*, but she wouldn't take it."

"I'll be back next week with more fabric samples." She folded the quilt and slipped it into her tote bag. Then she set her notebook and colored pencils into the tote bag and carried her glass to the sink. After pouring the remaining tea into the sink, she began to scrub the glass.

He leaned against the counter beside her as he recalled how much quilts cost at the Bird-in-Hand quilt shop. "Will you let me know how much I owe you after you find the fabric? Or do you want money now?"

"You don't need to give me any money." She dried the glass and then set it in the cabinet beside the sink. Then she pointed to the table. "Would you like me to wash your glass?"

"No, *danki*. I can wash it." He pointed toward the tote bag. "So, you'll give me a price after you find the fabric?"

"No, please, I don't need your money."

"But what about the cost of your fabric?"

"I think I have enough fabric at home to make the quilt. If not, then I won't have to buy much."

"But I do need to pay you for your time."

She tilted her head. "Are you listening to me, Colin? I can cover this."

"Why would you want to do this for free?" He eyed her with suspicion.

She lifted her chin. "Because some people *do* want to help you and your *mammi*."

Colin pressed his lips together as a mixture of embarrassment and irritation threaded through him.

"How has your *mammi* been sleeping?" Her pleasant expression returned.

"Some nights are better than others."

"Have you tried warm milk to calm her before bedtime?"

He shook his head. "I'll have to try that."

Tires crunching on his driveway and the hum of an engine sounded outside the window.

Joanne glanced out the window behind her. "*Mei dat* is here." She hefted her tote bag onto her shoulder. "Are you coming to youth group tomorrow?"

"No. I have to take care of *mei mammi*." He blinked, surprised by the question.

"My parents could sit with her so you could enjoy an afternoon with *freinden*."

Once again, he was confused by her concern. "Why would your parents want to do that?"

"Like I said, because, believe it or not, people want to help you and Hettie. You just have to let the members of the community know what you need."

"I think I'd rather rest, but *danki* for the offer."

She actually looked disappointed. "That's a shame. Well, I'll talk to you soon."

He followed her to the door and walked out onto the porch with her.

"*Danki*, Joanne," he said as she walked down the steps.

"*Gern gschehne*," she called after him before hurrying to the truck and climbing into the back seat.

Colin waved at her father, Ezra, and the driver in the front seat before the truck began backing down the driveway. Then he stepped back into his house and tried to comprehend why Joanne felt moved to help him.

As he peeked in on his sleeping grandmother, he wondered if the night ahead of them would be more peaceful than the last.

FOUR

I think I have all the supplies we need to work on Colin's quilt," Joanne said as she sat in a booth at the Bird-in-Hand Family Restaurant Tuesday afternoon with her sister and friends. "I appreciate all of you shopping with me today."

Lena smiled across the table at Joanne. "I'm excited to see how it turns out."

"I am too," Mary Ellen said.

Joanne took a bite of her roasted turkey sandwich and then sipped her glass of water.

Barbara Ann grinned over at Joanne. "Do you like Colin?"

"What?" Joanne shook her head. "No."

Mary Ellen snorted. "Why not? He's so handsome."

"And he's cold." Joanne popped a french fry into her mouth.

Barbara Ann swallowed a bite of her roast beef sandwich. "If you think he's cold, then why are you helping him?"

"We're supposed to help each other regardless. Besides, I'm doing this for Hettie, not for Colin. My heart breaks for her when I think of her sobbing for her quilt. Why wouldn't

I want to help her after hearing that story?" Joanne took another bite of her sandwich.

"It's really kind that you're doing this," Becky said as she picked up a potato chip. "*Mammi* would be proud."

Joanne felt a tug at her heart. How she missed her grandmother who had passed away last year. She ate another fry as she tried to swallow her grief. "He gave me his quilt to use as a sample for the type of stitching Hettie's quilt had. It's a star pattern with beautiful shades of blue and gray. I'm going to fix it for him."

"So, you *do* like him." Becky elbowed Joanne in the side as their friends laughed.

Joanne glared at her sister. "Ouch, and no I don't." Then she felt her glare fade. "Will you go with me to see him tomorrow so he doesn't get the wrong idea?"

"Of course I will." Becky grinned. "But you do like him."

Joanne sighed. Sometimes her younger sister was incorrigible.

"How is your wedding ring quilt going, Barbara Ann?" Annie asked.

When Joanne glanced over at Annie, her best friend gave her a wink. Joanne felt herself relax as the conversation turned away from Colin and toward less embarrassing chatter.

———•◆•———

Later that evening, Joanne sat in the sewing room and mended Colin's quilt. She took in the intricate stitching and worn fabric and smiled as she imagined Hettie creating this beautiful blanket for Colin, quilting love into every stitch.

As she worked, she recalled Colin sitting across from her at the table and watching her while she colored in the blocks on her drawing. The intensity in his blue eyes had made her feel uncomfortable, as if she had forgotten her prayer *kapp* and sat across from him with a naked head.

Lena was right when she'd said Colin was handsome with his sandy-blond hair, sky-blue eyes, angular jaw, tall stature, and trim waist. But the bitterness and resentment that radiated from him overshadowed his good looks.

Joanne finished mending one corner and then moved on to the next as her thoughts continued to focus on Colin. She hoped she could be a blessing to him, but she could not imagine being romantically involved with him.

Lord, I'm doing my best to follow your lead. I feel you working in my life, guiding me toward helping Hettie and Colin. I'll do my best to be a blessing to them.

"Is that Colin's quilt?"

Joanne glanced toward the doorway as Becky walked in, wearing a powder-blue nightgown, her thick, light-brown hair hanging to her waist. "*Ya*, it is."

"Let me see it." Becky took a seat on a chair across from her and ran her fingers over the stitching. "It's lovely."

"It is. I'm fixing it before I get back to my Christmas quilts." Joanne finished fixing the corner and then started working on a tear near the center of the quilt. "When we go back to Colin's *haus*, would you please keep Hettie busy while I talk to him?"

"I'll do my best. Why?"

"Colin doesn't want her to know I'm working on the quilt in case it doesn't work out."

"Okay." Becky's expression turned devious. "You can tell me the truth, and I won't tell anyone. Do you like Colin?"

Joanne huffed a breath and glared at her sister. "What makes you think I like him?"

"You're going out of your way for him." Becky pointed to the quilt. "You're doing much more than he expects."

"But he doesn't have anyone to help him. Why wouldn't I offer to help?"

"Good point." Becky stood and yawned. "Anyway, don't stay up too late. We have chores to do before we go to Colin's farm tomorrow."

"I won't. *Gut nacht.*"

"Gut nacht." Becky gave a little wave before disappearing into the hallway.

Joanne kept her eyes focused on the quilt as she began to pray once again.

Lord, please let Hettie and Colin have a restful night.

———•—•———

Colin awoke with a start later that evening. He sat up and gasped as he glanced around his dark bedroom. The digital numbers on his battery-operated clock read 2:09.

He rubbed his eyes and sighed. Perhaps he'd had a bad dream. Then he rolled onto his side and adjusted the pillow. He closed his eyes just as a howl crashed through the quiet house.

"My quilt! I can't find it!" *Mammi* hollered.

Colin pushed himself out of the bed, feeling as if the weight of the world squeezed his chest.

After grabbing his flashlight, he trudged toward the doorway and started out toward *Mammi*'s room. Then he stopped as Joanne's advice filled his mind.

"Warm milk," he whispered, hurrying toward the kitchen. He retrieved a saucepan, set it on the stove, and poured milk in before turning on the burner.

Mammi's cries tore through the air as he grabbed a glass from the cabinet. After a few moments, he poured the milk into the glass, and then rushed down the hallway to her room, where she laid in bed, sobbing and crying for her quilt.

"Mammi. Mammi!"

When he raised his voice, she stopped and stared at him, wiping her cheeks with the back of her hand.

"Drink this. It will help you feel better."

Mammi sniffed and then took a sip of the milk. She blinked and stared down at the cup.

"It's warm milk to help you sleep."

She drank some more and then her lip began to tremble. "I need my quilt."

Colin sighed. So much for Joanne's idea. "I know. I wish I could help you."

As *Mammi* began to cry, Colin gazed at the cot he'd picked up at a secondhand store in town yesterday. He'd set it up in her room when her crying spell began last night, and he'd tossed and turned before sleeping a few hours and then waking up with a backache. But it was still a better option than the floor.

Mammi's cries escalated, and Colin touched her hand as his heart sank.

"It's okay, *Mammi*. You don't need the quilt to sleep."

"I do." Her voice trembled. "I need it now."

"I'll stay with you." Colin pushed the cot over beside her bed, switched off his flashlight, and then reached up and held *Mammi*'s hand.

Tonight would be another night spent on that lumpy, old mattress listening to his grandmother cry herself to sleep. He stared up through the blackness toward the ceiling as *Mammi* continued to sob. His thoughts spun like a tornado as he shifted on the cot, trying in vain to get comfortable.

He recalled when Joanne had first come to visit him, and he cringed. He had to apologize for being so short with her. She didn't deserve to be treated that way—no one did— especially when she was going above and beyond for him and his grandmother. He needed to say he was sorry when he saw her again.

He hoped she would keep her promise and come back with an update on the quilt. Until then, he'd hold on by a thread as his exhaustion seemed to grow more overwhelming every day.

"Please, Lord," he whispered, his voice barely audible over her weeping. "Please help *Mammi*, and please guide me to a solution. I'm not sure how much more I can endure."

———————◆———————

On Wednesday afternoon, Joanne held her tote bag and Colin's quilt in her arms and knocked on Colin's back door with a free hand. The mid-September sky above her was bright azure, and birds sang in the nearby trees as the familiar aroma of animals overtook her nostrils.

After a few moments, she turned to her sister beside her. "Maybe they aren't home."

"I wonder if he's in the barn." Becky balanced a casserole dish and cake plate in her hands as she nodded toward the large dairy barn.

Just then, the storm door creaked open, and Hettie smiled at them. "Joanne. Becky. What a nice surprise. What brings you here today?"

Hettie remembers us today! Joanne breathed a sigh of relief.

"We wanted to bring you a meal." Becky held up the disposable dishes. "I hope you like bacon ranch macaroni and cheese casserole and Rice Krispies treats."

Hettie clapped her hands and then opened the door wide. "Oh my goodness. That sounds heavenly. Come in."

"Where's Colin?" Joanne asked her.

Hettie pointed toward the row of barns. "He's working out there."

"Excuse me, but I need to speak with him before I come in to visit."

"Take your time," Becky said with a wink. "Hettie and I will have fun getting caught up."

"*Danki,*" Joanne said before scurrying down the porch steps toward the large dairy barn. She peeked around, taking in the cows and diesel-powered milkers, and then walked through to the back entrance. When she moved outside, she spotted Colin walking toward the barn from the rolling green pasture.

He stopped, and when he looked out toward the neighboring farm, she admired his profile and his handsome face.

Then he looked back toward her, meeting her gaze and lifting his arm in a greeting. As he made his way toward her, he looked haggard, his eyes swollen with exhaustion.

"*Wie geht's?*" he asked as he approached.

"I'm worried about you." The words slipped past her lips without forethought, and embarrassment warmed her face.

Something unreadable flickered across his features. "Why?"

"You look like you haven't slept. I suppose your *mammi* is still keeping you awake."

"*Ya.*" He cupped his hand on the back of his neck. "I tried the warm milk last night. It worked, but it took a while. I put a cot in her room, so I got some sleep."

"I'm glad to hear you slept."

"*Danki.*"

An awkward moment passed between them, and she cleared her throat. "I brought you a few things. Do you have some time to talk?"

"*Ya*, of course. Do you want to go inside?"

"Becky is inside keeping your *mammi* occupied so that we can discuss the quilt. We brought a casserole and Rice Krispies treats."

"That's very kind of you." He smiled, and when his face lit up, her stomach dipped.

For a heartbeat, something magnetic pulled her to him.

"Why don't we sit on the porch?" he asked.

"That would be nice."

They walked side by side toward the house. When they reached the steps, he slowed and motioned for her to walk up onto the porch first. She ascended the stairs, stunned by his manners.

She reached the porch and then stopped, finding only a porch swing and a rocker. She glanced over at him, and he held out a hand toward the swing.

"Have a seat."

She sank down onto the swing, setting the tote bag and quilt on her lap.

He sat down beside her, and the swing shifted under his weight as his leg brushed against her. His nearness sent her senses spinning.

"What did you want to talk about?" he asked.

"Here's the quilt you let me borrow." She set it in his lap. "I fixed where it was torn." She pointed out the corners and the place where the seam had come open.

He smiled as he moved his fingers over the quilt. *"Danki."*

"Gern gschehne." She pulled the pieces of fabric out of her tote bag. "I found this fabric in my piles at home and then I picked up another sample too. Do these look close to the colors that were in Hettie's quilt?"

He examined the fabric pieces. "I think they'll work."

"Gut. I also redrew the pattern since you said it's a single bed size." She pulled her notebook out of her bag and turned to the new pattern. "I put the colors in the order you remembered."

He examined it and then nodded. "That looks spot-on to me."

"I'll start on it right away." She breathed a sigh of relief.

"I have some money I'd like to give you."

"This was my idea, so I can't accept any money from you." She closed up the notebook and slid it into the bag.

His brow furrowed. "But you've fixed my quilt and now you're going to make a new one so that *mei mammi* and I can sleep. I can't take advantage of you that way."

"How about you consider it a Christmas gift for you and your *mammi*? Would that work?"

He studied her. Then he smiled, and she was once again caught off guard by the brightness in his eyes and the warmth in his face.

"I don't think it's right, but I'll find a way to repay you." He glanced down at his lap and then back up at her. "Look, Joanne, I owe you an apology. I was rude to you the first time you came over to see me, and you didn't deserve it. Even more, I was rude to you at church when I stepped on your foot and kept walking. I hope you can forgive me."

She opened her mouth and then closed it, her mind swirling with shock and confusion. "Of course I forgive you. You've been under a tremendous amount of stress."

"That's no excuse." He frowned, shaking his head. "You've been so kind to me, even when I didn't deserve it. And I want to thank you."

Feeling awkward, she stood, anxious to change the subject. "You're welcome. Did you want to come inside? Becky and I made a bacon ranch mac and cheese casserole as well as the Rice Krispies treats. I hope you like them both."

"They sound *appeditlich*."

"Great."

Colin held the storm door for Joanne, and she walked

through the mudroom into the kitchen, where Becky and Hettie sat at the table.

Hettie smiled over at Joanne and Colin. "Well, there you are, Joanne! I was wondering where you'd gone off to." She pointed at Colin. "Is that the quilt I made you when you were five?"

Colin held it up. "*Ya*. Joanne fixed it for me."

"How nice." Hettie's smile was wide. "Becky was just telling me about the time her father watched one of their cows open the gate and lead out the rest of the herd." She chuckled. "You have to hear this story. Start over, please, Becky."

As Becky started to talk, Joanne peeked over at Colin and found him smiling at her. Her knees wobbled, and she placed her hand on the counter to right herself.

Turning her attention back to Becky, Joanne dismissed her body's reaction to Colin's smile. He wasn't even her friend—barely more than an acquaintance.

Joanne waited until Becky finished her story and then walked over to her sister. "Well, Hettie, we really need to go. Thank you for keeping *mei schweschder* company. We have chores to do before supper."

"Oh, right. I completely lost track of time." Becky stood. "It was so nice seeing you, Hettie. I hope you enjoy the food we brought."

Hettie reached a wrinkled hand across the table and placed it on top of Becky's. "Oh, we will. *Danki* for coming to visit me." Then she waved good-bye to Joanne.

"Take care, Hettie," Joanne told her and then turned to Colin. "I'll be in touch."

His expression became intense. *"Danki."*

"Gern gschehne," Joanne told him before opening the back door and rushing out toward her father's horse and buggy.

"Wait up!" Becky ran after her. "What's the hurry?"

"I just don't want *Mamm* to worry about us." Joanne hustled to the buggy, trying to leave her strange new feelings for Colin behind.

"How did your talk go with Colin?"

"It went well. I think he's appreciative of the quilt. I need to stop at the fabric store on the way home and then I'll get started on it." Joanne climbed into the buggy.

"Hettie is so funny. I was glad she recognized us today. We had a hilarious discussion about dairy farms."

Becky chattered while Joanne guided the horse to the road. As her sister talked on, Joanne silently marveled at her new and confusing feelings for Colin. Joanne had dated a few men, but none of her relationships had lasted more than a few months. She was certain she'd never fallen in love, and she hadn't put much effort into dating of late. She was busy enough with her chores at home and her quilting bees—but even more, no man had piqued her interest enough to distract her from her daily life.

This new attraction for Colin had come out of nowhere. What should she do with this feeling?

She banished her questions and tried to concentrate on her sister's discussion of Hettie, but Colin still lingered in the back of her mind. She needed to focus on the quilt, not Colin. After all, he was being nice to her only because he needed her. After she gave him the quilt, they would be nothing more than acquaintances, and he would ignore her at church. If she set her heart on him, he would only hurt her.

But maybe they could be friends. That was all she could hope for.

FIVE

Mammi smiled across the table at Colin later that evening. "This casserole is *appeditlich*."

"It is." Colin spooned another bite into his mouth.

Not only was it delicious but it was a relief not to have to cook tonight. Although *Mammi* used to cook, Colin—now worried that *Mammi* might hurt herself—had taken on kitchen duty as well. Lately *Mammi* would forget to turn off a burner or grab a hot pan without a pot holder, so Colin had taken over a few months ago when her dementia had worsened.

Mammi took another bite and smiled. "That Becky is so funny. She tells the best stories."

She got a faraway look in her bright hazel eyes. "That reminds me of when your *dat* was maybe sixteen, and your *daadi* was trying to teach him how to use the milkers. He thought he had them set up right, but he had gotten a little too sure of himself. He walked away, and next thing you know, there was milk all over the barn floor. Your *daadi* was so angry!"

Amy Clipston

Colin chuckled. "*Dat* and *Daadi* never told me that story." He had a difficult time imagining his grandfather angry. *Daadi* had always been so easygoing, but everyone seemed to have their limits.

"How about the time your *dat* had gone to see the *maedel* who lived at the next farm over, and he didn't make sure the gate was latched? Most of the cows got out. Your *daadi* was even more furious that time." She laughed, the happy noise echoing through the little kitchen.

Colin chuckled along with her as he felt his body relax and happiness rush through him for the first time since the fire. His grandmother was lucid and content as she shared stories without tears of grief.

And he had Joanne to thank for this. Not only had she and her sister visited today and brought food but they also made his grandmother happy.

He recalled their brief conversation while sitting on the porch swing. After he'd apologized, she'd seemed almost nervous around him, which he found peculiar. Why had she stood so abruptly and suggested they go into the house?

Perhaps he had said something wrong, but he couldn't remember uttering anything inappropriate or rude. He inwardly cringed. If he had, he hoped she would forgive him and realize he hadn't meant to hurt her again.

On the other hand, she had graced him with a beautiful smile before she left. Maybe he hadn't ruined things after all.

"That was so sweet of Joanne to fix your old quilt." *Mammi*'s comment pulled him back to the present.

"*Ya*, it was."

"She's a *schee maedel*. Isn't she your age?"

"She was a year behind me in school."

Mammi's smile became mischievous. "She'd be a lovely *maedel* to date. I wonder if she has a boyfriend."

"I'm not sure if she does or not. But either way, I'm not looking for a relationship."

"Why not? You're almost thirty, Colin. You need to settle down and have a family."

"I'm only twenty-six, *Mammi*, which means I'm not quite thirty. I still have time."

"But I might not. I want to see some great-grandchildren before I'm gone."

He sighed. "What makes you think Joanne would even consider dating me?"

"Well, she and her *schweschder* seem to like visiting you, and she fixed your quilt. That has to mean something. Have any other *maed* come by to visit you or offered to help you like that?"

Colin shook his head. *Mammi* had a point, except that Joanne had visited him solely because she'd heard about *Mammi*'s insomnia battle through Marcus. But he couldn't share that information with *Mammi*.

"You know I'm right." *Mammi* leaned forward and grinned conspiratorially. "When are you going to ask her *dat* if you can date her?"

Colin shook his head. "Now's not the right time. I have so much to do here on the farm."

"And a *fraa* could help with that. When you're married, you and your *fraa* are a team, dividing up the chores and running the farm together."

"I know that, but dating takes more time and energy than I have."

Mammi snorted. "If it's a burden, you're doing it wrong." Then her expression became solemn. "Do you want to spend your life alone, Colin?"

"Of course not." He took another bite of casserole.

"You need to realize that once I'm gone, you'll be here alone with your work and your animals. That's not what I want for you." She reached over and set her wrinkled hand on his. "I want you to find love and happiness. Everyone deserves a happy life."

He took in her serious expression, and his heart clenched. "I'm sure I'll find a *fraa* when the Lord's timing is right."

"Just make sure you're paying attention." She wagged a finger at him. "Joanne could be that *maedel*. Don't be so focused on rejecting her that you miss what the Lord intends for you."

Colin stopped chewing as his grandmother's words twirled through his mind. Surely, she was wrong about Joanne. She was pretty, smart, talented, and thoughtful— not to mention a really good cook and quilter—but now wasn't the right time for him to start dating. With caring for *Mammi*, he barely had enough energy to run the farm, let alone be an attentive boyfriend to a special woman. Trying to date right now would just invite more stress to his already chaotic life.

Besides, Joanne deserved a man who could focus on her and nurture a relationship with her, not someone like Colin who was hanging by a thread most days.

Mammi shared more memories of Colin's father and

grandfather while they finished their servings of casserole and then enjoyed a few Rice Krispies treats for dessert.

"I can help you clean up," *Mammi* said as Colin carried their dishes and utensils to the sink.

He set the dishes and utensils in the sink and then started filling one side of the sink with hot water and dish detergent. "I don't mind doing it."

"I know you're afraid I might forget what I'm doing and get hurt, but I feel like myself today. You carry the load around here, and I want to be more help to you." *Mammi* sidled up to him. "Please, Colin."

Colin turned off the water and pulled in a deep breath through his nose. He wanted to trust *Mammi* to help in the kitchen, but memories of her accidents engulfed his mind— when she had left the water in the sink running and flooded the kitchen, causing her to fall and bruise her hip. Or the time she turned the water on too hot and scalded herself. And then there was the time she forgot she had put knives in the water and sliced her palm open so badly that they needed to go to the emergency room for stitches.

Allowing her to help put her at risk, and he wouldn't be able to live with himself if something happened to her that he could have prevented. It was his job to protect her, just as she had protected him when he was a child.

But instead of reminding her of her mishaps, Colin forced his lips into an easy smile. "Why don't you take your bath while I finish up the dishes? I'll make you some warm milk so you can relax and hopefully sleep better tonight."

"You're such a *gut* man." She patted his cheek before shuffling out of the kitchen toward the bathroom.

Colin sighed as he carried the serving platters and drinking glasses to the counter and set them in the soapy water. While he scrubbed the dishes, he gazed out the window toward the birdfeeder and wondered what it would be like to have a wife by his side, helping him run the farm and care for his grandmother. Oh, how wonderful it would be to have a partner, confidante, and companion, who would also help carry the load and love him for the rest of their lives together.

In that moment, it seemed an impossible dream. After all, he had nothing to offer a *maedel* except his tiny farm. Even more, the other men in the community were more prosperous and didn't have the complication of an ailing grandmother. Colin knew he would never be a woman's first choice.

And that realization sat like a block of ice in his chest.

———◆———

When a knock sounded on the doorframe that evening, Joanne looked up from her sewing table toward her mother. Then she glanced over at the clock on the wall and grimaced when she found it was five thirty. "Is it suppertime already?"

"*Ya*, it is." *Mamm* smiled as she stepped into the room. "You've been busy ever since you came home. How's it going?"

Joanne pointed to where she had started cutting out fabric. "It's going okay. I'm just getting started on piecing Hettie's quilt." She ran her fingers over the fabric and then looked up at her mother. "I've been thinking and praying while I work, and I feel led to help Colin by doing more than just making the quilt."

Mamm's forehead crinkled. "What do you mean?"

"I want to check in on him and Hettie more often—maybe offer to help with some chores. He has his hands full, and I can tell how exhausted he is just by looking at him. It might make him feel like the community cares about him if someone offers to help out with the day-to-day burdens."

"He thinks the community doesn't care?"

"He said as much when I first went over to see him. At first I was insulted by the comment, but then I realized that maybe he just doesn't know how to ask for help. If I go over and offer my help, then he'll see that there are people who want to help him and Hettie."

Mamm smiled. "I like that idea."

"*Gut.*" Relief swept through Joanne. "Would you consider sitting with Hettie on Sundays so that Colin can go to youth group?"

Mamm tilted her head. "Do you care for him?"

"Only as a *freind.*" Joanne fingered the edge of her sewing table. "I think he needs to spend time with *freinden*, but he can't even go to youth gatherings because he's afraid to leave Hettie alone."

Mamm patted Joanne's hand. "You're a very thoughtful *maedel.* Of course your *dat* and I would take care of Hettie. Have you suggested the idea to Colin?"

"*Ya*, I did. He didn't think it was necessary, but I thought maybe I could ask him again at church and try to change his mind."

"That's a *wunderbaar* idea. I'm sure Colin would appreciate some time for fun." *Mamm* moved toward the door. "Supper is getting cold. Come down to eat."

Excitement bubbled through Joanne as she followed her mother down the stairs to the kitchen. She couldn't wait to see Colin on Sunday and ask him if he would join her at the youth gathering.

She just hoped he would take her up on her offer.

———◆◆———

"Did I tell you Joanne Lapp is making *mei mammi* a new quilt?" Colin asked Marcus while they sat across from each other in the Riehl family's barn after the church service Sunday afternoon.

Marcus's dark eyebrows lifted. "She is?"

"*Ya.* She and her *schweschder* have come to visit a couple of times so that Joanne could discuss the quilt with me while Becky visited with *mei mammi*." Colin smothered a piece of bread with peanut butter spread.

"That's fantastic. Maybe you'll get some sleep."

"I'm praying she can duplicate the quilt, and it works."

"How did Joanne find out about the quilt?"

"I thought you'd know the answer to that question," Colin quipped, and Marcus looked confused. "You told your *mamm*, your *mamm* told Joanne's *mamm*, and then Joanne came to see me." He folded the bread in half and then took a bite.

"Oh." Marcus hesitated and then grinned. "I guess it all worked out." He popped a pretzel into his mouth.

Colin swallowed and wiped his mouth with a paper napkin. "I'm hoping so. She seems determined to get it right. She was precise about the size of the old quilt, the color of the fabric—all of those details."

"It doesn't hurt that she's *schee*."

"*Ya*, I've noticed."

Marcus grinned. "You like her."

"Not in that way." Colin placed a couple of pieces of salami and cheese on another piece of bread and folded it in half.

"Why not?"

Colin sighed. "My life is too complicated to date right now. It's all I can do to take *gut* care of *mei mammi* and also manage to run the farm."

"That's a shame. She must care for you if she's putting so much effort into the quilt."

"No, I think she's doing it out of pity for *mei mammi*. I can tell she and her *schweschder* feel sorry for *Mammi* by the way they interact with her, which is fine. I feel sorry for her too." Colin glanced down the table just as Joanne approached them with a coffee carafe. "*Shh!* Here she comes."

When Joanne's gaze caught his, he felt a strange stirring in his chest. "Hi, Colin."

He nodded. "Joanne."

"Hi, Joanne." Marcus's smile was a little too bright. "How are you today?"

She smiled as she filled Marcus's cup. "Fine. You?"

"*Gut*. Colin and I are just having a nice conversation here." Marcus grinned at Colin, who shot him a warning look.

"And what are you discussing?" Joanne held her hand out to Colin, and when her hand brushed his as he gave her his cup, his skin tingled at her touch.

"Nothing really," Colin said quickly. "We were just talking about work."

Joanne handed him his cup. "That's nice." She hesitated. "Colin, could I speak with you after lunch?"

"Of course."

"*Danki*. I'll look for you later." Then she moved on down the line to fill more cups.

"She likes you," Marcus sang under his breath.

Colin shook his head. "No, she doesn't."

"But she wants to talk to you after lunch."

"She probably just has a question about the quilt. That's all we ever talk about." Colin looked down the table to where Joanne smiled and served more *kaffi*, and he wondered what it would be like to date her.

Who was he kidding? She would never be interested in him.

Still, the idea of being more than her friend took hold of him, and once again, he felt a rousing in his heart that he'd never felt before.

SIX

Later that afternoon, Joanne hurried out of the kitchen after helping the other women with cleanup. She spotted Colin leaning against a fence post talking to Marcus. He gazed over at her, and when his lips turned up in a smile, her heart thumped against her rib cage.

Colin said something to Marcus, who looked over at Joanne before giving her a wave and strolling toward a group of their mutual friends from youth group.

"*Danki* for waiting for me," Joanne said as she approached Colin.

"It's no problem. I had to wait for *mei mammi*."

"Right." She felt her expression become embarrassed.

"What did you want to discuss?"

"I wanted you to know I started working on the quilt. I'll keep you posted on how it's going."

"Oh. Right." His expression flickered with something that resembled disappointment. "I appreciate it very much."

She bit her lower lip and then squared her shoulders. "Colin, I have a suggestion, although you already said no, but I want to ask again."

"What is it?" His brow pinched.

"I talked to my parents, and they said they would be *froh* to stay with Hettie so that you can come to youth group." When he opened his mouth to respond, she held her hand up. "Please—will you hear me out?"

He looked resigned. "I'm listening."

"We're going to play volleyball today, and you need a break. You work so hard running your farm and caring for Hettie, and you need to be around people your own age. Just come with us. You'll have fun, and my parents will take *gut* care of your *mammi* for the day."

To her surprise, he smiled. "I appreciate your concern, but I don't expect anyone to do that for me."

"But we want to help you."

He looked past her, and she turned to where Hettie spoke with another elderly woman from their congregation.

"Here she comes," Colin said. "I'm going to take her home, but *danki* again for the offer. I hope you enjoy your afternoon."

"I'll stop by soon and give you an update on the quilt."

"I look forward to it." He smiled and then started toward his grandmother.

Joanne waved at Hettie, but disappointment curled through her as her plan to visit with Colin at a youth gathering dissolved.

"What were you and Joanne talking about when I walked out of the barn with Gladys?" *Mammi* asked as Colin guided his horse toward their home.

He kept his eyes focused on the road while trying to think of a believable response. "We were just talking about the weather, and she asked how my week had been. That's all."

Mammi patted his arm. "She fancies you."

"I don't think so." He chuckled. *I should be so blessed!*

"I do." She sang the words.

He needed to change the subject. "How's Gladys doing?"

"Better. She still has problems with her hip, and she said that her knee hurts now. She had another great-grandchild born last week, which means she's up to six now. Oh, how I'd love to have a great-grandchild." *Mammi* grinned at him. "She said she hopes to go visit the new *boppli* next week if her *sohn* agrees to take her out to see the family."

As *Mammi* talked on about her friend's news, Colin gripped the reins and recalled Joanne's conversation and her promise to stop by. He couldn't wait to see her again, and he wondered if they could forge a special friendship that was based on more than the quilt. But was hoping for something more setting him up for disappointment?

———•◆•———

Joanne sat on a hill surrounded by friends at the King family's farm while watching teams play volleyball at the makeshift courts set up on the grass. The bright-blue sky above her was cloudless, and when a cool mid-September breeze moved over her, she breathed in the fresh scent of grass, moist earth, and flowers. It was the perfect day for a youth gathering!

Annie leaned over to Joanne. "Did you invite Colin to come today?"

Before the church service began, Joanne had shared her plan with Annie. "I did, but he turned me down." She bent her knees and hugged them to her chest.

"I'm sorry. I'm sure he appreciated the offer."

"I suppose so." But she doubted it. Maybe Colin considered her offer too forward, and he assumed she was trying to ask him out. She swallowed a groan and cringed at the idea. She didn't need Colin misinterpreting her offer of help and telling other men in the church district that she was desperate for a date.

One of the volleyball games broke up, and when new teams began to form, Annie stood. "Want to play?"

Joanne tented her eyes from the sun as she looked up at her best friend. "No, *danki*. I'm enjoying just watching today."

"Suit yourself." Annie trotted down the hill toward the net, passing a group of friends who made their way up the hill.

Marcus walked over to the group and sat down beside her. Joanne smiled over at him. "How was the game?"

"I'm a little worn-out." He chuckled.

She tilted her head as questions about Colin came to mind. She considered asking Marcus but feared giving him the wrong idea about her feelings for Colin.

On the other hand, Marcus was Colin's best friend. He might have some useful insight.

"Colin told me you're making his *mammi* a quilt," he said.

Joanne angled her body toward him and tried to conceal her delight that Marcus had opened the door to discuss Colin. "*Ya*, that's true. Your *mamm* told *mei mamm* about how Hettie has been suffering, and I felt led to help them."

"He appreciates it."

Warmth swirled in Joanne's chest. "He hasn't been to a youth group gathering in a couple of years, right?"

"*Ya*, that's true." Marcus leaned back on his palms. "He stopped coming after his *dat* died and he felt more responsibility over the farm. He said he was too old for youth gatherings." He snickered. "He acts like he's forty sometimes."

"It's a shame he has so much weighing on him."

"It is, but he also has a tough time asking for help."

"I've noticed that." Joanne picked at a blade of grass and then tossed it.

"What you're doing for him and Hettie is fantastic, and he needs you more than he would care to admit."

Joanne's gaze snapped to his. "You think so?"

"I know so. *Danki* for helping him and Hettie."

"*Gern gschehne.*" She looked out toward the volleyball game.

Lord, help me be a blessing to Colin and Hettie.

———◆———

Colin heard a knock on the door on Friday of the following week. It was the middle of the morning, and he had just

come in from the barn to check on *Mammi*, who was reading in her favorite recliner in the family room.

He pulled the door open and happiness poured through
him when he found Joanne smiling up at him. "Hi, Joanne."

She gave a sheepish expression. "I'm sorry I didn't visit
last week like I promised. Is it okay if I come in?"

He opened the door wide, grateful for the company. "Of
course. How are things at your family's farm?"

"Busy. *Mei mamm* decided we needed to clean out the
attic and the basement last week, and that turned into a
weeklong project. I never realized how many boxes we had
from my grandparents." She pulled a container out of her
tote bag and handed it to him. "I made oatmeal raisin *kichlin* for you and Hettie yesterday. I hope you like them."

"I do. *Danki.*"

"Great." She set her tote bag on a kitchen chair. "Is
Hettie around?"

He nodded toward the family room. "She's reading in
the *schtupp.*"

"Oh." She took a step toward him and lowered her voice.
"I'm making progress on the quilt."

"That's fantastic. *Danki.*" The scent of her flowery sham-
poo filled his senses, and he suddenly felt too close to her.
He took a step back.

"I thought I might visit with Hettie and do some chores
for you since you have so much to do on the farm. *Mei dat*
doesn't stop working until it's time to go to bed, so I know
you're busy."

"Oh, that's not necessary. I don't expect you to—"

"Nope," she cut him off and held her hand up. "I won't

accept no for an answer. I'm here to help." She jammed her thumb toward the family room. "I'll go see how she is and then find something to do around here. Do you need me to sweep or maybe mop?"

Colin examined her pretty face. Joanne seemed much more stubborn than he recalled from when they were in school. Or perhaps he never paid attention to her, which baffled him. He had to have been blind to never have noticed her adorable face with that petite nose and those charming freckles.

"You win." He sighed. "How about mending some clothes for me? *Mammi* can't see well enough to sew anymore, and I honestly don't trust her with scissors. She's had some accidents just washing dishes, so I can't give her anything that's sharp."

"What happened when she did the dishes?"

He shared how his grandmother had cut herself with a knife, scalded herself, and also flooded the kitchen on three separate occasions. "That's why I handle all of the chores now."

Joanne wagged a finger at him. "And that's why you need my help. Where are those shirts and trousers that need mending?"

"I'll get them for you." He started toward his bedroom.

"Would you please find your grandmother's sewing basket too?" she called after him.

Colin located his three torn shirts and two ripped pairs of trousers and then picked up *Mammi*'s sewing basket in the extra room before returning to the family room. Joanne sat on his wing chair across from *Mammi*, and both women smiled at him.

"Colin!" *Mammi* exclaimed. "I'm so delighted we have a visitor today!"

"I am too."

Joanne stood and closed the distance between them while reaching for the shirts, trousers, and sewing basket. "I'll mend these while we visit."

"Danki."

"I'm *froh* to help." She gave him a sweet smile before returning to her chair. Then she set the pile of clothes on the footstool and examined the first shirt until she came to the rip.

"Tell me more about when you were growing up on your *dat*'s farm, Hettie." Joanne opened the sewing basket and located a needle and thread.

"Well, *mei mamm* and I always liked to sew together. Back then, I had near perfect vision. She taught me how to sew and quilt."

Colin lingered in the doorway for a moment while *Mammi* continued talking, and an unfamiliar longing overcame him. He tried to imagine Joanne as a part of his family, interacting with *Mammi* and him daily, but the thought fizzled out as he wondered if he possessed the emotional strength for a relationship. Perhaps having her as a friend would be enough.

He stepped out of the doorway and continued through the kitchen and out the back door toward the barn. Relief swirled through him. For the first time since he'd lost his father, he could focus on his chores without worrying about his grandmother's welfare.

Thank you, God, for Joanne's friendship.

———•◆•———

Joanne mended Colin's clothes while Hettie talked on about her childhood. When Hettie announced she was ready for a nap, Joanne walked her to her bedroom and helped her get settled before carrying Colin's mended clothes into the bedroom next door.

She glanced around the large room with its plain white walls, double bed, two dressers, and empty bookshelf, and she tried to imagine what the house looked like before the fire. Had his former room been just as empty? Had he lost all of his favorite things—perhaps his favorite books or mementos from his beloved parents, such as special letters or birthday cards?

Her chest clutched at the thought of losing all of her special things in a fire. But worse than that, Colin had lost so much over the years—his parents and then his childhood home, and now Hettie was the only family member he had left. Joanne couldn't fathom losing her parents, her sister, *and* her home. Her heart went out to Colin.

She moved to the closet, where she hung up his shirts and trousers, stopping to breathe in the familiar scent of soap, detergent, and something that was uniquely Colin.

Joanne walked to the kitchen, where she glanced around at the breakfast dishes in the sink and the counters that looked as if they hadn't been wiped down in a few days. She peeked behind a nearby door and found the utility room, complete with a wringer washer, dustpan, broom, mop, and other cleaning supplies.

"This is just what I need," she whispered with a smile.

Then she set to work, first washing, drying, and stowing the dishes in the sink before scrubbing the counters and sweeping the floor.

Joanne had just finished dumping the contents of the dustpan in the trash can when Colin walked into the kitchen and gave her a surprised look. "Hettie wanted to take a nap, so I helped her to bed and then looked for some chores I could do for you. I started cleaning, and I got a little carried away. I washed the dishes, cleaned the counters, and swept the floor."

"You didn't have to do that, but I sure do appreciate it."

"I was going to mop too." She pointed to the mop and bucket sitting by the utility room door. "I can do it before I go."

"I wouldn't feel right if you did that. You've already done so much. You gave me peace of mind while I worked outside because I knew *Mammi* was safe. Besides, I'm sure you have more important things to do at home."

"I don't mind." She looked up at him and took in the dark shadows under his eyes, suddenly overcome by a twinge of pity. "I guess the warm milk isn't helping much?"

He shrugged. "Some nights are better than others. Last night was tough, but I think she settles down faster with the milk."

"*Gut.* I'll finish the quilt as quickly as I can."

"Okay." He seemed to study her.

She shifted her weight on her feet. "Well then, if you won't let me mop today, I should really get going." She pointed to the counter, where she'd transferred the remaining cookies into one of his refrigerator jars before putting her container in her tote bag. "I left the *kichlin* there for you."

He took a step toward her. "I really don't know how to properly thank you for all you've done today. I'm feeling at a loss for words right now."

"There's no need to thank me. We take care of one another in our community, right?" She shouldered her tote bag.

"Do you need to call your driver for a ride home?"

"*Ya.*" She started for the door.

"Let me walk you out to the phone."

They strolled out together, making small talk about the farm on their way to the phone, which was located in the barn. He waited outside for her while she called her driver, and then they ambled to the driveway together. While they waited for her ride, she racked her brain for something to say.

"Tell Hettie," she began as he said something at the same time.

They both laughed, and happiness filled her as she enjoyed his attractive smile.

He pointed toward her. "You go first."

"I was just going to ask you to please tell Hettie I said good-bye."

"I will."

Just then her driver's truck motored up the driveway, and she felt a pang of disappointment.

"I'll see you soon," she said.

"I look forward to it."

As she climbed into the truck, she waved at Colin and hoped she was the blessing that he'd needed.

SEVEN

How's Hettie's quilt going?" Lena asked the following Thursday afternoon.

Joanne nodded at her quilting bee friends while they sat together in her family room and stitched their Christmas quilts. "It's coming together well. I think Hettie will be pleased with it."

Excitement bubbled through Joanne. She had stayed up late every night piecing together the quilt, and she could see the progress! While she worked, she prayed for Hettie and Colin, asking God to give them a good night of rest and to help Hettie with her dementia.

"What's that smile for?" Mary Ellen sang. "Are you and Colin getting close?"

Joanne shook her head. "No. Well, I think we're becoming *freinden*. I went to his *haus* last week and helped him with some chores and then we spoke briefly at church. We've never been more than acquaintances until now."

"And that's a start," Becky said. "It could turn into something romantic."

"No, no." Joanne focused her attention on her red and green Lone Star quilt and tried to ignore the flush that flooded her cheeks.

The truth was that he had become important to her. She enjoyed their talks now that she understood why he had been so brusque at first. She admired his work ethic, his kind heart, and how he cared for his grandmother. Not to mention his laugh and his rugged good looks.

Still, she could never imagine that he would care for her in return. Although he had thanked her again for her help with the chores when she saw him on Sunday, he had also declined joining her at youth group again. If he cared for her, he would have allowed her parents to visit with Hettie while he enjoyed an afternoon with her and the other young adults.

On the other hand, he had been really kind to her, and perhaps he finally considered her a friend—maybe even a good friend. That thought made her stomach quiver.

"You need to show everyone how far you've gotten on the quilt." Her sister's suggestion yanked Joanne from her thoughts.

"*Ya*, I will." Joanne sat up straighter. "You can come upstairs to the sewing room before you leave."

"Oh, I can't wait to see it," Barbara Ann said.

Mary Ellen rubbed her hands together. "I bet it's *schee*."

Annie touched Joanne's arm. "I'm sure the quilt will mean a lot to Hettie and Colin."

"*Ya*." Joanne hoped the quilt would be enough to sustain a friendship—and if she was fortunate, maybe something more.

———◆———

A knock sounded on the back door late the following Wednesday afternoon. Colin cupped his hand to his mouth to shield a yawn as he walked through the family room and past *Mammi*, who was napping in her favorite chair.

As he trudged along, he felt as if the weight of the world was pressing down on his shoulders. He'd barely slept last night while his grandmother whimpered for her quilt, and it was all he could do to drag himself through the motions to complete his chores today.

When he opened the door, he felt the muscles in his shoulders relax as Joanne smiled up at him. *"Wie geht's?"*

She held up an aluminum pan. "I brought supper. Do you and Hettie like beef noodle casserole?"

He grinned and leaned against the door. "As a matter of fact, I like any dish that contains beef, and I'm sure *Mammi* would agree."

"Great!" Then her smile wobbled. "But it's after four. Have you already cooked?"

He shook his head. "To be completely honest, I haven't even thought about supper. It's been one of those days."

"Has something happened?" Her pretty face clouded with a frown.

He blew out a deep breath. "We had a bad night last night and then she was confused this morning. She kept calling me Elvin."

"I'm so sorry." She shook her head. "If it's a bad time, I can leave the casserole with you and go."

"No, no." He opened the door wider. "I think company might be just what *mei mammi* needs." *And it's exactly what I need!* "I hope you will stay. Please come in."

She stepped past him into the kitchen and set her tote bag on a kitchen chair before placing the pan on the counter. "May I preheat your oven?"

"Of course." He leaned against the end of the counter as she flipped knobs on the stove. He took in her profile and admired how sunlight streaming through the nearby kitchen window highlighted her adorable freckles and made her brown eyes look like chocolate.

He once again wondered if she had a boyfriend, and longing hit him square in the chest. However, at the last church service, Marcus had mentioned that he'd never witnessed Joanne talking to any of the men at youth group. Colin held on to the hope that Joanne was single, even though he knew in his heart that a young woman wouldn't be interested in a man with so much stress and baggage in his life. Colin would never be able to give Joanne the attention she deserved when his grandmother required so much care.

"I was going to make something for dessert, but I ran out of time. So I stopped by the market on the way here and picked up some *kichlin*." She gave him a tentative smile as she pulled the box from her tote bag and set it on the table.

"*Danki*, but I'm sure they're not nearly as *gut* as yours. However, I'll eat them just the same."

She chuckled. "I doubt mine are better."

"What can I do to help?"

"It will take a little bit for the casserole to warm up. Do you have any chores to finish while I set the table?"

"I do, actually. I had come in to check on *Mammi*, and she's sleeping in the *schtupp*."

"Why don't you finish your chores while I get supper ready? It should be ready in about thirty minutes or so."

"*Danki*," he said, his heart lifting as he rambled through the mudroom and out the back door to the barn.

The mid-October sky was deep blue as he took in the leaves on the trees that had seemed to turn beautiful shades of red, gold, orange, and brown overnight. He breathed in the cool fall air and the scent of a wood-burning fireplace in the distance.

While he loved this time of year, he was even more thankful for his unexpected guest. The Lord had sent Joanne over today just when he needed a friend.

"Thank you, God, for my friendship with Joanne," he whispered as he stepped into the barn. He couldn't wait to finish his work and enjoy supper with Joanne.

———•—

After completing his chores in the barn, Colin hurried back to the house and inhaled the delicious aroma of the casserole when he stepped into the kitchen.

Mammi carried a basket of bread to the table and then grinned over at Colin. "Wait until you try this *appeditlich* casserole Suetta made for us! It's fantastic."

Colin grimaced when *Mammi* called Joanne by her mother's name. He stole a glance over at Joanne standing by the counter holding a pitcher of water, and she graced him with a warm smile and a wink. Thank goodness she wasn't bothered by *Mammi*'s mistake!

Colin moved to the sink and began scrubbing his hands. "I can't wait to try it."

Joanne filled their glasses with water and then they sat down to eat.

Mammi spent their suppertime sharing stories of when she was a girl while they enjoyed the casserole and bread. After supper, they drank coffee and ate cookies before Joanne cleared the table.

"I'll help you clean up," *Mammi* told Joanne as she carried the utensils to the counter.

Joanne shook her head as she set the utensils in the soapy water. "I'll take care of it. Why don't you get your bath?"

Mammi wagged a wrinkled finger at Joanne. "Don't you leave before I get a chance to say good-bye."

Joanne chuckled. "I promise I won't, Hettie."

Mammi seemed satisfied and headed toward the bathroom.

Colin sidled up to her at the sink. "Let me clean up. You did all of the cooking, so it's only fair."

She looked up at him and her eyes seemed to sparkle in the low light shining in through the kitchen window. "How about we both clean up, and then once we're sure Hettie is settled, we can sit on the porch and talk before I leave?"

"That sounds perfect." Colin's heart thudded with delight. "I'll take care of the dishes."

"How about you wipe down the table and sweep?"

He grinned at her bossiness. *"Ya, Mamm."*

She laughed.

They made small talk about the weather while they

worked, and it struck Colin that chores seemed to go so much faster when done alongside good company.

Once the kitchen was spotless and sparkling, Joanne hurried out to the barn to schedule her driver. Meanwhile, Colin helped *Mammi* settle into her chair to read a novel. "Call for me if you need me," he told his grandmother, laying a blanket over her lap.

She peeked at him over her reading glasses. "Where are you going?"

"Joanne and I are going to sit on the porch until her driver comes."

Mammi's grin was mischievous. "Oh, it sounds like it's getting serious. *Gut* for you." She patted his hand.

"No, *Mammi*. It's not like that."

"Oh, but it will be," she sang before opening her book.

He shook his head as he started for the back door.

"I'll be sure to not need you," *Mammi* called after him.

Colin couldn't help but laugh at his mischievous grandmother. How he loved this side of her, along with her great sense of humor. She could always make him laugh, no matter how bleak a situation seemed to be. He kicked the cylinder on the storm door, setting the button to keep it open, then walked out onto the porch just as Joanne climbed the stairs. "Did you reach your driver?"

"I did. He'll be here in an hour."

"Perfect." He motioned toward the porch swing. "Would you like to sit here?"

Her expression was shy. "*Ya*, I would." She sank down onto the swing and then patted the seat beside her. "Join me."

He sat down, and the swing moved under his weight.

When his leg brushed hers, a shiver raced up it. "Supper was fantastic."

"I'm so glad you liked it." She looked out toward the pasture as the sun began to set, painting vibrant streaks of red, orange, and yellow across the sky.

He admired her profile, wondering if she had any idea how effortlessly beautiful she was.

"Hettie was a little confused when she woke up from her nap."

He felt his expression fall. "I'm sorry she called you by your *mamm*'s name."

"Not to worry. I've heard it's best to just let someone with dementia live in their world when they get confused. If I had corrected her, I could have made it worse."

Appreciation whipped over him. "I'm glad she didn't upset you."

"Of course she didn't. I enjoy spending time with her. I understand that Hettie gets confused sometimes, and I'm just glad she recognized *mei mamm* in me." She angled her body toward him. "Does she talk much about the fire? I haven't heard you say much about it . . ."

He stared out toward his small pasture as memories washed over him. "Well, after the lightning hit the roof above the *schtupp*, it all happened so fast. You brought food over when your *dat* came to help rebuild the *haus*, so you saw the damage for yourself. We lost almost everything." He shrugged as if seeing his family's home go up in flames hadn't gutted him.

"Yes, but . . . What was it like being in the house? It must have been terrifying."

He glanced over at her warm expression and felt something inside of him crack open. He trusted her, and he suddenly wanted to tell her everything.

"I heard the thunderclap. It shook the *haus* like a freight train, and it woke me out of a deep sleep. My clock said it was almost two in the morning. Then I smelled the smoke, and I jumped up and ran to *Mammi*'s room. My first thought was to take care of her. I got her out of the *haus* as quick as I could. I couldn't even fathom the thought of losing her. She's my only family—all I have left in this world. Once *Mammi* was safe, I called nine-one-one. It was like a living nightmare." His voice sounded gravelly.

Her eyes were full of a tenderness that almost stole his breath. "I can't imagine."

"The fire department was here in minutes, but the *haus* was just about engulfed in flames by then." He swallowed and turned away from her concerned expression. "They were able to save the back part of the house, but the smoke damage was already done."

He hesitated as his throat thickened. "We lost nearly everything. I was born here, I grew up here, but it's all gone— just like my parents. I had kept some of my parents' favorite things, like *mei mamm*'s Bible, and *mei dat*'s favorite fishing pole, but they were both destroyed. I feel like I've been robbed of more of their memories, you know?"

"How awful, Colin." Her voice was so soft it was barely audible.

He looked out toward the road, afraid that the emotion in her pretty face might break him apart. "*Mammi* and I stayed with one of our neighbors while we waited for our new *haus*. The men in the community built it quickly. It's smaller, but it's just what *Mammi* and I need. And we had more casseroles and groceries than we could eat."

Silence stretched between them.

"If everyone pitched in, then why do you feel like no one helped you?" Her question was soft, tenuous.

He sighed as he faced her again, guilt slithering under his skin. "It wasn't that they didn't help us initially, but it was as if they forgot about us after the *haus* was done."

"Which was when you needed help the most because Hettie's dementia had gotten worse." She finished his thought as if she'd read his mind.

He nodded. "It was as if the fire triggered something in her mind. At night she reverts more and more to a child since we lost the *haus*. She constantly talks about when she was a *maedel* and then she cries and calls me by *mei dat*'s name. Sometimes she calls me by *mei daadi*'s name or *mei* great-*daadi*'s. I think losing the *haus* and the memories it held was too much for her."

"That has to be so difficult for you." She cocked her head, looking as if she were wading through something in her mind.

"What are you thinking?"

She hesitated.

"You can be honest with me."

"When Hettie got worse, did you ask anyone for help?

"No, I didn't share what was going on until I told Marcus, and his *mamm* told your *mamm*."

She smiled. "I'm glad you finally told someone. I'm praying that my quilt helps. I want to be a blessing to Hettie."

You already have been a blessing to us both.

They talked about their friends in the community as the darkness crept in, bringing with it cooler air and the aroma of wood-burning fireplaces.

When headlights bounced off the barn doors, disappointment clutched his chest. Their time together had ended too soon. He wished he could take her home in his buggy, but he couldn't risk leaving *Mammi* home alone.

"Where did the time go?" she asked as she stood. "I need to get my tote bag and say good night to Hettie."

While the truck parked at the top of the driveway, she rushed into the house and then returned a few moments later with her tote bag balanced on her shoulder.

"I enjoyed our visit." She held her hand out to him.

He shook it and once again felt sparks zip up his arm. "I did too. *Danki* for coming over and bringing the *wunderbaar* meal."

"*Gern gschehne.*" She trotted down the stairs, then turned to wave good-bye before climbing into the truck.

Colin leaned forward on the porch railing as the truck motored down the driveway. For the first time since he lost his father, he longed to have a relationship. Specifically, he wanted Joanne in his life. He wanted to call her his girlfriend and possibly even more.

But he knew in his heart such a dream was too much to hope for.

EIGHT

Joanne found her mother and sister sitting at the kitchen table when she got home. They both greeted her with wide grins.

"Did Colin and Hettie like the casserole?" *Mamm* asked as Joanne set her tote bag on a kitchen chair.

Becky patted the chair beside her. "Sit down and tell us everything! How did it go?"

"Calm down." Joanne dropped into the chair. "There's not much to tell. I warmed up the casserole and visited with Hettie. Then Colin and I sat on the porch until it was time for me to come home." She absently drew circles on the faded mahogany wood grain as she recalled how much she enjoyed sitting beside Colin on the porch swing.

For a moment, she had imagined that they were a couple, enjoying each other's company as the sun began to set. She felt comfortable with him, and the conversation seemed to flow easily between them. She was honored that he had opened up to her, sharing his intimate feelings about the fire. He was the first man who had truly warmed her heart, and she craved a meaningful relationship with him. Did he feel the same way about her?

She assumed the answer was no. Tonight would have been the perfect time for him to say he wanted to be more than friends. But as the night wore on, he never broached the subject. She was just an acquaintance to him—a friend who wanted to help him and his grandmother.

"*Was iss letz?*" her sister asked.

"Nothing is wrong." Joanne looked up at her mother's and sister's concerned expressions. "I had a nice time. Hettie was in a great mood, but she was a little confused when she first saw me. She kept calling me Suetta."

Becky shook her head. "*Ach*, that's so *bedauerlich*."

"How did you react when she called you by my name?" *Mamm* asked.

"I just went with it. I didn't want to upset her or confuse her more. We had a really nice supper. Hettie talked about her childhood." Joanne recalled the sweet smiles Colin had shared while they ate, and her heart did a little dance.

Becky leaned forward, her grin back. "What did you talk about on the porch with Colin?"

"Not much." Joanne returned to drawing circles on the table. "I asked him about the fire, and he shared what they went through." She contemplated how he had seemed to open up to her, but still, there was something holding him back. Perhaps she would never be good enough for a man as handsome as he was.

"What's bothering you?" *Mamm* asked.

Becky tapped Joanne's arm. "You care for him."

"*Ya*, I do, but I don't think he likes me that way . . . Anyway, I'm going to work on Hettie's quilt until it's time for bed. We have a lot to do tomorrow since we're hosting the service on Sunday." Joanne pushed her chair back, stood, and lifted her tote bag.

"Wait." *Mamm* held her hand up. "Sit and talk to us. Why don't you think he cares for you?"

Joanne blew out a sigh as she sat down again, letting her tote bag drop to the floor. "He's nice to me, but I feel like he's holding back. I can't explain it. I just don't think he'd ever like me as more than an acquaintance."

"An acquaintance doesn't bring you meals and do your chores." Becky's nose scrunched.

Mamm nodded. "Becky's right."

"Fine. Then I'm more of a *freind*, but that's it." Joanne frowned. "And don't worry—I'll get over it. If I concentrate on finishing Hettie's quilt, then I can do my good deed and move on."

Joanne stood and padded up the stairs to the sewing room, then hung her bag on a hook on the wall before walking over to Hettie's quilt. She was nearly halfway done with it, and her heart sank when she imagined handing it over to Colin. Once the quilt was done, she wouldn't have an excuse to visit him and Hettie. It would likely be the end to her friendship with him too.

She scanned the piles of fabric on her worktable, and her gaze landed on a gray, blue, and green block pattern quilt she had started before the Christmas order rush began. She pulled it out and ran her fingers over it as an idea formed in her head. If she hurried, she could finish this quilt for

Colin as a way to show him how much his friendship meant to her.

Joanne sat down at her sewing table and held the quilt on her lap. Yes, she would complete this quilt after she finished Hettie's—a Christmas gift for Colin! She just prayed he would understand the significance of the quilt. And perhaps he'd feel the emotion that she stitched into it for him.

Colin walked out into the sun Sunday afternoon after attending the service at Joanne's family's barn and then eating lunch with Marcus and the other men. The mid-October sky was clogged with fluffy white clouds as his shoes crunched the leaves peppering the ground.

He glanced over at the cheerful autumn flowers that seemed to smile at him from Suetta's garden as he imagined Joanne helping her mother and sister plant them.

He had a difficult time keeping his eyes from darting over to Joanne during the service. She looked lovely today wearing a bright-pink dress that was the perfect contrast to her dark hair and eyes, and when she graced him with a sweet smile, his heart lifted. He'd hoped to have a moment to talk to her, but she'd been busy delivering the meal and making sure the members of the congregation had what they needed during lunch. Perhaps she'd visit him again this week, and they'd have a chance to talk.

"Colin!"

He turned as Joanne, Becky, and Suetta walked over toward him, each of them carrying an empty serving tray.

Joanne's expression was hopeful as she approached him. "We haven't had a chance to talk today. Would you and Hettie like to stay and visit this afternoon?"

"Oh." Colin pressed his lips together as he considered the offer. "I wouldn't want to impose."

"You wouldn't be imposing," Suetta said.

Becky shook her head. "Not at all. In fact, we insist."

"That's right," Joanne added, lifting her chin.

"Okay." He gave a nervous laugh. "Let me tell *mei mammi.*"

Becky nodded toward the barn. "She's eating now. I just brought food to her table, so I can tell her you're planning to stay."

"Why don't you come inside?" Joanne gestured toward the back door of their house. "You can talk to *mei dat* while we finish the meal and clean up."

"That sounds nice."

Colin walked into the house and found Ezra, Joanne's father, in the family room reading the Amish newspaper, *The Budget,* while sitting in a recliner.

Ezra looked up and smiled at him. "Colin. Have a seat."

"Danki." Colin sank down onto the sofa across from the recliner.

"How's the farm?"

Colin rested his right ankle on his left knee. "Keeping me busy."

Soon he and Ezra fell into an easy conversation about their farms while a flurry of activity sounded from the kitchen. He peeked out toward the doorway leading to the kitchen and spotted Joanne and the other women in the community rushing around. She had changed from her pink church dress to a blue work dress, but she still looked lovely.

For the first time in a long time, Colin felt himself relax while he and Ezra discussed their work. Oh, how he'd missed having these conversations with his father!

After a while, the kitchen noise diminished, and when Colin looked out the window, he spotted a line of buggies heading down the driveway. The congregation members were finally making their way back home.

When Colin heard *Mammi*'s voice in the kitchen, he stood. "Excuse me, Ezra. I need to check on my grandmother."

"Take your time."

Colin walked to the doorway and stopped when he found Hettie sitting at the table with Suetta, drinking a cup of tea.

Joanne stood at the counter, setting serving dishes in the cabinets. She turned and smiled at him. "I was going to make pork chops for our supper. Does that sound *gut*?"

"*Ya*." He nodded. "*Danki*."

"Perfect."

Colin took in the scene as Suetta and *Mammi* talked about recipes, and Joanne and Becky prepared the meal. Suddenly an overwhelming desire squeezed his heart—he longed to be a part of Joanne's family.

Dismissing his thoughts, Colin returned to his seat on the sofa. "So, Ezra, what do you think of the rising cost of diesel? We need it to run our milkers. It's really affecting my profits. How about you?"

"Absolutely," Ezra agreed.

Colin smiled as Ezra continued to talk. He was grateful Joanne, Becky, and Suetta had convinced him to stay.

———◆———

Later that afternoon, Joanne couldn't stop smiling. Oh, how she had enjoyed her time visiting with Hettie and Colin! Not only had Hettie been lucid this afternoon but Joanne had seen Colin enjoying himself while they had eaten an early supper with her family. She cherished the sound of his deep, rich laugh!

Now the kitchen was cleaned, and Colin and *Dat* sat on the porch talking, while Hettie, *Mamm*, and Becky remained at the kitchen table with Joanne and drank tea.

Joanne had hoped to speak to Colin alone to show him the quilt, but she hadn't figured out how to do so without Hettie seeing it too. Since taking him upstairs alone would be inappropriate, she had to find a way to sneak the quilt downstairs.

She rolled the idea around in her head until a solution filled her mind. Then she stood. "Excuse me. I'll be right back."

Joanne hurried up the stairs and folded the quilt into her large tote bag. Then she carried it down to the family room and hid it behind the sofa before stepping out onto the porch, where Colin and *Dat* sat side by side in rocking chairs. The late afternoon temperature had dropped, and she shivered and rubbed her arms as a chill permeated her dress.

Dat turned toward her. "Hi, Joanne. Colin and I were just discussing the weather. It certainly feels like fall."

"It does." Her gaze entangled with Colin's, and his smile sent a jolt to her heart. "I was wondering if I could speak to Colin for a moment."

"Of course," *Dat* said as Colin stood.

"I'll bring him right back," she promised, and *Dat* chuckled.

Joanne and Colin walked into the mudroom and through the kitchen, where *Mamm*, Becky, and Hettie gave them curious looks.

"Is *mei dat* boring you to tears?" she asked when they reached the family room.

"Not at all. I've missed talking to *mei dat* about the business and other issues like that."

"Well, I'm glad to hear it. I'm sure he gets tired of having only women to talk to." She walked over to the sofa. "I wanted to show you something, but I didn't want Hettie to see." She waved him over to her and then peered toward the doorway. Finding it empty, she pulled out the quilt. "Here's the quilt."

Colin gasped as he ran his hand over the quilt top, which had been pieced together with fine stitches. "Joanne. It's perfect." His voice was reverent, sending a chill down her spine. "It's so *schee*."

"I'm glad you like it. I just hope that it works. What if Hettie can tell the difference, and it doesn't help you? I mean—Hettie and you," she added quickly.

"It looks just like it. I'm sure it will work." He met her gaze, and his blue eyes became intense. "I can't thank you enough. Please let me pay you."

"No." She shook her head.

"At least let me pay you for the supplies."

"Please don't trouble yourself. I had most of the fabric already."

To her surprise, he touched her hand, and her skin warmed

at the contact. The air around them felt charged—as if striking a match would cause it to explode.

"Joanne?" *Mamm* asked.

When she found *Mamm* in the doorway to the family room, Joanne jumped and stepped away from Colin, her hand suddenly cold. *"Ya?"*

Mamm looked curious as she walked over to them. "Are you showing him the quilt?" She craned her neck over her shoulder and glanced at the doorway before touching the quilt. "Isn't it gorgeous?" she asked Colin.

"It is," Colin agreed before looking at Joanne once again. *"Mei mammi* is going to love it."

"I hope so," Joanne said.

Mamm turned toward Joanne. "Why don't you take the quilt back upstairs while I get out that apple pie you made yesterday? I'll warm it up, and we can serve it with vanilla ice cream."

"That sounds amazing," Colin said.

Joanne slipped the quilt back into the tote bag and started up toward the sewing room. As she stowed the quilt, her shoulders sank. Her excuse for visiting Colin and Hettie would soon come to an end.

She hoped she wouldn't lose Colin's friendship when she gave him the quilt. If so, then her heart would surely break.

———— ◆ ————

"Danki for a *wunderbaar* visit," Colin told Suetta and Ezra as he stood on the porch with *Mammi*, Joanne, and her family later in the afternoon.

Ezra shook Colin's hand. "We're so glad you could spend time with us."

"You're welcome here anytime," Suetta said before sharing a look with Joanne, who seemed embarrassed.

"You all have a nice evening. *Danki* for the *wunderbaar* food and fellowship." *Mammi* shook hands with Joanne's parents and then gripped the railing as she started slowly down the porch steps. "Let's go, Colin. It's getting late."

Joanne laughed as Colin shook his head. "She's the boss."

"That she is." Colin held his hand out to Joanne, and she took it. He held on to her hand a moment too long before releasing it. "Have a *gut* evening."

"You too. Be safe going home," she told him.

Colin jogged down the steps and toward his waiting horse and buggy, which he had hitched up before saying good-bye. He opened the passenger door and helped *Mammi* in before waving to the Lapp family once more. Then he climbed into the driver's side and guided the horse toward the road.

"I had a great time," *Mammi* announced. "That Lapp family is so funny."

Colin grinned as he recalled Joanne's beautiful smile. "They're a joy to be around."

"You should marry Joanne."

Colin guffawed. "She's not even my girlfriend."

"Well, she should be. You're not getting any younger, Colin James. You need to propose to her now. I mean it when I say I expect to see some great-grandchildren before I die."

"It's not that simple. I need to have time to cultivate a

relationship with a *maedel* before I can propose. Right now, I don't have that kind of time."

Mammi's smile wobbled. "I'm sorry I'm such a burden to you."

"You're not a burden to me, *Mammi*. I love you, and you're my family." Colin reached over and placed his hand on hers. "You took care of me after *mei mamm* died, and I'm grateful the Lord has allowed me to care for you. You're my best friend. I'm so grateful that you raised me, and it's my honor to be here for you. I'm so thankful to have you in my life, and I hope to have many more years with you."

Mammi sniffed, then patted his hand. "You still need a *fraa*."

Colin chuckled and shook his head, even though having a special *maedel* to share his life with was his heart's greatest desire.

NINE

A month later, Joanne shivered as she walked up Colin's driveway on Wednesday evening with Hettie's finished quilt in her arms. Her driver's truck sat near the top of the driveway, the engine humming. The cold November air whipped over her, sending the ties to her prayer *kapp* fluttering behind her while she made her way toward his back porch.

During the past month, Joanne had visited Colin and Hettie once every week to help with chores. She had also spoken to him at church services, but she had been disappointed that their relationship had not seemed to progress. While they talked about their lives and even shared some personal stories with each other, Colin hadn't made any effort to move beyond friendship. And to make matters even worse, Joanne had realized that she loved him.

Since the Christmas Bazaar had been last week, Joanne had turned her attention to working on Hettie's quilt, along with helping Becky create their Christmas cards and starting to make her list of gifts she needed to buy since Christmas was a little more than a month away.

After finishing Hettie's quilt earlier in the afternoon, she had felt a peculiar sadness overtake her. The end of the project would mark the end of her regular visits, and since Colin didn't seem eager to date her, she decided it was time to move on. She was twenty-five and wanted to get married and have a family someday. Pinning her hopes on Colin was breaking her heart when it was clear he didn't care for her as more than a friend.

She reached the back door and knocked before hugging the large, black garbage bag that held the quilt against her chest.

The back door opened, and Colin stepped out onto the porch, his smile wide. "Joanne. Hi."

She held out the bag. "I finished the quilt for Hettie. I thought you might want to try it tonight. Maybe you'll finally be able to get some *gut* sleep."

He took the bag from her and peeked inside. "*Danki*, Joanne. You don't understand how this will change my life if it works. She's cried every night since Sunday." He pointed toward the kitchen. "I was just putting on a roast. Would you like to join us for supper?"

"No, *danki*. I need to get home. Becky and I are working on our Christmas cards. She decided we should make them this year, and we have a long list of addressees."

"Oh." His expression clouded. "Are you sure you don't have an hour to spare?"

Sadness swirled in her chest. "I'm sorry, but I don't. I hope the quilt blesses you and Hettie. I enjoyed making it."

He swallowed as he stared at her, looking as if he had pieces of words in his mouth that he was trying to fit together.

She held her breath. *Tell me you love me. Tell me you want to see me even though I'm done with the quilt. Tell me you want to be more than my friend.*

"Have a *gut* evening," he finally said.

Joanne took a step away from him as gloom settled in the pit of her stomach. "You too."

Then she rushed down the stairs, her heart breaking with each step, before climbing into the passenger seat of the truck. As her driver backed down the driveway, Joanne stared at her lap and hugged her arms to her chest, feeling heavy, hollowed out by Colin's lack of care.

———— ◆ ————

Later that evening, Colin walked into *Mammi*'s room and found her sitting on her bed. "I have something for you."

"What's that?"

He pulled the quilt out of the bag and handed it to her. Then he held his breath. *Please, Lord, let* Mammi *accept this quilt.*

Mammi gasped as tears sparkled in her eyes. "You found my quilt!"

He released the breath he'd been holding as *Mammi* hugged the quilt to her chest, her lips turned up in a smile.

His heart turned over in his chest. *Thank you, God!*

She snuggled down onto the bed.

"Would you like me to cover you?" he offered.

"*Ya*, please."

He spread the beautiful hand-sewn quilt over her and then turned off the lantern by her bed before flipping on his flashlight. "Sleep well, *Mammi*."

"You too," she called after him.

Colin padded into his room and sat down on the edge of the bed. He stilled, waiting for *Mammi* to start crying; however, the house remained silent.

"You did it, Joanne," he whispered into the night air as warmth surged through him.

Crawling into bed, he switched off his flashlight and settled down under his covers. He rested his forearm on his brow and stared up through the darkness toward the ceiling as Joanne's beautiful face filled his mind.

He had enjoyed their time together during the past month, as he'd found himself growing more and more attached to her. For the first time in his life, he realized he was in love—and he didn't know what to do about it.

Mammi's suggestion of asking Joanne to be his girlfriend had floated through his mind each time he saw her, but fear kept him frozen in place. Today when she'd handed him the quilt, he once again longed to ask her if she'd ever consider being more than his friend—but he couldn't find the courage to form the words.

You're a coward, Colin.

He groaned and closed his eyes.

"Lord, I'm in love with Joanne," he whispered. "Please give me the strength to ask her how she feels about me. Help me find the words to ask her to be my girlfriend. And if she rejects me, please heal my heart—and help me find joy again in places you see fit."

He rolled over to his side and listened, waiting to hear *Mammi* cry out. When the house remained quiet, he smiled, opening his heart to God once again. "Thank you, Lord, for bringing Joanne into my life. Now please help me keep her in it."

———•◆•———

Mamm stepped into the doorway of the sewing room that same evening. "Joanne, it's after eleven. Why are you still up?"

Joanne looked up from the quilt she'd been stitching. "*Ach* no! Did I wake you?"

"No." *Mamm* sat down on the chair beside her. "I went to the bathroom and saw the lantern on in here. I thought maybe you'd left it on." She seemed to study Joanne. "You hardly said a word at supper, and you rushed up here after we cleaned up the dishes. Are you okay?"

Joanne shook her head as her throat suddenly felt thick.

"*Ach, mei liewe.* What is it?"

"I'm in love with him, and it's obvious he doesn't feel the same way about me."

"Colin?"

Joanne nodded and sniffed as she ran her fingers over the quilt she'd been finishing for him. "When I went to give him the quilt, I thought maybe he'd finally tell me he cared for me, but he didn't. Now that I've given him Hettie's quilt, he has no reason to see me. I'll just be an acquaintance who sees him at church every other week, and that's going to hurt. So now I'm trying to figure out how to mend my heart."

"I'm so sorry." *Mamm* rubbed her shoulder. "He and

Hettie seemed to have such a *gut* time with us when they visited after church last month. How do you know he doesn't care for you?"

"If he cared for me, then he would have told me by now. He would have asked *Dat* for permission to date me." She paused. "Has he asked *Dat* to see me?"

"Not that I know of." *Mamm* sighed. "I know it hurts when you love someone who doesn't love you back, but you're young. God has the perfect plan for you. You just have to be patient and wait for his perfect timing."

Joanne yanked a tissue from a nearby box and wiped her eyes and nose. "I know you're right, *Mamm*. But I'm going to miss Colin and Hettie. They both have become important to me."

Mamm touched the quilt. "This is so *schee*. Are you going to sell it?"

"I had started it a while ago and planned to sell it. Then I decided to finish it for Colin." Joanne's eyes filled with tears. "I feel led to give it to him, even though he doesn't seem to share my feelings."

Mamm's expression was hopeful. "Maybe if you give him the quilt, he'll understand the heart you have for him. What if he cares for you, but he's afraid you don't care for him in return?"

Joanne snorted. "Isn't it obvious how I feel? I've made time to help him and Hettie, and I also made her the quilt."

"But what if Colin has the same insecurities you do? What if he's afraid you could never love him?"

The thought settled over Joanne's heart, and a tiny seed of hope began to grow. "Maybe it wouldn't hurt to try."

Mamm pointed to the clock on the wall. "It's late. Why don't you finish up tomorrow?"

"I'm almost done. I won't be long."

Mamm smiled and stood. *"Gut nacht."*

"Gut nacht."

After her mother left, Joanne turned her focus back to the quilt—and the hope that perhaps one more act of kindness would truly demonstrate her love.

———•◆•———

Colin wiped his sweaty hands on his trouser legs as he climbed the Lapps' porch steps the following afternoon. He cleared his throat and tried his best to remember the speech he'd practiced on his way over to the farm. He stepped toward the door just as it opened, and Joanne stepped out, a look of shock overtaking her face as she walked toward him on the porch.

"Wh-What are you doing here?" She adjusted the large bag on her shoulder.

"I came to talk to you."

She looked past him toward his driver's van. "Is Hettie home alone?"

"No. She's waiting in the van."

"How funny . . . I was coming to see you too. I was just about to call the driver." Her expression became expectant. "What did you want to talk about?"

He heaved out a trembly breath and swallowed. *Guide my words, Lord.*

"After the fire," he began, "I felt alone, and I lost faith in my community. But then you came to see me and offered your help. You changed everything with your kindness, Joanne. You made me realize that I had closed myself off from everyone and expected people to ignore *mei mammi* and me. The truth was that I was too focused on what was wrong with my life to see what was right. And you were right to point out that I had never asked for help. I was too concerned with myself to consider that other people had no idea what I was going through."

He took her hands in his and her face flickered with surprise. "What I'm trying to say is that you brought happiness and joy back into my life. You're so kind and talented and lovely, and I have no idea how to express to you just how important you've become to me. I can't stop thinking about you. In fact . . . I'm pretty sure I'm in love with you, Joanne."

She gasped and tears sparkled in her eyes.

"I've loved you for a while, but I was afraid to tell you because I didn't think you'd ever want to get involved with me."

"Why would you think that?" her eyes searched his.

"My life is complicated because *mei mammi* needs a lot of care. If you dated me, you'd wind up helping me care for her."

"I love Hettie and enjoy spending time with her. Besides, being with her reminds me of my own *mammi*. I would love to help care for her, especially if it meant having more time with you."

He felt his back and shoulders relax. "Does that mean you'd consider dating me? I need to speak to your *dat*, but—"

"I thought you'd never ask," she said, smiling through tears. "*Ich liebe dich*, Colin, but I was afraid you'd never see me as more than a *freind*. I was on my way over to give you this in hopes that you'd realize just how much I love you."

She released her hands from his and let the tote bag drop from her shoulder. Then she handed him the bag. When he opened it, he drew in a sharp breath as he took in the gorgeous quilt.

"You made this for me?" His voice came out in a rasp.

"*Ya*, I stayed up late last night finishing it."

"I-I don't deserve this."

"You do." She cupped her hand to his cheek. "You've made me *froh* too."

"I'm sorry it took me so long to find the courage to tell you how I feel."

"Please don't apologize. God's timing is perfect." She pointed toward the house. "Why don't you and Hettie come in, and you can talk to my father?"

He smiled as excitement flowed through him. "I'd consider it an honor."

———— • ◆ • ————

"Are you warm enough?" Colin asked Joanne as they sat together on a glider on her back porch later that evening while her parents, Becky, and Hettie visited in the kitchen.

She hugged her coat closer to her body. "I am. You?"

"*Ya*." He threaded his warm fingers with hers. "*Danki* for inviting *Mammi* and me to stay for supper. That fried chicken was *appeditlich*."

"I'm glad we had enough and that you and Hettie could join us."

"So, I talked to your *dat* while you cleaned up the kitchen."

"And?" Her pulse fluttered.

"And I have a question for you." He angled his body toward her. "Would you consider being my girlfriend?"

"I thought you'd never ask." Happiness bubbled through her.

"Is that a yes?"

"Of course it is."

"I've never been so happy in my life," he said as he ran his finger down her jaw, the sensation sending chills down her spine.

He leaned over, and when his lips brushed hers, she closed her eyes, savoring the feel of his mouth against hers and losing track of everything. She felt as if she were floating as she kissed the love of her life.

When he pulled away, she rested her head on his shoulder.

"*Ich liebe dich*, Joanne," he said, his voice sounding thick.

She looked up at him. "I love you too."

As they both gazed out toward the setting sun, Joanne thanked God in her heart for making something beautiful out of this special, once-in-a-lifetime friendship.

EPILOGUE

*F*rehlicher Grischtdaag!" Hettie announced as she and Colin walked into Joanne's kitchen on Christmas Day.

"Merry Christmas," Joanne responded as Colin walked over to her.

Hettie walked over to the counter and handed *Mamm* a portable pie plate. "Colin and I made a pumpkin pie last night."

"How nice," *Mamm* said.

Joanne pointed to the table, which was ready for six. "You're right on time. Becky and I just finished setting out the food."

Colin threaded his fingers with Joanne's. "Will you sit next to me?"

"I'd love to."

Joanne's heart lifted as she and Colin sat together across from Becky and Hettie. She glanced at her parents at either end of the table and then she looked beside her and took in Colin's handsome face. Oh, how blessed she was to have Colin and Hettie join her family for Christmas!

Joanne bowed her head in silent prayer and thanked God for all of her blessings during the past month as she and Colin fell into a routine. Not only did Colin and Hettie join them for supper two or three times per week, but Joanne and Becky went to visit them and help with chores as well.

Becky and Joanne had helped Hettie write her Christmas cards and decorate their house with greenery and a poinsettia. They also invited Colin and Hettie to join them for Thanksgiving dinner. Hettie and Colin had become a part of their family, and Joanne had never been happier.

She just hoped that someday soon Colin might ask her to be his wife. Her stomach fluttered at the thought of living with him and Hettie on their farm and spending the rest of her life by his side.

When her father shifted in his chair, Joanne looked up and breathed in the delicious scent of the bountiful Christmas meal she, her sister, and her mother had prepared—the roasted turkey, stuffing, mashed potatoes, green beans, and salad.

Soon the sounds of utensils scraping the plates and murmurs of conversations filled the kitchen as everyone began talking at once, sharing stories and laughing.

After supper, Joanne, Becky, and *Mamm* cleaned up the kitchen, while Colin, *Dat*, and Hettie sat in the family room. Joanne had just set a clean tray in the cabinet when she felt a hand on her back.

"Could I please speak to you for a moment in private?" Colin's voice was husky in her ear and sent a shiver trilling along her spine.

Joanne turned toward her mother, who smiled and nodded. "*Ya.* Let's go into the mudroom," Joanne answered him.

She followed him to the mudroom, and her heartbeat ticked up as his expression became serious. "Is everything all right, Colin?"

"*Ya*, it is. In fact, it's perfect." He pressed his lips together as if gathering his thoughts. "Joanne, you are the greatest blessing in my life, and ever since I told you I love you, I haven't been able to stop thinking about our future together."

He took a deep breath. "I've been racking my brain for the perfect gift for you this Christmas, and I realized that there are two things I want to give you. The first is this." He took her hand in his and then laid it flat against his chest. "My heart. You've had my heart ever since the day you came to visit me and told me that you wanted to help me and *mei mammi*. It's only right that I tell you it's yours."

She sniffed as her eyes stung with tears.

"You made me realize that I had built a wall around myself after losing my parents and my home, and you brought my heart back to life."

"Oh, Colin." She cupped her hand to his cheek.

"I'm not done." He paused for a moment. "You, your parents, and Becky have become important to *mei mammi* and me. You're our family, and I'd like to make that official. So, I asked your father's permission for the second part of my gift." He took a deep breath. "Joanne, I love you with all my heart and my soul. Will you marry me?"

"Yes, yes! Of course I will!" She launched herself into his arms with a dizzying happiness.

He brushed his lips over hers, sending electric pulses singing through her. When he pulled away, her lips tingled from his touch. "I'm so grateful God used *mei mammi*'s quilt to bring us together."

"I am too. That quilt represents how much you mean to me. It's a patchwork of promises from me to you. I promise to stand by your side and love you for the rest of my life."

"I promise to do the same for you." He ran his finger down her cheek, making her feel momentarily light-headed. "This is the best Christmas ever."

"*Ya*, it is."

As he hugged her, she closed her eyes and looked forward to what God had in store for their future.

ACKNOWLEDGMENTS

As always, I'm grateful for my loving family, including my mother, Lola Goebelbecker; my husband, Joe; and my sons, Zac and Matt.

Thank you to my mother and my dear friend Maggie Halpin, who graciously read the draft of this book to check for typos.

I'm also grateful for my special Amish friend, who patiently shares stories and answers my questions about her community.

Thank you to my wonderful church family at Morning Star Lutheran in Matthews, North Carolina, for your encouragement, prayers, love, and friendship. You all mean so much to my family and me.

Thank you to Zac Weikal and the fabulous members of my Bookworm Bunch! I'm so grateful for your friendship and your excitement about my books. You all are awesome!

To my agent, Natasha Kern—I can't thank you enough for your guidance, advice, and friendship. You are a tremendous blessing in my life.

Thank you to my amazing editor, Jocelyn Bailey, for your

friendship and guidance. I'm grateful to each and every person at HarperCollins Christian Publishing who helped make this book a reality.

Thank you to editor Becky Philpott for polishing the story and connecting the dots. I'm so grateful that we are working together again!

Thank you most of all to God—for giving me the inspiration and the words to glorify you. I'm grateful and humbled you've chosen this path for me.

DISCUSSION QUESTIONS

1. Joanne is determined to help Colin and Hettie after she hears about Hettie's trouble sleeping. Why do you think Joanne felt led to make the quilt?
2. Colin is convinced the community forgot about him and his grandmother after they rebuilt their house. Do you think he was right to feel abandoned?
3. Hettie suffers from dementia. Have you ever known anyone who suffered with that disease?
4. Colin is afraid Joanne would never love him because he has his hands full caring for his grandmother. Do you think his feelings are valid?
5. Which character can you identify with the most?
6. Which character seemed to carry the most emotional stake in the story? Was it Joanne, Colin, or someone else?

A Common
Thread

———◆———

KATHLEEN FULLER

To James. I love you.

ONE

That couldn't be him . . . could it?

Butterflies danced in Susie Glick's stomach as she watched the man search for an empty seat on the crowded bus. She tried not to stare at him. For some reason, he reminded her of Alex Lehman. And that was why this man couldn't be someone she recognized. Alex had left their Middlefield community a little over two years ago. Two years and three months, to be exact. He had wanted to travel the US, and everyone assumed he would never come back home, including her.

She dared another glance, then stared at her lap, the butterflies now crashing into one another. Whoever this man was, he made her feel the way she used to when she was around Alex. How confusing. She'd thought she'd gotten over him.

But did anyone really ever get over their first love?

"Mind if I sit here?"

Her head jerked up, and she met his gaze. His eyes were the same honeyed brown color as Alex's, and so was his

117

auburn hair. But that's where the similarities ended. This man looked like he'd lived in the wilderness for the past decade. He wore a plain white T-shirt and faded blue jeans, a far cry from broadfall pants and an Amish shirt. His long hair hung past his shoulders, the sides pulled behind his ears. He also had a full russet beard and mustache, and his skin was golden tan, as if he'd spent years out in the sun.

Although she rarely gave Yankee men a passing glance, she couldn't ignore this handsome one, and her heartbeat kicked into overdrive knowing he wanted to sit next to her. Then she remembered there wasn't another empty seat on the bus, and that tempered her emotions. It also made more sense. Good-looking men—or men in general—didn't just plop themselves down next to Susie for no reason, especially in public. Her Amish clothing and shy demeanor usually kept them away, and normally she was fine with that.

"*Hallo?*"

He spoke Amish? That was a surprise.

"Are you saving this seat for someone?"

She was still caught off guard by his Amish greeting and couldn't find the words to respond.

He looked around the bus. "I guess they overbooked the trip," he mumbled.

His comment made her realize she hadn't answered him, and when he looked at her again, she nodded and quickly pointed to the empty seat.

"*Danki.*" He smiled and sat down as the driver shut the door and shifted the bus into gear. He set his backpack underneath the seat in front of him. "For a second there I was worried I'd have to get off the bus and wait for the next one." He turned to her. "I'm running late as it is—" He stopped short and his eyes grew wide. "Susie?" Before she could say anything he added, "Wow, what a small world. Remember me? Alex Lehman?"

She could barely breathe. It really was Alex. *And he's sitting next to me!* She almost laughed at the idea that she wouldn't remember him. She had never forgotten.

Her mouth felt like she'd gargled with sawdust. He was still looking at her, as if waiting for her to reply. But she couldn't find her words. Any words would do, but her lips wouldn't move.

Then his brow started to furrow, a look she recognized and not just from him. She was waiting too long to respond to a simple question, something that happened to her when she was nervous. Alex wasn't just making her nervous. She was also giddy in a way she hadn't been since she last saw him before he left Middlefield. Not a good combination. Attempting to act nonchalant, she gave him a quick nod, then turned to look out the window as if the bus station was the most interesting place she'd ever seen.

"Uh, Susie? You've got something on the back of your *kapp*."

Surprise overcoming her nerves, she touched the back of her white prayer *kapp* . . . and felt something sticky on the fabric. When she looked at her fingers, she gasped. Oh no. They were covered in melted chocolate.

Alex frowned. "Lean forward." When she complied, he said, "Great. Some kid must have wiped his fingers on the back of the seat during the last ride. Let's just be glad it's only chocolate and not something worse." He grinned.

But Susie didn't return his smile. She had leaned back against the seat when she first got on the bus, exhausted from her two-day trip to Berlin, and hadn't thought to look at her seat to see if there was anything on it. Didn't bus drivers wipe down the seats between stops anyway? Apparently not this driver. She opened her purse and took out a handkerchief and wiped her fingers, but what was she supposed to do about her *kapp*? How could she walk around with a big brown splotch on the back of her head? She also couldn't take the *kapp* off. An Amish woman's head must always remain covered, especially in public.

As she tried to figure out what to do, she turned to wipe the chocolate off the back of the headrest. The bus suddenly lurched forward, and she fell against Alex, almost landing in his lap.

"You okay?" He put his hands on her shoulders, then helped her back to her side of the seat.

"Sorry," she squeaked out. Here she was sitting next to her teenage crush, a man she never expected to see again, her *kapp* and her dignity in ruins. She couldn't be making a worse impression.

"*Nee* worries." He smiled again.

She nearly melted in the seat, her attraction to him growing stronger. She was glad to see he hadn't changed. He had always been in a good mood, always smiling, and always ready to help someone in need. Those qualities and more were why she had fallen for him when she was sixteen, even though he was five years older than her and one of her brother Ben's friends. His good looks were a bonus.

Ach, she had to get it together. They had a two-hour-plus

bus ride to Ashtabula, and they hadn't even left the station lot yet. She needed to focus on the problem at hand—her chocolate-stained head covering. *Never mind* mei *racing heart*. She tried to rub out the spot again, a difficult task since she couldn't take off the *kapp* and see what she was doing.

Alex picked up his backpack and unzipped the front pocket. Then he pulled out a bright-red handkerchief. "You can use this. Don't worry, it's clean."

She wasn't worried about whether the handkerchief was clean or not. She marveled that he knew exactly what she needed—a hair covering, or else she would have had to wear her chocolate-stained *kapp* all the way home to Middlefield. Then again, he did have seven older sisters, so she shouldn't be that surprised that he'd thought about offering her his handkerchief.

"*Danki*," she said, taking the handkerchief from him. He was rummaging in his backpack for something else while she slipped down in the seat, quickly pulled the clips from her *kapp*, and then removed it. She glanced at the back of the *kapp*. Ugh. The spot definitely could be confused for something else other than chocolate. Grateful he'd given her the kerchief, she tied it over her hair, getting a whiff of the outdoors from the red cotton fabric. As she sat back up and settled into her seat, the full force of what just happened hit her. *I'm wearing his handkerchief. I'm wearing Alex Lehman's handkerchief.* She couldn't keep from smiling.

"Glad *yer* taking this so well." He handed her a small bottle of hand sanitizer, which was what he must have been searching for in his backpack while she attended to her head covering. "Martha would have flipped out if her *kapp* had been messed up like that."

He sounded more English than Amish, and she didn't mind as she squirted some in her palm. She didn't mind anything about Alex, other than the fact he had left Middlefield so long ago and hadn't been back for even a visit. She did know that he was still in touch with his family, as their mothers were friends.

Then she realized something. Maybe he wasn't returning to Middlefield. He hadn't said where he was going, and there were several bus stops on the way to Ashtabula. He could get off at any one of them and disappear . . . like he had two years ago.

"You should probably rub that sanitizer into your hands," he said, his smooth voice diving into her train of thought.

Blinking, she looked down at the glob of sanitizer in her left hand. "Oh. Right." She handed him the small bottle and quickly rubbed her hands together until her palms started to heat.

Alex put the sanitizer back into his backpack. He started to lean against the back of his seat, then stopped. He did a quick check of his headrest, which was clean, and he sat back, relaxed. "How crazy is it seeing you here after all this time," he said, turning his head toward her.

"*Ya.*" Why couldn't she speak more than one-word sentences?

"Ah, Susannah Glick. Still quiet as always."

Her cheeks heated. He had noticed that about her? He had *noticed* her? She didn't think that was possible, considering their age gap. When he left, he'd been twenty-one years old at the time—a real man in her eyes. But now that she was this close to him, she could see there was a difference. He had changed, at least physically, and even through the wild hair and full beard she could see that he had matured. "Now this is a man."

"Excuse me?"

Oh nee. Had she really said that out loud? *What is wrong with me?* She tried to come up with something that wasn't as embarrassing as her previous statement. "I—I can't wait to see *mei mamm*," she blurted, then wished she could disappear into the bus seat. Way to sound like a mature woman. For sure he thought she was *ab im kopp* by now.

But his expression grew serious. "Me too. To see *mei mamm*, I mean. It's been a while since I've seen her."

His words made her forget her embarrassment. "You're going to Middlefield?"

He nodded. "*Ya.* I've been away long enough."

A warm feeling of joy came over her. She'd been right all along. After two long years. Alex Lehman was coming home.

———— •◆• ————

Alex didn't believe in luck, so the fact he was sitting next to Susie Glick on the final leg of his return to Middlefield had to be providential. When he'd jumped on the bus at the very last minute, he hadn't realized how full it was, and when he saw that the only empty seat on the bus was next to an Amish woman, he wasn't thrilled. He looked like a disheveled mess since he'd lost the one ponytail holder he left somewhere between his hotel room and the bus station. Even though he'd given his hair and beard a quick brush before he hopped on the bus, he didn't want to make the young woman nervous when he sat next to her. Then he'd realized it was Susie, and he said a short silent prayer of thanks that he would be sitting next to someone he knew from home.

He glanced at her again, their conversation screeching to a halt when he told her he was coming back to Middlefield. He wasn't surprised they had stopped talking. Susie had always been a shy, cute girl, and he could see that hadn't changed. Well, the shyness hadn't. But she wasn't a cute girl anymore. She was downright pretty, with the biggest, softest brown eyes he'd ever seen. The round cheeks she used to have had thinned out a little but were still as rosy as he remembered. Odd, he hadn't paid any attention to Susie when she was a teenager, but he could barely keep his eyes off her now. Hopefully, she hadn't noticed.

"Susie?" That name suited a kid. She wasn't a kid anymore.

"*Ya?*"

"How are things back home?" The question was only partly necessary. He knew a lot about his community, thanks to regular correspondence with his mother—mostly phone calls. They never talked long, since idle chitchat was frowned upon, and even though he wasn't Amish, he respected her adherence to the faith. He also made sure to send lots of postcards to his sisters and their kids during his travels around the country. There were times when he had stayed in one place long enough to have an address, and then he would exchange letters. Because of his commitment to keeping in touch, he had been kept in the loop. But it would be nice to get another perspective.

Susie looked at her lap and fiddled with the hem of one of the long sleeves of her light-green dress. "Things are *gut*." She didn't look at him.

"Just *gut*?"

Her gaze jumped to his for a split second, then she fixed her eyes on her sleeve again. "*Nix* has changed much lately."

But you have. Oh boy. This wasn't good. What was he doing thinking about Susie—Susannah—Glick like this, and after all these years? His nerves must be getting the best of him. Even though his parents had remained understanding about his need to travel before he joined the church, that didn't mean he wasn't anxious about coming back. So anxious he hadn't told them about his arrival. Partly because he wanted to surprise them, and partly because he needed a little more time to get himself together. Once he stepped into his parents' home, there was no turning back. He had made the mental commitment to join the church, and he was determined to see it through.

Still, there was a tiny part of him that held back. Not from being baptized, but from facing the rest of the community, who he was 100 percent sure weren't going to be as understanding as his parents. That was the one thing he dreaded. While he'd kept in touch with his parents, he hadn't done the same with his friends, and he wasn't sure how they would react after not hearing from him for so long. Ben was one of those friends. "How's your *bruder* doing?"

"Okay. He's married."

"To Priscilla Mast?"

"*Nee*. He married a woman from Lancaster."

He was a little surprised Ben hadn't married Priscilla, the girl he was dating when Alex left. But as long as he was happy, that's what mattered. "Is he still living in Middlefield?"

"*Ya*. One street over."

Getting information out of her was like trying to open a locked door without a key, but he didn't have a problem being patient with her. He also didn't blame her for being guarded with him. Leaving for two years was unusual to say the least.

"How long are you visiting Middlefield?" she suddenly asked.

Glad that she finally asked him a question, he quickly answered, "Permanently."

Susie's large eyes grew even wider, something he didn't think was possible. "You're staying for *gut*?"

"*Ya*." The hum of the bus and the low chatter of the rest of the passengers faded away as he continued to talk to her. "I'm joining the church in two weeks. I already talked to the bishop about it."

"That's wonderful. I know *yer mamm* and *daed* will be so happy." She smiled.

Had she always had such a pretty smile? He settled his emotions and cleared his throat. "I hope so."

The smile disappeared. "You haven't told them yet? Don't they know you're coming?"

He shook his head, wondering for the dozenth time if he had made the right decision not to tell his folks. "I wanted to surprise them," he said, feeling the need to explain. "I'm staying at a bed-and-breakfast close by on Route 86 for a couple of days. I have to get some Amish clothes and get rid of all this." He gestured to his hair and beard. "I can't show up looking like a hermit."

"That wouldn't be a *gut* idea." She looked at his hair. "When was the last time you cut it?"

"Almost two years ago. I think it was when I was in Montana."

"You went all the way to Montana?"

"I went all the way to Alaska."

Excitement sparked in her eyes. "Oh, how was Alaska? Is it as cold as everyone says it is? Did you see a bear?"

He almost laughed. Her enthusiasm was genuine, and her shyness had disappeared. He didn't want her to turn silent again, and she would surely do so if she thought he was making fun of her. He remembered she could be sensitive. "*Ya*, it was cold. *Nee*, I didn't see a bear, thank goodness. Although it was a possibility when I was camping outside Fairbanks."

"Where else have you been?"

The bus ride flew by as he told her about his adventures traveling the fifty states, which had been his dream since he was a young child. "I would spend hours looking at travel books at the library," he said, explaining what had started off his interest. "Fortunately *Mamm* and *Daed* were supportive."

"They didn't mind you leaving and not joining the church?"

"*Ya*, they did mind, but they also knew they couldn't stop me. It helped that I didn't leave because I wasn't sure about being Amish. I always knew I would come back and join the church. But before I joined, I wanted to get the wanderlust out of *mei* bones."

"Did you?" She touched the side of the kerchief, as if checking to see if it was still in place.

The red color looked good on her, even though it was a unisex handkerchief. "*Ya.* I'm done traveling. I saw what I wanted to, and I filled out a bunch of journals with my traveling adventures. When I have *kinner*, I'll share those with them."

"Ah." She looked down at her lap again. Her cheeks turned cherry red.

The sound of the bus driver announcing they would be arriving in Ashtabula soon diverted his attention. Susie gazed out the window, and Alex became lost in his own thoughts. They didn't say anything else for the next fifteen minutes or so until their ride ended.

When the bus jerked to a halt, Alex's nerves shifted into high gear. This was it. He was home, or at least he would be in a day or two. He had to get ready to meet his parents before that. He turned to her.

"Do you know where I can get some Amish clothing? And an Amish haircut?" He couldn't go to a regular store and buy the clothes or to a barber to get the proper haircut. If he could, he would have done that before returning home. While he had gotten on the bus in Berlin, he'd arrived only a few hours before his connection to Ashtabula. Before that he'd been in Cincinnati, and there weren't any Amish settlements close by where he was. He hadn't planned his trip home too well. Then again, he hadn't planned anything for the past two years.

She paused, then said, "What about Ben's clothes? He left a few things at home after he got married, and I guess he's forgotten about them. *Mei mamm* was supposed to pack them up but she hasn't gotten around to it."

Alex nodded. "How is *yer mamm*?" He knew better than to ask about her father. It wasn't a secret that he had abandoned Susannah, Ben, and their mother over fifteen years ago. His jaw clenched. How could a man leave his family like that? That was something he would never, ever do, and another reason why he had wanted to finish traveling before he settled down and got married.

"*Mamm's* doing fine. Still working at Jane's."

"The Yankee seamstress?"

"*Ya.* When *Mamm* first took the job, she thought business would eventually slow down, and Jane would have to let her go. Instead, they keep getting busier. *Mamm* said the other day Jane might have to hire a part-time seamstress soon." She looked at him. "You're welcome to borrow Ben's clothes if you want."

"That would be great, but how would I get them? I don't want anyone to know I'm here." He didn't even have to ask her to keep that information to herself. For some reason, he trusted she would.

"I can bring them to you." She pressed her teeth against her bottom lip. "I, uh, can also give you a haircut."

"You would do that for me?"

She nodded. "If you're okay with that."

This was better than he expected. "I'm totally okay with it." Then he looked around at the empty bus. He'd been so busy talking he hadn't realized everyone had left. "We should leave before they kick us off."

He grabbed his backpack and stood, then slid out from

the seat and gave her room to move to the aisle before they headed toward the head of the bus.

After disembarking, they went to get their luggage. Although it was late June, the day was cooler than usual, with a few warm rays of sunshine peeking through thick, fluffy clouds. "I'm staying at the Concord Inn," he said. "Do you know where it is?"

"*Ya.* I can meet you there sometime after ten tomorrow."

"*Danki*, Su-Susie." He almost said Susannah. "I owe you one."

"You're welcome. And you don't owe me anything." She looked down at the ground. "I better get *mei* suitcase and get going," she said. "See you tomorrow."

Before he could offer to get her suitcase for her, she disappeared into the crowd of passengers fighting to get their luggage. He knew from experience to wait until the rush died down before getting his bags. When the crowd cleared, Susannah—he couldn't bring himself to call her Susie anymore—had disappeared.

He smiled. It didn't matter, though. He would see her tomorrow, and she would help him get ready to reenter the Amish community. Suddenly he wasn't as nervous as he had been. He was excited to get home.

TWO

You picked out some lovely fabric, Susie." *Mamm* ran her hand over a bolt of sage-green fabric covered with tiny, pale-pink flowers.

Susie smiled, but not because her mother was complimenting her on her color choices. She was still thinking about Alex. Although she had been home for a few hours, she was still replaying every part of their conversation. He'd led an exciting life over the past two years, and a part of her envied that, even though she never gave much thought to traveling any farther than around Northeast Ohio. The most exotic place she had ever been was the Cleveland Science Museum, which had been educational, but not adventurous. She'd enjoyed living vicariously for three hours while Alex told her about the different states he had visited.

She also enjoyed simply sitting next to him on the bus, whether they were talking or not.

"The group is going to love quilting with these." *Mamm* set the bolt of cloth next to a stack of folded yards of fabric. "Are you sure you don't want to join us?"

Mamm paused, then shook her head. "I wish I had time, but I just don't. You know how busy I am with *mei* job at Jane's."

"But, *Mamm*, you're the best quilter out of all of us. And you can sew circles around everyone in our district. Everyone in the group misses you. They say the circle isn't the same without you."

Mamm's cheeks turned pink as she brushed her hand over another bolt of fabric, and Susie knew that her mother was pleased by the compliments, even if she couldn't outright accept them. "Did you enjoy your stay in Berlin?" *Mamm* asked, deftly switching the subject from herself.

Susie nodded, Alex's image appearing in front of her again. It wasn't easy to focus on fabric and Berlin while she was thinking about how thick and luxurious Alex's hair looked. Hair she would be touching tomorrow when she gave him an Amish haircut. Butterflies fluttered in her stomach again. She still couldn't believe she had offered to cut his hair. She'd never been so bold in her entire life.

"*Ya*," she said, pushing thoughts of Alex and his hair to the side. "But it's a busy community. Too busy for me."

Mamm rose from her chair. "I agree. Very touristy if you ask me. But the Helping Hands Quilt Shop always has such pretty fabric. Would you like another piece of chocolate pie?"

Tempted, she almost said yes. She hadn't eaten much at supper. She was still floating from her bus ride with Alex. Her mother had prepared a simple meal for the two of them, and Susie noticed they were all her favorites—chicken turnovers, glazed carrots, and fresh salad with early vegetables from the garden. But her mother's chocolate pie was the best she'd ever had, and she would never skimp on dessert. Still, she shouldn't be greedy for another piece. "*Nee*, not right now."

"All right." *Mamm* covered the pie with aluminum foil. "I thought tomorrow morning we could have bananas Foster pancakes for breakfast before I *geh* to work."

"That sounds *gut*." Susie thought about telling her mother that she would be leaving after breakfast but changed her mind. She wouldn't betray Alex's confidence, and her mother would ask questions, especially since Susie rarely went anywhere during the week. Because *Mamm* worked, it was up to Susie to do the household chores and cooking, which she didn't mind. She would be back from Alex's before her mother would know she was gone.

Mamm turned to her and smiled. "I missed you while you were gone." She walked over to Susie and put a hand on her shoulder. "Benjamin stopped by twice. He said it was because he was close by, but I know he was checking up on me. I enjoy his company, but it's not the same as having you here."

Susie nodded, putting her hand over her mother's. She understood. For more than twenty years it had been the three of them, and it had taken Susie a while to get used to her brother not living in the same house anymore. He lived only a few streets over and she and *Mamm* saw him at least once a week besides church, but he had his own family to focus on now. His wife, Sadie, was from Lancaster, and Susie was still getting to know her. One thing she did know was that Sadie and Ben wanted children. That hadn't happened yet, but Susie prayed that, God willing, it would happen soon.

"I'm pleased, though." *Mamm* squeezed Susie's hand. "You traveling all the way to Berlin by yourself. Like I said before you left, that was a surprise." *Mamm* let go of her hand.

"What else did Benjamin have to say?" Susie asked.

"He and Sadie are going to Lancaster tomorrow to visit her family. They'll be gone for a week." *Mamm* frowned. "I'm going to darn a pair of socks before I turn in for the night. I brought them home with me since we were so busy today."

Susie started after her, then stopped. *Mamm* might be happy about her going to Berlin, but it had been difficult for Susie to travel by herself. She was confident when it came to buying fabric, but leaving the comfort of home was a different story, and there were times when her shyness had almost gotten the best of her, like when she had checked into the small inn where she stayed overnight. But when the ladies at their last quilting circle had said they wanted some new fabric, she volunteered. How else was she going to get over her bashfulness unless she faced it head-on? So after a lot of prayers for courage, she had left and accomplished her mission.

Unlike her, Benjamin didn't have any trouble traveling or making friends. When he and Sadie had met at a wedding in Walnut Creek, he hadn't hesitated to go visit her whenever he could. *Mamm* said she understood, but Susie knew she wasn't happy about it. She always got the same look on her face anytime Benjamin left Middlefield. But she couldn't expect him not to visit Sadie's family.

She got up from the table and looked at the fabric again.

If she hadn't made the trip to Berlin, she wouldn't have spent all that wonderful time with Alex. She smiled as she placed the bolt back into one of the two large, fabric tote bags she had taken with her on the trip. As soon as her mother went to bed, she would go upstairs and pack up some of Ben's clothing. She thought he might have a hat in his closet too. But before she did that, she would have to go to the phone shanty and schedule a taxi for tomorrow morning. The Concord Inn was too far away for a quick buggy ride.

She put her hand over her stomach, trying to calm her nerves, although she couldn't stop grinning. Was it possible to be nervous, happy, and excited at the same time? Must be, because that was exactly what she was feeling. *I'm seeing Alex tomorrow . . . for the second day in a row!*

Now that he was back, she let her thoughts travel a path they hadn't dared go in two years. *What if he ends up liking me as much as I like him? What if we fall in love? What if we got married?*

Susie closed her eyes, basking in the dream for a few seconds. Then she returned to reality. She was being silly. Alex had just arrived home. The last thing he would be interested in was pursuing a relationship. And even if he was, it wouldn't be with her. She was sixteen when he left. Surely he still saw her as a young girl.

Tomorrow she would take Alex his clothes, cut his hair, and that would be the end of things. She wasn't the only girl who had a crush on him before he left. Julia Yoder was twenty-three—the same age as Alex. She was also pretty and newly single after breaking up with Jonas Miller last year. Susie was sure once Julia knew Alex was in town, she wouldn't hesitate to let him know her interest. Unlike Susie, Julia was bold, and always went after what she wanted.

Susie didn't stand a chance.

———•◆•———

"They fit pretty *gut, ya?*"

Susie gulped as she watched Alex turn around after he put on Benjamin's clothes. She had arrived at the inn fifteen minutes ago, and he'd met her in the lobby. When she gave him the clothes, he disappeared upstairs to his room, then came back down. Fortunately, the lobby was empty, or else any witnesses would have thought they were both out of their heads, him with his loose-fitting Amish clothes and shoulder-length hair, and her barely able to speak and unable to take her eyes off him.

He faced her, his mouth forming a slight frown. "Is something wrong with the clothes?"

She shook her head, still grasping for her words. The happiness and excitement she felt the night before had disappeared on the taxi ride over here, leaving her nerves wound up in a tight ball in the pit of her stomach. In a few minutes she would be giving him a haircut, and the thought of being so close to him made her clam up more.

"Susannah?"

Why was he calling her by her full name? No one called her that, except for her mother when she wanted to get Susie's attention. "They look *gut,*" she finally said, glad to see the relief on his face.

"Great. One item down, one more to *geh.*" He shook out

his hair until it was covering his face. "Or maybe I should just show up like this."

She couldn't help but laugh. He looked ridiculous, his hair a thick curtain in front of his face. "*Yer mamm* will have a heart attack, Alex."

He pushed back his hair, revealing his handsome grin. "Nah. She would take the scissors to me herself." His expression sobered. "I want her and *Daed* to know I'm serious about staying and joining the church. I don't want to give them any room for doubt."

"That's very kind of you," she murmured. Although he had said his parents understood his need to travel the country, their only son leaving had to have been stressful for them. What if he had decided to never come back? She understood the pain of losing someone she loved to the outside world. She also witnessed firsthand what that had done to her mother and brother too.

"It's the least I can do." He moved a few steps toward her as the front door of the inn opened and a middle-aged couple with two huge suitcases walked in. They went to the front counter, which was just a few feet away from them, and tapped the small silver bell on the counter. A Yankee woman appeared from the office behind the counter.

Susie looked at Alex. "This inn isn't run by Amish?"

He shook his head. "*Nee.* But the family that owns this place has lived in Middlefield their entire lives, and they understand our ways. When I explained everything to Mrs. Stone, she didn't bat an eye. She's already set us up outside for *mei* haircut."

Susie almost breathed a sigh of relief. On the way to the

inn, she worried about being alone with Alex in his room. Not that she thought he would do anything ungentlemanly. But if anyone found out they had been in his room together, especially when they didn't know he had returned home, the community grapevine would light up with gossip. A little more confident now, she patted the quilted fabric tote bag still slung over her shoulder. "I have *mei* scissors right here."

"I'll run upstairs and change. I don't want to get hair all over these clothes. Be back in a second."

She watched him run up the stairs, taking them two at a time. Then she sighed.

"He's a nice young man."

She jerked around and saw the woman who had helped the Yankee couple standing next to her. "He is," Susie managed to say, hoping the innkeeper didn't hear her sighing over him.

"When he said one of his friends was coming over to cut his hair, I thought he meant a male friend." She smiled. "You must be glad he's come back home."

She nodded again, this time not saying anything. Alex considered her a friend. How disappointing. But what did she expect? He was Ben's older friend and had no idea about her feelings. At least he hadn't called her some girl or a kid. That would have been awful.

Alex bounded down the stairs, wearing a navy-blue T-shirt and jean shorts that hit just above his knee. "Last time for this outfit," he said as he walked over to her and Mrs. Stone. "Thank you for helping us take care of my mop." He touched one of the messy locks. "I can't wait to get rid of all this."

"No problem." Mrs. Stone smiled, revealing a row of straight, top teeth in contrast to several crooked bottom ones. "I'm glad to do it. Everything is ready for you behind the garden shed. You'll have a little privacy there in case any of our guests want to go outside."

He turned to Susie. "Ready?"

Taking a deep breath and hoping neither he nor Mrs. Stone noticed, she gathered her courage. "*Ya,*" she said, determined to give him the best Amish haircut he'd ever had. "I'm ready."

———•—•———

Alex sat down in the wooden chair Mrs. Stone had placed behind the garden shed. He was glad to see that the shed was large enough that he and Susannah were well hidden. He was also surprised how his nerves suddenly jumped. He'd told the truth when he said he was ready to get rid of all this hair. It was easy to manage when he'd been traveling. After washing it, he would gather it in a ponytail and be on his way. But it was also heavy and tangled easily, and he was tired of it. His transformation into an Amish man would be one step closer to completion after Susannah cut it.

But she would be touching his hair. Now he knew why he was so nervous.

Stop being dumb. If Susannah knew he was having any kind of thoughts about her, she would take her scissors and go home. She would definitely run if she knew he'd thought about her last night—a lot. Despite her warming up to him on the bus yesterday, by the time they parted, she had reverted to Ben Glick's shy younger sister. He didn't want her to feel bashful or uncomfortable around him. Even now she was standing to the side, as if she were unsure what to do.

He reached around for the large towel that Mrs. Stone had laid over the back of the chair. "Guess I better tie this around *mei* neck," he said, whirling it over his shoulders like a cape. Good, that made her smile. "Just call me Captain Amish."

Now she was giggling. "I don't think the bishop would approve of Amish superheroes."

"I'm sure he wouldn't." Alex tied two of the ends around his neck into a loose knot.

That seemed to spur Susannah into action. She set down her bag on a small, round wrought iron table that he guessed Mrs. Stone had brought from the inn's patio, then fished out her scissors. "Wow," he said, eyeing the long blades. "That's a big pair."

"*Mamm* has had them for years. She cut Benjamin's hair with these, and before that *mei* . . ." Her head shook almost imperceptibly. "I sharpened them before I came over. You have more hair than Benjamin ever had."

"That's the truth." He kept his tone light, seeing the touch of sadness in her big brown eyes. Anyone could tell that she still harbored pain from her father's abandonment. He wondered if she even knew where he was or had ever heard from him after he left the family and the community. But he wouldn't ask her. This wasn't the time, and her relationship with her father wasn't his business.

When she moved behind him, he held his breath. This

was it. Good-bye, hair. But she didn't do or say anything for a few seconds. Finally he said, "Susannah?"

"Your hair is tucked into the towel."

"Oh. *Geh* ahead and pull it out then." He felt gentle tugging as she moved his hair from the back of his neck. He relaxed, knowing he was in good hands.

A few seconds later, she said, "Ready?"

Alex closed his eyes. "Definitely."

THREE

Once Susie conquered her anxiety, she became engrossed in cutting Alex's hair. First, she had decided to twist all of his hair into a ponytail at the nape of his neck, then shear the ponytail off. It wasn't easy since his hair was so thick, but once she cut through it, she smiled and walked around to him. "Do you want to save this for posterity?" she asked, holding the long length of hair in front of him.

He took the ponytail from her hand and held it, then bounced his hand up and down as if to guess the hair's weight. Then he shook his head and handed it back to her. "*Nee*. This is part of *mei* old life."

She took the hair from him, then set it in the plastic bag she had brought to keep his cut hair. She hadn't been sure where she would be cutting his hair, and she didn't want to leave a mess for Alex or anyone else to clean up. When she looked at him, he was shaking his head again.

"I can't believe how light it feels," he said, grinning as

he glanced at her. "I didn't realize how much *mei* hair was weighing me down."

Susie sort of understood what he was talking about. She had never had a haircut, and she guessed that her long hair was heavy, but she didn't have anything to compare it to like Alex did. But she did know how events in the past could weigh a person down. Maybe he was thinking about something bad that had happened to him during his travels. She didn't know, and she couldn't ask him. She was a friend cutting his hair, and not even a close friend. But that didn't keep her from wondering.

When he stilled, she went back to snipping his hair. The task was much easier now that the bulk of it was gone. She trimmed up the back into the standard Amish haircut, cutting it to the nape of his neck and up to the middle of his ears. She walked around to make sure that the sides were even.

"You never did tell me why you were in Berlin," he said as she walked around to fix the right side of his hair, which was at least an inch longer than the left.

"There's a quilt store *Mamm* and I like to visit from time to time." She used the tip of the scissors to carefully cut only a few hairs at a time. "We're starting a new quilt with the group to donate to the special needs auction in September, and we wanted to get new fabric. *Mamm* had to work, so I volunteered to *geh* by myself."

"I remember going to that auction over the years. I'm glad they're still having it. Lots of kids have benefited from the clinic."

Susie nodded. "I look forward to going every year, but this is the first time I'll be taking a small part in the auction. We're going to start the quilt this week." She smiled, thinking about how wonderful it would be to know that her handiwork was going to an excellent cause.

"How long have you been in the group?"

"I joined last year." *Snip.* "But I've been quilting since I was eight years old."

"You enjoy quilting, *ya*?"

"I do. *Mamm* taught me the basics, but now I'm learning new techniques."

"*Mei mamm* never quilted. *Mei schwesters* never caught on to it either."

"Not everyone likes to sew," Susie said. "If they did, *mei Mamm* and Jane would be out of business." She stopped snipping. "There, I think I've evened it all up."

"I'm sure it's fine. *Mamm*'s haircuts were never perfectly straight. I remember one time she was in a hurry and had to cut *mei* hair." He laughed. "It was so lopsided I looked like I'd been sitting on the side of a hill when she gave me the haircut. But she didn't have time to fix it before I went to school. I was the laughingstock of the day until I got home and she cut it some more. It ended up on the short side, but it was better than it was before."

Susie didn't know what Alex was talking about, so it must have happened when he was in one of the elementary grades. Their district's school was in one building, but the lower and upper grades were separated by an accordion divider. The two levels rarely interacted with each other except before and after school.

"I've never had trouble growing hair, that's for sure." He moved the remainder of his long hair to the front of his face until it was completely covered. "This part is the last to *geh*."

She'd been fairly relaxed up until this point, mostly because Alex was easy to talk with. But now the tension was back, settling into her shoulders. It was one thing to cut his hair while she was standing behind him. But she couldn't very well do that when cutting his bangs. She would have to be in front of him, looking at his face, still handsome even with the beard and mustache, remembering all the times she had wished she could be this close to him . . . and none of those thoughts had ever included a haircut.

"Susannah." He turned slightly in the chair and held out his hand.

He'd been calling her by her full name since she arrived, and although she didn't know why he did, she was pleased. While he looked funny with his hair hanging over his face, she could see his eyes. They were filled with encouragement. Something stirred inside her. He seemed to know she was struggling, and instead of getting impatient with her, he was showing her he understood. If she hadn't had a crush on him before, this moment would have been the tipping point. Not that she needed any prodding.

Her nerves disappeared and she slipped her hand into his. She was surprised at how warm it was, and her palm rested against what she thought were two callouses. That also surprised her. Obviously, he had done hard labor while he was gone.

When she was in front of him, Alex let go of her hand

and settled back in the chair, his hands resting on his knees, his shoulders back. Then he closed his eyes.

Snip. Snip. Snip.

A few minutes later, she stood back and regarded her finished work. "Wait," she said, taking a step forward. "Don't open your eyes yet. I need to get the hair off your face." After quickly and lightly brushing the excess hair from his brow, eyes, and cheeks with the clean hand towel she brought, she said, "Done."

He opened his eyes and smiled. "*Danki*," he said softly.

His voice sent a shiver down her back. *Uh-oh.* She was in big trouble. He might think of her as a friend, but she was still crazy about him, even more so now. Then she noticed he had one more stray hair above his left eyebrow. She started to brush it off, her fingers lightly touching his brow.

He jerked her hand away from his face. "I can get the rest," he said, his tone turning rough. Then he jumped up from the chair. "I've got to get rid of this beard anyway. Don't worry about the mess. I'll clean it up." He flung off the towel and tossed it on the chair. "Thanks again, Susie." Then he went back to the inn.

She stood there, dumbfounded. He'd called her Susie again, instead of Susannah. And the way he left so quickly, it was as if he couldn't wait to get away from her. What had she done wrong?

A sinking sensation filled her chest even though she was trying to be rational. Alex leaving so fast was for the best. She was falling harder for him than she had before, but he only saw her as a friend.

Alex slammed the door to his room and leaned against it, his heavy breathing having nothing to do with him running up the stairs at breakneck speed. He was in trouble. Big trouble. When he opened his eyes after Susannah had finished his haircut, he'd never seen anything so beautiful in his life—and he had seen some breathtaking things on his travels. Those big brown eyes gazing at him, reaching into his soul. This wasn't what he had expected when he planned to come back to Middlefield. He hadn't even seen his parents yet or joined the church or even been in town for twenty-four hours, but here he was, sweaty palms and all, falling hard for Susannah Glick.

He glanced up at the ceiling, but that wasn't his focus. *God, what's happening here?* He wasn't confused about joining the church or leaving the Yankee life behind. He was as sure of his faith as he was about the ground he'd been standing on outside. But these feelings? They were blowing his mind. Even when he had held out his hand to her, his intentions were innocent. She was retreating into her shyness, and he wanted to help her. What he was experiencing now was far from helpful, and that's why he had hightailed it away from her.

He went to the bathroom and splashed cold water on his face, then looked in the mirror. His image shocked him, and then he had to laugh. The haircut was perfect, as he expected it to be. Susannah had taken plenty of time and care. But he'd never seen the combination of shaggy beard and mustache with the traditional Amish bowl cut before, and he looked ridiculous. Yet he was thankful for the break in his thoughts. He needed to concentrate on starting his new life, and that didn't include romance—something he'd never had time for anyway. He picked up one of the razors from the pack he had purchased before leaving Berlin, knowing he would need more than one to vanquish his facial hair.

Once he was done, he stared at his reflection again, running his hand over his smooth face. Now he not only looked right but he also felt right.

He went to the phone in his guest room and picked up the receiver, then called for a taxi to his parents' house. He was surprised he remembered Max's number, one of the Yankees who for years had operated a taxi service. As he waited for Max to pick up, he vowed to keep Susannah—Susie—out of his mind.

———— • ————

Two days after giving Alex a haircut, Susie went to the weekly quilting bee at Ida Mae Erb's house. For the past four years *Mamm* had met with her friends at Ida Mae's house. Ida Mae was the mother of eleven children, now all grown and moved out of their large house. She had the biggest living room where they could set up the large quilt frame when they were ready to quilt the pieced-together fabric motifs. Susie was invited to the group last year when *Mamm* had to drop out, and even though she was the youngest one, she always enjoyed being around the older women as they exchanged stories and taught her quilting techniques. Today she was excited to show them the new fabric she bought in

Berlin, hoping they were as pleased with her purchases as *Mamm* was.

Ida Mae lived a short walk from Susie's house, so it didn't take long for her to arrive promptly at 10:00 a.m., when the quilting bees always started. She saw Velda Kauffman's buggy parked near the barn, Velda's horse already in the pasture and snacking on timothy grass. The other two women, Malinda Mast and Norma Hershberger, were always dropped off by their husbands.

When Susie walked into Ida Mae's house, the scent of vegetable soup simmering hung in the air. That was another fun part of the quilting circle—lunch afterward. She set down the tray of fresh rolls she had baked this morning next to a white bowl of colorful fruit salad covered with plastic wrap, courtesy of Norma, who was always watching her weight but never actually losing any. Malinda, who was thin as a rail, always brought a rich dessert, and today was no exception as Susie spied what looked like a vanilla pound cake sitting next to the fruit salad. Velda must have brought the chowchow, since she was always bringing something canned to their lunches.

Susie followed the sound of women's voices from the kitchen to the living room. Since they were starting a new quilt today, the frame wasn't set up, and in its place was a long table filled with quilting supplies—rulers, cutting mats, scissors and wheeled cutters, pincushions, and of course lots of pins. Ida Mae sat at the head of the table, and the rest of the ladies filled in the sides. Susie took her place in the empty chair at the opposite end of the table.

Ida Mae held up her hand. "We better get started. But

first—Susie, how is your *mamm*? Other than church service, we never get to see her anymore."

"She's very busy at work," Susie said.

Velda sighed. "She's going to work herself to the bone."

Susie thought her comment was odd, considering hard work was valued among the Amish.

"I saw the bags under her eyes." Malinda clucked. "I don't think she's getting enough sleep."

Norma nodded. "I'm a little concerned about her." She turned to Susie. "Please tell her she's always welcome to come back to the group, even if it's every once in a while. I would talk to her myself, but she leaves right after church."

Susie nodded, deliberating whether she should tell the group that she had already talked to her mother about returning. But before she could say anything, Ida Mae cut in.

"Susie, what did you find at Helping Hands?" she asked.

Glad for the reprieve, Susie stood and unpacked the bolts of fabric she'd bought, pleased as the women oohed and aahed over her choices.

"I love the green with the pink flowers," Velda said.

"The lavender with the pale yellow dots is *mei* favorite," Norma added.

"Baby blue is always a practical choice," Malinda chimed in.

"I'm glad you chose plain cream." Ida Mae nodded her approval. "A neutral fabric will set off the rest of the fancier ones."

Susie almost laughed. The other fabrics were far from fancy, with their muted designs and colors. But there was enough of a variety of colors that the quilt wouldn't be too plain but would be neutral enough for any décor in case a Yankee decided to buy it. Last year Alex's mother, Frannie, had purchased the quilt the group made, which was made of cream, beige, and light cocoa-colored fabric.

"Here are the templates," Ida Mae said, passing several cut pieces of paper around the women. "We're making the Broken Star pattern."

"One of *mei* favorites." Norma smiled, her white marking pencil tucked behind her ear.

Soon everyone was busy pinning their pattern pieces and cutting out the fabric. The rest of the women talked while Susie focused on making sure her pieces were cut exactly right. This was her first auction quilt, and she didn't want to make a mistake.

"I suppose everyone has heard that Alex Lehman is back," Velda said.

Susie's scissors ripped through both the fabric and the template. *Oh* nee. Not only had she not wanted to think about Alex, she also ruined her first quilt piece. Fortunately there was a roll of clear tape nearby. The tape was always part of the supplies on the table, but as far as she knew, no one ever used it. She grabbed it and repaired the pattern.

"I always thought that situation was strange." Norma made a mark on the lavender fabric. "Frannie being just fine with her son galivanting all over the country. She even has a photo album of all the postcards he sent to her."

"I heard he called her every Sunday afternoon." Malinda sniffed. "I wonder if the bishop knew about how much time she spent on the phone during the week."

"Oh, I'm sure Josiah would be fine with it," Ida Mae

said. "If you ask me, he's a *gut sohn* to keep in touch with his parents the way he did."

"If he were a *gut sohn*," Velda said," he would have joined the church and never left to begin with."

Susie gripped her scissors so hard her knuckles ached. How dare these women gossip about Alex? "He *is* joining the church," she said.

The women all hushed and looked at her. "How do you know?" Malinda asked.

Uh-oh. She shouldn't have opened her big mouth. "I, uh, saw him on the bus when I was coming back from Berlin. He mentioned he was here to stay." No need to tell them any other details. She was annoyed enough that they were talking so poorly about him.

"See?" Ida Mae said. "He's making things right. I'm sure Frannie and Lonnie are happy to have him home after all this time."

"Oh, of course." Norma smiled.

"Let's just hope he doesn't decide to leave again," Malinda said. "We all know not everyone keeps their vow when they join the church."

"Malinda," Ida Mae hissed.

"Ow!" Malinda glared at Ida Mae.

But it was too late. Susie knew they were talking about her father. She kept her head down, unable to face any of them. What could she say? Her father had left them. Everyone in the district knew what he'd done.

Norma scowled. "Malinda, why did you say that?" she hissed.

"It's the truth . . . Oh." Her haughty expression disappeared. "Oh *nee*. I forgot about Marvin."

The women looked at Susie. Her hands were shaking. She was even angrier now than she had been when they were discussing Alex. "Excuse me," she said, and she fled the quilting circle.

FOUR

More chicken potpie?"

Alex looked at his mother, who was holding up a huge serving spoon full of the delicious potpie. "I've had two servings already, *Mamm*," he said, chuckling. "I can't fit any more into *mei* belly."

"She aims to fatten you up." *Daed* wiped his mouth and sat back in his chair. The noonday sun streamed through the kitchen window, and warm summer air came through the screen covering the lower half of the pane.

"And I aim to work it off." He grinned, pleased when he saw his father's look of approval. His homecoming two days ago had been everything he'd hoped for. His parents welcomed him with open arms, his mother making all of his favorite foods and his father catching him up on his bookbinding business. *Daed* knew Alex wasn't suited for sitting at a desk, and he'd never said anything about training him to follow in his footsteps. He was grateful to God for having such understanding parents. Not all children, Amish or Yankee, did.

"I'm not used to eating so much for lunch, *Mamm*," he added, turning to her with a smile, not wanting to hurt her feelings.

"Neither am I," *Daed* said. "But I have to admit, it's been a nice treat. *Appeditlich* too."

"Now, you both know I'm not the only one who's been cooking. Abigail and Amanda have been doing their fair share of making meals for their little *bruder*."

That was true. Last night Amanda and her husband, Dale, brought over sauerkraut casserole, and the day before that Abigail and her husband, Paul, had joined them for supper. Taco salad was his eldest sister's contribution to the meal. Tonight both families, including his three nephews and two nieces, would be here for a steak dinner. The steaks would be cooked on their outdoor grill, and Alex planned to make a small fire and roast marshmallows with the kids.

"Have you given any more thought to carpentry?" *Daed* asked.

Alex nodded. During his travels, he'd spent extended time with Amish families all over the country. Those ended up being his most important and special adventures because he had learned so much about the differences between districts and communities in different states. He'd had no idea how much of a variety there was in *Ordnungs* and customs from one part of the US to the other. During one of those stays, he had apprenticed as a carpenter, and enjoyed it so much he made sure to keep up his skills doing various odd carpentry jobs as he traveled. "Dale said Roy Nisley might be hiring."

Daed nodded. "His business has grown a lot over the

past two years. I'm not surprised he might be needing extra help."

"When do you meet with Josiah?" *Mamm* asked, cutting a thick slice of triple layer mocha cake from the cake in the middle of the table.

"Later this afternoon." He couldn't wait to discuss his upcoming baptism with the bishop. His eagerness to join the church caught him by surprise. He didn't have any hesitation he was doing the right thing, but the fact he was so happy to be an official member of the congregation and community was unexpected. Besides, focusing on his baptism, his employment prospects, and even the thousand-calorie piece of mocha cake his mother was pushing on him kept him from thinking about Susannah—Susie—again. For the most part, at least.

"Well, I better get back to work. Those books don't bind themselves." Laughing at his own lame joke, his father smoothed his hand over his balding head before standing up. He clapped Alex on the back. "Glad to have you home, *sohn*. Did I tell you that?"

"A few times." Alex smiled, but his heart was full. Ya, *Lord, I'm exactly where I'm supposed to be.*

Once his father left the kitchen, *Mamm* looked at him, her eyes watery, as they had been several times over the past two days. He reached for her hand. "I'm not going anywhere, *Mamm*."

"I know that. It's just that we missed you so much, even though we talked to you every week." She squeezed his hand. "*Danki* for letting us know where you were all the time. That eased some of *mei* worry."

"But not all of it."

She shook her head. "I know the Lord says we're not to be anxious, but a mother's heart can't help it. I didn't want anything to happen to you while you were still apart from us."

"He kept me safe." Looking back, Alex knew that was true. He was always careful not to take too many risks, but there were times when he couldn't resist doing something that could end up with him in danger, like mountain climbing in the Rockies or hiking the Appalachian Trail by himself. He would always treasure all those experiences, but he was smart enough to realize he hadn't been alone during them.

"The *kinner* are excited to see you tonight." *Mamm* wiped a drop of chocolate frosting from the edge of the white serving platter that held the cake. "Abigail said that when she told the *maed* they were toasting marshmallows with *Onkel* Alex tonight they squealed."

Alex laughed, but it was tempered with regret. He didn't have many regrets, but the one thing was that he had missed so many years of his nieces' and nephews' lives. They were babies and toddlers when he left, and now they were all school age. Which made them fun to be around, but he was also acutely aware how fast the time had gone.

Mamm got up from the chair and started to clear the table. Alex joined her, then said, "I'll wash the dishes."

"You don't have to do that," *Mamm* said.

"I know, but I want to. I'll even dry them."

His mother laughed. "I've missed your good humor. I'll take you up on the offer."

A few moments later he was wrist deep in soap suds. He

ran a dishcloth over one of the plates and looked out the window. Two smoke-gray squirrels were chasing each other across the front yard. Suddenly Susannah came to mind, as she did when he was alone or not distracted. He wondered what she was doing on this beautiful day. Over the past two days, especially at night when he was lying in bed before he fell asleep, he couldn't figure out why he was so smitten with her. He'd met a lot of single women over the past five years, both Amish and Yankee, and he'd never felt this way about any of them. That wasn't a slam against them, more of a testament to his strong feelings. Feelings he shouldn't be having, considering he and Susannah hadn't spent much time together. He didn't even bother to mentally correct her name anymore. She was Susannah to him.

But another thought had come to his mind, one he was dwelling on more and more. His life was changing. God had changed him by exchanging his desire to travel with a desire to stay home, get a steady job, and eventually have a wife and family. He hadn't expected the latter to happen anytime soon, but he was sure that sitting by Susannah on the bus ride home to Berlin was providence. *God, is she a part of your plan for my life too?* Instead of thinking of all the reasons they shouldn't be together, maybe he should pay attention to why they could.

There was only one way to find out for sure.

He finished the dishes and pulled the plug out of the sink. As the water swirled and gurgled down the drain, he made a decision. He had other obligations to fulfill, like spending more time with his family and studying for his baptism. But when the time was right, he would seek out Susannah again and ask her on a date. If he wasn't meant to be with Susannah, God would let him know. *But if I am* . . .

He grinned and picked up the dishtowel.

———•———

Susie stood at Ida Mae's kitchen sink wondering what she should do. The vegetable soup bubbling on the gas stove was the only sound in the kitchen. Should she leave? If they were going to continue to talk about her father and Alex, she definitely should. But she was so excited to be a part of this group. She didn't want to go . . . but she also couldn't stay, not when they were gossiping about Alex and her father.

Malinda hurried into the kitchen. "Susie, I'm so sorry," she said, tears in her eyes. "I didn't mean to hurt your feelings. Please forgive me."

Malinda sounded sincere, and even though Susie couldn't refuse her because of the Amish belief in forgiveness, she would have forgiven her anyway. "It's all right," she said. "We all misspeak sometimes."

"*Nee* more idle talk," she said. "Let's *geh* back and do what we do best—quilt." She smiled.

Somehow Susie managed to return it. "I'll be right there."

Malinda touched her arm and went back to the quilting room. But Susie was unable to move. Was Alex just like her father? She refused to believe that. Alex had returned to Middlefield. Her father hadn't, and after twenty-one years, she knew he never would. But the seed had been planted, and she couldn't shake off the idea.

Not wanting to make anyone wonder what was taking

her so long, she went back to the living room and rejoined the group. Conversation now focused around the time line for finishing the quilt. Everyone would take their quilt pieces home and piece as many of them together as they could, and when they came next week, they could put the larger pieces together.

Susie remained silent, keeping her head down as she cut out her pieces. For once being shy was in her favor, and the other women didn't try to draw her into their conversation.

When they broke for lunch, Ida Mae took Susie aside while the rest of the women went into the kitchen. "I wanted to make sure you were all right," she said.

"*Ya.*" But she wasn't. She was still embarrassed, and still wondering about Alex. Quilting wasn't enough of a distraction, and she wondered if anything would be, at least for a while. But she didn't want to get into all that with Ida Mae. "I'm fine."

"*Gut.*" Ida Mae smiled. "Malinda didn't mean any harm. We were all at fault anyway. We shouldn't have been gossiping about the Lehmans in the first place."

On that point Susie agreed. She also noticed that both Ida Mae and Malinda hadn't mentioned her father again. *Thank God.*

Ida Mae patted Susie's arm. "I'm so glad you're a part of our group. I didn't have a daughter to share my love of quilting with. You and your *mamm* are blessed to have each other. Don't let us gossipy hens get in the way of your enjoyment. Now, I'm starving and ready for some vegetable soup." She gave Susie one more smile, then headed for the kitchen.

Ida Mae was right. Susie shouldn't let her mixed emotions get in the way of her love of quilting—or a good lunch. Malinda had apologized and no one had said anything further about Alex or her father, and that showed they really were apologetic. Besides, the delicious scent of the vegetable soup was making her stomach growl.

"Susie?" Ida Mae called from the kitchen.

"Coming." She left the room, determined to enjoy lunch and friendship—and to put the morning behind her.

FIVE

For the next four weeks, Alex focused on launching his new life. At the end of July he had been baptized in the church, and two days after that he started working for Roy in his carpentry shop. He was starting from the bottom, basically cleaning up the shop, sanding wood, and running errands. He was glad for the work, but not because he needed money. He had plenty saved from all the odd jobs he had worked during his travels, plus what he had saved from his various jobs he'd held before he left Middlefield. But Roy was open to teaching Alex more about carpentry. He'd gotten only a rudimentary education from his friend Stan Raber back in Holmes County, and he was eager to learn the craft, even though he was getting a late start compared to most Amish carpenters.

He had also started reconnecting with his old friends, all of whom were married and had started families. That included Ben Glick, but Alex never mentioned Susannah to him. Turned out that his worries about not being accepted back in the community or having anyone thinking poorly of him for leaving were for nothing. *Thank you, Lord, for that.*

One night he was having supper with Dan and Anna Nisley at their home. Dan was Roy's cousin, and although he didn't work with Roy, he was in construction and helped build Yankee houses. Dan and Anna were a few years older than Alex, had four kids, and were expecting another. He was in the living room with Dan, talking about the new housing development that had sprung up just outside of Middlefield, when someone knocked at the door.

Anna poked her head into the living room. "Dan, can you get that? I'm busy getting the *kinner* settled. Supper's almost ready." Before he could respond, she went back to the kitchen.

Dan rose from his seat. "I don't know who that could be. Anna didn't say we were having extra company."

Alex stood as Dan opened the door. When he saw who was standing there, he inwardly groaned. Julia Yoder. *Great. Just great.* She'd dropped by three times last week where he worked, bringing him a sweet treat each time. She was nice enough. Pretty enough. *But she's not Susannah.*

"Hi, Julia," Dan said, sounding uncertain. "Ah, did Anna know you were coming?"

"Of course." Julia entered the house like she owned it. "She invited me. Didn't she tell you?"

"*Nee*," Dan said, but Julia was already in front of Alex.

"Fancy meeting you here." Julia smiled, looking at him beneath her eyelashes. "I brought Peanut Butter Dream Bars for dessert." She leaned forward. "I made them especially for you."

"Um, *danki*." Alex took a step back. Growing up, he hadn't interacted with Julia too much, and he had no idea she liked to be so close to people when she talked. Too close.

"I hope you're not allergic to nuts." Julia laughed and tapped Alex playfully on the shoulder. Then she turned to Dan. "Is Anna in the kitchen?"

"*Ya*. Supper's almost ready," he added, still looking dumbfounded.

"I'll help her finish." She turned to Alex and winked, then dashed off to see Anna.

"Oh boy." Dan rubbed the back of his neck. "This isn't *gut*."

"Why?" Alex still couldn't believe Julia had winked at him.

"I think Julia's on the prowl." He looked at Alex and held out his hands in surrender. "She and Anna have been friends for years, and I've been getting an earful about Julia since she and Jonas broke up."

"Jonas Miller? He and Julia were together?"

"They were engaged. Trust me, all the single fellas around here were relieved when they started dating. They actually make a decent pair. Jonas barely says two words and Julia never stops talking."

Alex would have laughed except he didn't like the idea that Julia might be here because of him. Now he knew why she had stopped by his work with so many desserts this week. "Is tonight's supper a blind date?"

Dan sighed. "I had *nee* idea she was coming over here, or I would have warned you. That's probably why Anna didn't mention it."

"Time to eat!" Julia shouted from the kitchen.

"If you want to leave, I'll make up an excuse," Dan said.

Spoken like a true friend. But Alex shook his head. "Don't worry about it. I'm sure everything will be fine. Besides, I'm not one to turn down a *gut* meal."

"*Danki* for taking this so well," Dan said. "Maybe she'll get an attack of laryngitis."

But Julia didn't have laryngitis. In fact, just the opposite, and by the time Anna brought out the Peanut Butter Dream Bars, even she was giving Alex apologetic looks. Dan and Anna's kids, all under eight, looked worn-out from the non-stop chatter.

"May we be excused?" asked Iris, the oldest child. The other three children, one boy and two girls, nodded.

"Don't you want dessert?" Anna asked.

"*Nee.*" Iris looked at her siblings, who all nodded again. "We're too full." She patted her stomach.

"*Ya,*" Dan said. "You can have dessert later. *Geh* outside and play until it's time for bed."

The children scurried from the table and ran out the back door.

"Huh. I've never seen *kinner* turn down dessert before," Julia said. "Maybe if you hadn't added so much pepper to the mashed potatoes, Anna, they wouldn't have stomachaches."

"More like earaches," Dan muttered.

When Anna stood up to get the dessert, Julia shot up from her chair. "Oh, Anna, let me get the bars for you." Julia pointed to Anna's empty chair. "Sit right down and rest. You worked hard, even though the pot roast was too tough." She walked to the counter and picked up the dessert platter, continuing to talk.

"Did I tell you all how much butter is in this recipe? Almost two cups! I thought that was too much but *mei* older *schwester* Rachel—you know, she's the one that has one foot bigger than the other, although she doesn't like people to know but everyone knows because it's so noticeable—she said all the calories were worth it. I hope so, because I don't like gaining weight. It's hard to lose the older you get. That's what *Mamm* says anyway, but how would she know, she's been skinny all her life. I hope I take after her and not Rachel, who's already getting fat. That's probably why she doesn't mind so much butter, because she's already overweight. I guess her husband, Wayne, doesn't mind having a fat wife, but I bet you would, right, Alex?"

Alex froze. The entire time Julia talked, she was placing bars on dessert plates and passing them around, giving Alex the largest piece. Now she was asking him the worst question a woman could ask a man. When he shot Dan a look, he saw that his friend was sinking in his chair.

"I don't think you should put Alex on the spot like that," Anna said. "That's not—"

"Oh, it's just a question. Why would Alex mind a question? You don't mind a question, do you, Alex?"

"Uh, usually I don't." He couldn't wriggle out of this one. Jonas was a saint, and he was starting to believe Anna was, too, for putting up with all this nonsense. Although he could tell Julia wasn't being rude on purpose. She was as clueless as she was loquacious. She was also expecting an answer. "To tell the truth," he said, measuring his words carefully, "I think a woman should keep herself healthy and not focus on what the scale says." There, that should shut her up.

"Oh, Alex, you're just perfect, did you know that?" She went over to him and hugged his shoulders. "You'll make any woman a wonderful husband."

"That's, uh, nice of you to say." Alex awkwardly patted her arm.

"You can let him *geh* now." Dan finally found his backbone. After Julia complied, he said, "Alex, how about we take dessert out on the patio? I like keeping an eye on the *kinner* while they play."

"You don't trust them to play by themselves?" Julia clicked her tongue. "Since Iris is eight years old, she should be responsible enough to mind her siblings. I guess it's all in how you raise them, isn't it, Anna?"

Anna shot a glare at Dan that could melt stone.

"Fresh air sounds *gut*." Alex grabbed the dessert plate and stood, the chair legs scraping against the floor.

Julia started to pick up her plate too. "I'll join you—"

"I need your help with the kitchen," Anna said, moving to stand in between Julia and Alex. "The men can handle watching the *kinner*."

"But—"

Anna nodded to Dan, and he and Alex went outside. They collapsed in two of the wooden patio chairs as the Nisley kids chased one another around the yard.

"That wasn't as bad as I thought," Dan said.

Alex's brows shot up. "You're joking, right?"

"It could have been worse. She could have proposed to you."

"You're right. It could have been worse."

"At least Anna learned her lesson. I don't think she'll

be setting up any more blind dates with Julia." Dan took a bite of his peanut butter bar. "Wow, these are really good. Rachel's right, the calories are worth it."

Alex and Dan spent the rest of the evening outside with the kids. Alex even joined in on a game of tag with the children. Somehow Anna kept Julia inside the entire time, and by dusk when they all went inside, Julia was gone.

"I'm so sorry, Alex," Anna said the minute he stepped inside the kitchen. "I didn't realize she was going to be so . . . so . . ."

"Julia?" Dan supplied.

Anna frowned, but nodded. "*Ya.* She's been out of sorts since her breakup with Jonas. I thought tonight would help keep her mind off it, but when she found out you were coming over she went a little *ab im kopp.*"

"It's fine," Alex said. "*Nee* harm done."

A look of relief crossed her weary face. "Want some more dessert? Julia left the rest of the bars here for the *familye.* She really is a nice *maedel.* Very generous."

"Especially with her conversation." Dan took another bar off the plate.

"Dan," Anna huffed.

But Alex chuckled. He even felt a little pity for Julia. Breakups weren't easy, although that was more from guessing than from experience. During his travels he made sure to keep all his relationships with the opposite sex polite and superficial. He didn't want to hurt anyone's feelings when he moved on to the next town, and he didn't want to get caught up in a relationship when he wasn't ready to settle down. But since he returned back home, he was starting to think he finally was ready to get married. Susannah came immediately to mind.

Alex hung around the Nisleys for a few more minutes, then headed back home. He'd come straight from work to Dan's, and as he walked back to his house, he realized he would be passing by Susannah's. His palms grew damp at the thought. He'd spent the entire evening with a pretty, single woman and had never once felt the intense spark he did just knowing he would soon be near Susannah's house. Whatever these surprising—and, admittedly, pleasant— feelings were, he couldn't deny them. Trouble was, he had no idea what to do with them.

The sky had turned dark, but thanks to a few street-lamps spread out along the road, he had plenty of light to see by. Middlefield wasn't like most of the Amish communities he'd lived in. Here the Amish and Yankees lived close together, and that was the case on Susannah's street.

As he approached her house, he heard the sound of running water, then he saw a woman using a hose to water flowers that circled the base of a large oak tree. Even in the dim light he could tell it was Susannah. Her back was to him, and as long as she stayed that way, he could hurry past and she would never see him. Instead he slowed his steps as he tried to come up with an excuse to talk to her. Then he remembered what he'd said after she cut his hair. He needed to return the favor of her loaning him Ben's clothes and cutting his hair. He'd been so busy he hadn't had a chance to return the clothes.

He walked up her driveway just as she turned around. "Hey, Susannah," he said. The streetlamps didn't give off enough light to see her expression. She was wearing a kerchief instead of a *kapp*, and he couldn't tell what color it was either.

"Hi," she said, staring down at the ground the way she usually did.

What a difference from Julia, who probably would have tackled him while telling him about the time her father got a hangnail. But now that he was here, he wasn't sure how to proceed. He stood in the driveway, but she stayed in the yard and hadn't looked at him yet. Which made him wonder if it had been a mistake to approach her.

"Nice evening to water flowers," he mumbled, sticking his hands in the pockets of his pants.

"*Ya*, it is—oh!" She looked at the hose, which was still running and now watering the grass instead of the flowers. "Just a minute, let me shut off the water."

"I can do that for you. Where's the spigot?"

She pointed to the side of the house nearest the driveway. "Right over there."

He followed the hose and found the faucet, then turned it off. "If you put down the hose, I'll roll it up for you."

Susannah complied and Alex quickly wound up the hose and set it on the wrought iron holder against the house. By that time she had walked up to him. "*Danki*," she said.

"You're welcome." He faced her. "That's the least I can do considering all you did for me."

"I didn't do much." She turned her bare feet inward until her toes met.

"*Ya*, Susannah. You did."

———◆———

Susie couldn't believe Alex was standing right in front of her. Other than church, she hadn't seen him since she had cut his hair. She'd heard he'd gotten a job with Roy Nisley, and she also assumed he would want to spend time with his family and his friends after being gone for so long. She had been busy, too, working on the quilt and taking care of the house, yard, and garden while *Mamm* worked. But that didn't mean she didn't think about him every day and remember the pleasant fluttering she'd felt when she was around him. In fact, she was wearing the kerchief he'd let her borrow. Usually she kept it under her pillow, but this afternoon she had put it on. She knew she should have returned it by now, but she hadn't been able to bring herself to do so. Hopefully he didn't notice.

He took a step toward her. "I'm sorry I haven't brought Ben's clothes back to you."

"That's all right. I figured you were busy." She couldn't very well be upset that he hadn't returned the clothes when she still kept his handkerchief. Glancing up, she was finally able to meet his gaze, even though it was too dark to clearly read his expression. She wished *Mamm* would agree to outdoor sensor lights. They were battery operated and came on whenever someone moved near the light. But *Mamm* said no every time Susie brought it up. *"They're unnecessary,"* she said. Susie would give anything to have those lights right now.

"*Nee*, it's not all right. I've been busy, but I should have brought them over by now. Can I stop by and bring them after work tomorrow?"

"I don't want you to *geh* to any trouble," she said. "There's *nee* hurry."

"Trust me, it's *nee* trouble." He cleared his throat. "Susie, I, uh . . ."

When he didn't continue, she looked at him again. She didn't have to see him in the light to know how handsome he was. As she always did when she saw him at church, she marveled at his attractiveness, more so now that he no longer had his shaggy hair and was wearing Amish clothes. She had to make sure she didn't get caught staring at him when she was supposed to be focusing on the service.

"I . . . well, I . . ." He fumbled his words again.

She frowned, beginning to feel concerned. He wasn't usually at a loss for conversation. "Is something wrong, Alex?"

"*Nee.*" He ran his hand through his hair and let out an awkward chuckle. "It's just that I've never done this before."

"Done what?"

"Asked a *maedel* out."

Susie's knees nearly buckled. "What?"

"I've never asked anyone out on a date. Sounds dumb, I know. I always knew I would leave Middlefield and travel around the country, and when I was doing that, I didn't want to get involved with anyone. More importantly, I hadn't met anyone I wanted to get involved with. Until now."

Her heartbeat started to gallop. Surely, he wasn't going to ask her out. But if he wasn't, why would he bring up the subject?

"*Gut* thing Julia isn't here now," he said, shaking his head.

Her pulse slid to a halt. "Julia?"

"*Ya.* She was at Dan and Anna's tonight. We had supper together."

"Oh." Bother. Her eyes started to burn. But hadn't she predicted this, that Julia would be after him once she found out Alex had returned?

Alex was rubbing the back of his neck now. "She's quite . . ."

"Pretty?" Susie supplied.

"*Ya*. She is pretty."

Now she was grateful for the darkness, so Alex couldn't see that she was on the verge of tears.

"I'm really bad at this, aren't I?"

She wasn't sure how to respond. She also didn't know why he was talking to her about dating and Julia. Maybe he was looking for advice. But she wasn't the one to give it since she didn't have any experience with relationships either. Still, despite her disappointment, she wanted Alex to be happy. And if he was happy with Julia, then she needed to support him. "I think if you want to ask a *maedel* out, just do it. Being direct is always best."

"Of course. You're right." He chuckled again, but he sounded more like himself now. "Su—"

"Susie!" *Mamm*'s voice sounded through the screened-in front window. "Are you finished watering the flowers? I need your help hemming this dress."

She was never more thankful for an interruption before. "I've got to *geh*," she said, hurrying to the house.

"But—"

Susie ignored him as she ran inside. She shut not only the screen door but also the wooden front door, then leaned against it. So much for her hope that someday she and Alex would be together. Then again, what did she have to offer him? Julia was bubbly and vivacious. She was also a talker, and obviously Alex liked that. Who would want to be around someone who was quiet all the time?

"Were you talking to someone outside?" *Mamm* came into the living room, a pincushion tied to her wrist. "I thought I heard voices, but they were very faint."

She nodded. "Alex stopped by."

Mamm froze. "You were talking to Alex Lehman?"

"*Ya*." Her mother's reaction set off Susie's alarm bells. "Why?"

"Stay away from him, Susie," she snapped. "Don't you ever see him again."

SIX

Alex stood in Susannah's driveway with his mouth hanging open. He couldn't have bungled that more if he'd tried, and he definitely wasn't trying. He hadn't intended on asking Susannah on a date, only to offer to return Ben's clothes. But when he was near her, he couldn't help himself. In retrospect he should have waited until he'd been sure what to say. Now what was he supposed to do?

He glanced at her house. The light in the living room was still on. He could knock on the front door and try again, but he wasn't so sure he wouldn't get tongue-tied a second time. Alex Lehman had always been confident in himself, and he'd never shied away from trying anything. But something as important as this? He couldn't make a second attempt without getting his thoughts and emotions together first. It was embarrassing enough that he couldn't do something as simple as ask Susannah Glick out on a date. He didn't need to botch it a second time.

Alex turned and headed home. Fortunately, his embarrassment was starting to fade, and instead of focusing on his failure he thought about what she had said. *Being direct is always best.* She was right, and he should have just posed the question without all the awkwardness. The next time he saw Susannah Glick, and hopefully he would tomorrow after work, he would be ready to ask her for a date. *I just pray she says yes.*

———•◆•———

Susie hadn't seen her mother this upset in a long time. "I don't understand," she said, going toward *Mamm,* who still hadn't moved from the middle of the room. "Why do you want me to stay away from Alex?"

"I shouldn't have to spell it out for you." *Mamm*'s mouth pressed into a tight, thin line that turned her lips white. "Have you seen him before tonight?"

She nodded, telling him about her ride home from Berlin. "The bus was full, and the only empty seat was the one next to me."

"You didn't tell me that when you came home."

"I didn't think it was important," she said.

"What did he want?"

"*Mamm,* I . . . he just stopped by to say hello." And talk about Julia. Her heart dipped again.

"Don't get involved with him, Susie."

"Why not?" she asked, forgetting that she was supposed to be nonchalant about him.

"Because you never know when he might leave again."

Susie couldn't believe her ears. "He said he's here to stay, and I believe him."

Mamm lifted her chin. "I believed your *vatter* too. Look where it got me."

"I thought you forgave him," she said softly.

Her mother blinked. Then she sighed, her chin and shoulders drooping slightly. "I have. But I haven't forgotten what he's done. He abandoned me and you *kinner*. I've forgiven him, but that doesn't mean I want him to return."

Susie nodded. She didn't want any harm to come to him either. He had left when she was a baby, too young to know him or have any feelings for him. But she wouldn't wish bad things for anyone, including Julia Yoder, even though at the moment Susie didn't like her that much.

She walked over to her mother. "Alex isn't *Vatter*," she said.

"I know." *Mamm* looked at her, pain evident in her eyes. "You care about him. I can tell." Then she sighed again. "Why couldn't you fall for someone who's stable?"

"He is stable, *Mamm*. He has a job. He joined the church."

"He left once before."

"That doesn't mean he'll leave again. He's even interested in dating someone. That's why he was here tonight."

"He asked you out?"

I wish. She shook her head. "He's interested in Julia Yoder."

Mamm scrunched her nose. "That chatterbox?"

"She's pretty, though."

"Looks don't last, and they don't matter in the long run. Character does. Julia's . . . let's just say she doesn't think before she speaks." But *Mamm* looked relieved. "I'm just glad he's not interested in you."

Ouch. That hurt almost as much as knowing Alex liked Julia. But she didn't say anything, and for the rest of the night she helped her mother and kept quiet, like she usually did. She also hid her feelings. Her mother wasn't the person she could talk to about her crush on Alex. And now that he was going to ask Julia out, she needed to get over him.

Later that night before she went to bed, she took off Alex's handkerchief, folded it into a neat square, and set it on her dresser. She would give it to him tomorrow when he dropped off Ben's clothes. Then she would get over him for good.

But instead of putting on her nightgown, she stared at the handkerchief. Her mother was right about a lot of things, but not this time. Alex wasn't anything like her father. He wouldn't leave someone he loved. Susie would stake her heart on that.

———•———

The next morning, Susie laid out her pieces of the quilt on the table. Tomorrow she was meeting with the quilting circle again and she wanted to double-check her stitches. Everyone in the group stitched with precision, and although her stitches for the most part were straight and even, she wanted to correct any errors. Since the quilt would be auctioned off for charity, she wanted it to be as perfect as it could be.

Checking her stitches also helped her keep her mind off Alex and Julia—for the most part. Despite her vow to get over him, she had struggled to not think about him last night. But when she woke up this morning, she was even more determined to set him and Julia aside. There was no point in pining for what she couldn't have.

By noon she had finished checking and ironing the triangles that made up part of the points on the Broken Star pattern. She was carefully placing them between pieces of freezer paper when she heard a knock on the kitchen door. She looked through the window and saw Alex waving. For some reason she thought he would be by later in the day, but she was glad he was here now while *Mamm* was working at Jane's. Her mother had been subdued this morning during breakfast, and Susie knew she'd had a restless night. If *Mamm* knew Alex was here, she would be furious, and Susie didn't want her mother to be angry with him.

She went to the door and opened it. "Hi," she said, glancing at the bundle of clothes tucked under his arm.

"Hi, Susannah."

Now that it was daylight, she saw the tension on his face that must have been there last night when he was talking about Julia. Was he going to ask her for more advice? Probably, knowing her luck. "Come on in," she said, unable to muster any enthusiasm.

He shut the door behind him. "Here are Ben's clothes," he said, holding them out.

"*Danki.*" She set them on the counter, and started to reach in her pocket for the handkerchief.

"Working on the quilt, I see." He walked over to the table and glanced at the sage-green quilt pieces.

"*Ya.*" She pulled out the handkerchief and looked at it, then rubbed her fingers over the fabric before joining him by the table. "Here."

He turned to her, then looked at the handkerchief. "What is this?"

"You let me borrow it on the bus."

"Oh yeah. I'd forgotten about that."

Her stomach sank further. All the time she had spent savoring their time together on the bus, and he didn't even remember. "I'm sorry I didn't return it earlier," she managed to say, thrusting it at him.

He looked at it again. "You can keep it."

"I have plenty of handkerchiefs."

But instead of taking it, he folded her fingers over the fabric and moved closer to her. "I need to talk to you about something."

Here it goes, more Julia conversation. She gripped the handkerchief. "What about?"

"Us."

Alex loosened his hold on her hand, and in her nervousness, the handkerchief dropped to the ground. "Did you say *us*?"

He nodded, moving even closer to her. "That's exactly what I said."

She wished she had at least a tiny bit of experience with men, because she could really use some right now. "I didn't realize there was an *us*," she whispered.

"There isn't." He wiped his hands on his broadfall pants. He was wearing his hat today and had on black suspenders over a light-blue shirt.

Now she was really confused. Forgetting her shyness, she put her hands on her hips. "Alex, what are you talking about?"

"Remember last night?"

She nodded, cringing inwardly. "You needed advice about asking Julia out."

His brow hit his hairline. "*What*?"

"You were having trouble figuring out how to ask Julia out, and I said—"

"Direct is best. Right." He shook his head. "But you're wrong about me and Julia."

"Huh?" Now it was her turn to be surprised. "But you two had supper last night."

"Because Dan invited me for supper and Anna had secretly invited Julia."

Susie listened as Alex explained what happened during the meal. Her pulse began to race again, just as it had last night when she first saw him. "So you're not planning to ask Julia out on a date?"

"*Gut* grief, absolutely not." One more step closer. "You're the one I want to go out with, but I made a fool of myself last night."

She let his words sink in. "You want to *geh* out?"

"*Ya*." He grinned.

"With me?"

"Yep." Then his grin disappeared. "But there's a problem."

Of course there was. Her dream of dating Alex Lehman— she still couldn't believe he actually wanted to go out with her—was within her grasp. At least he had made it sound like it was. But nothing had been easy about her and Alex. Why should it be now?

"There's a carpenter I apprenticed with in Millersburg last year—Stan Raber. His wife called me last night after I got home. He fell off the ladder cleaning the gutters. Tried to break his fall with his hand and ended up shattering both wrists and he broke his leg. Obviously he can't work."

That sounded like a horrible accident. "I'm so sorry to hear that."

"Me too. Carrie asked if I could help out until he's healed up. Stan and his family are *gut* people, and I didn't hesitate to tell them that I'd be there as soon as possible, after I took care of some personal business. I'd planned to ask you on a date today when I brought over Ben's clothes, but I can't." He swallowed. "I would like to ask you for a future date, when I get back from Millersburg, though. If you want to."

Susie couldn't move. All she could do was stare into Alex's eyes. He was serious. Not only that, but she saw something in those brown depths that made her heart sing.

"I know this is sudden," he said, not moving away from her. "But I haven't been able to stop thinking about you since our bus ride together. I hope you don't think I'm being *seltsam* or too forward. I just want to get to know you better. What do you say, Susannah? Will you *geh* out with me after I come back home?"

"*Ya*," she said, her voice barely above a whisper. "I'll *geh* out with you."

He grinned. "Now, I'm holding you to it. Don't *geh* falling for some other guy while I'm gone." His tone sounded teasing, but his expression was serious.

"I won't." She smiled. "I promise."

Alex blew out a breath, still smiling. "I better run. I've got to catch the bus this morning so I can be at Stan's this afternoon. I'll write to you while I'm gone if that's all right."

His words finally sank in. Alex liked her, enough for a date and to write letters to her. She had to fight the urge to squeal with delight in front of him. "Of course," she said, trying to keep her tone even. "And I'll write you back too."

"I would hope so." His gaze shifted to her shoulder. "You have a thread or something stuck to your dress." He reached out and started to pull it off.

The kitchen door opened, and her mother walked inside. *Oh nee!* "*Mamm*," she said, stepping away from Alex at the same time he jumped back. "What are you doing home?"

"I thought I'd have lunch with *mei dochder*." *Mamm* turned to Alex, then looked back at Susie, her gaze cool. "But I see you have company."

"I was about to leave," Alex said, giving Susannah an apologetic glance.

Mamm didn't say anything, and Alex quickly dashed out the door.

Susie went to her mother but *Mamm* wasn't looking at her. Instead she walked over to the sink and took a glass from the cabinet, not uttering a word.

Susie rushed to her. "*Mamm*, I'm sorry. I didn't invite him over, he dropped by. He had something to ask me . . ." Oh no. She had said too much.

Mamm whirled around. "What did he ask you?" When Susie didn't answer, *Mamm* added, "Never mind. I already know. I thought I could trust you, Susannah."

"You can. It's just . . ." She paused. "I like him, *Mamm*. I really do. I liked him before he left."

"You were sixteen then." *Mamm* waved her hand. "A childhood crush."

"It's not a crush anymore." She lifted her chin. "And you're right. He did ask me out. But he's leaving for Millersburg—"

"See? I told you he wouldn't stay long. Barely more than a month!" *Mamm* set the glass on the counter so hard Susie was surprised it didn't break. "And he had the nerve to ask you to wait for him, *ya*?"

"*Ya*," she said, feeling three inches tall.

"Well, I hope you told him you wouldn't."

She thought it best not to correct her *mamm* for now. "He's helping a friend with his business while he's recuperating from an accident. As soon as he can, he's coming back."

Mamm's expression wasn't quite as tight as before, and Susie went into more detail about Stan's misfortune. "I'm sorry for his friend," *Mamm* said. "But I'm also grateful. This will give you time to get over Alex."

"But, *Mamm*—"

"It's for your own *gut*. Trust me." *Mamm* headed for the door.

"Where are you going?" Susie asked.

"Back to Jane's. I lost *mei* appetite." She walked out, slamming the door behind her.

Susie flinched. She'd have to apologize to *Mamm* tonight when she got home from work. But a part of her didn't want to. She was an adult now, and she knew her own heart. *He'll be back. I know he will.*

SEVEN

Dear Susannah,

I arrived at Stan's this afternoon. Boy, he's in bad shape. I'm worried about him, but Carrie assured me that the doctor said if he rests and doesn't do any work he will heal, but it will take a long time. After seeing him, I went to his workshop and spent the rest of the day there getting familiar with everything again. He has a lot of orders to fill, but his son-in-law can help out a few times a week in the evenings. David isn't a carpenter, but he does have some experience in woodworking. A few other people have said they will pitch in, too, but the bulk of the work will be my responsibility. I'm fine with that—it's the reason I'm here.

I miss you, Susannah. I hope I'm not being too forward in saying that. But it's true. Maybe you can come here for a visit in the near future. I'll even take you to the quilt shop in town.

Alex

———— •◆• ————

Dear Alex,

I was so happy to get your letter so soon. I'm sorry you have to do so much work, but I know Stan and his family are grateful that you're willing to. I would love to go to the quilt shop again. Right now we're finishing up the quilt for the auction, so I don't want to leave until that's done. Then I'll have more time to come for a visit.

I miss you too.

Susannah

Three weeks later . . .

Dear Susannah,

Here I am writing another letter to you. I think I've written to you every night since I arrived in Millersburg. I can't tell you how much your letters mean to me. I feel we've gotten to know each other so well since I've left. It's not quite the same as going out on dates, but that time will come. I'm glad to know that you feel the same way about me that I do about you. For the first time in my life I'm really homesick. I can't wait to see you.

Stan is steadily improving, and that's both good and bad. He's getting cranky now and insisting he can at least go to the workshop and supervise. But we know better—he'll have a saw in his hand the minute we turn our backs to him. Carrie's doing a good job keeping him on a fairly even keel, and several of his friends have stopped by regularly to visit.

Speaking of visits, have you figured out when you can come to Berlin? I know you said things are tense between you and your *Mamm*. A part of me wishes you would tell me why, but I also respect your privacy. Anytime you're ready to visit, I'll be available. I already told Stan and Carrie about you, and they're eager to meet you.

Alex

ONE WEEK LATER . . .

Dear Susannah,

You haven't replied to my past three letters, and I'm starting to get worried. I talked to my mother on Saturday. I wanted to ask her if you were okay, but you said you didn't want anyone to know we were writing to each other, and I don't want to break that confidence. But if I don't hear from you soon, I'll have to call you. I can't stand the thought that something has happened to you.

If you're not writing back because of something I wrote or did, please let me know. I miss getting your letters. I miss you.

Alex

———•◆•———

Dear Alex,

I don't think it's a good idea for us to write to each other anymore. I also can't go out with you when you come back to Middlefield. I'm sorry. Please don't send me another letter, and please don't call me. I'm fine.

Susannah

———•◦•———

THREE MONTHS LATER . . .

S usie, would you like to *geh* with me to the grocery store?"

Susie looked at *Mamm*, shook her head, and looked down at the magazine in her lap. The pages were open, but she had no idea what the articles were about. She hadn't been able to concentrate on much of anything since she had last written Alex. Her heart squeezed. She had to write the letter three times because her tears had stained the paper. She glanced out the living room window. Light snowflakes floated to the ground outside the window. It was the first snow of November. The gray, cloudy sky mirrored her dismal mood.

Mamm sat down on the sofa across from her. "How long are you going to mope?"

"What?" Susie said, turning to her.

"All you've done lately is spend your time at home sulking. You don't even *geh* to your quilting circle anymore."

"We finished the quilt for the auction," she said.

"I know that. I used to be a part of that group, remember? I also know that as soon as they finish one project, they start another."

"I didn't want to do a wall hanging." That was the project the circle had decided on, at Malinda's suggestion. The pattern was beautiful—a lovely dahlia consisting of various shades of pinks and creamy white. But her heart wasn't in quilting anymore. Alex still held it, and there was nothing she could do about that.

"You don't want to do anything." *Mamm* frowned, her hands folded in her lap. "I sense that you're trying to punish me for doing what's best for you."

Susie almost rolled her eyes. Ever since *Mamm* had found out that she was writing to Alex, she had been impossible to live with. She forced Susie to stop writing to him. Not only that, but she had also made her permanently cut off all ties with him. She tried to plead her case, but *Mamm* stood firm. "You can *geh* live with Ben and his wife if life is so difficult here. I can manage living alone."

"At least he was able to date and get married," Susie had muttered.

"He takes his family responsibilities seriously. I raised him to be faithful and loyal."

She had started to argue that Alex possessed those qualities, too, but she gave up. *Mamm* wasn't going to budge, and she'd even tried to set up Susie on dates with some of her friend's single sons, not just ones who lived in Middlefield but also some who resided in nearby Mesopotamia. She'd even suggested Jonas Miller, Julia's ex-boyfriend, of all people. But Susie had refused to entertain him or any other probable dates. Jonas was soon out of the picture anyway. He and Julia had made up and were getting married next Tuesday. *At least they got their happy ending.*

"Is this how things are going to be between us?" *Mamm* said, her knuckles turning white. "You pouting because you're not getting your way, and me having to live with it?" Before Susie could answer, *Mamm* added, "One day you'll see that I'm right. You can't trust a man who leaves at the drop of a hat. He's been gone almost four months now. So much for his promises that he's coming back."

"I'm sure his friend is still recuperating.

"Hmmph. A likely story."

Susie closed the magazine and glared at *Mamm. I would know exactly what was going on if you hadn't interfered.* But it was pointless to say those words out loud.

"Why can't you understand that I'm trying to spare you pain?"

"I'm in pain now, *Mamm*." She got up from the chair and walked to the window. The snow was falling a little harder now, but it barely stuck to the road, much less the grass. Why couldn't her mother understand how much she was hurting right now? How much she cared about Alex? He had been right about them getting to know each other through their letters. Before her last terse note to him, she had written him a ten-page letter, revealing things to him she hadn't told anyone. She had cared for him before he left for Millersburg. She was in love with him now.

"That will ease. Time heals all wounds."

"Like it has yours?" Susie bit her lip, continuing to stare out the window. The words had slipped out.

Mamm didn't answer right away. Finally she said, "Are you going to the store with me or not?"

"*Nee*. I'm staying here."

"Suit yourself."

Mamm left the room, and Susie hung her head. She didn't want her relationship with her mother to be this way. But she couldn't just act like everything was normal either. Her heart hurt, and her mother wouldn't budge on the subject.

There was also something else that added to her pain. Alex never wrote her back. He never called her. He did exactly what she asked him to. If he cared about her as much as he'd said, wouldn't he at least want to know why she was cutting him off? *Wouldn't he fight for me?*

She knew she was being unfair. But a small part of her wondered if *Mamm* was right—that all along he was just telling her what she wanted to hear. Maybe he was toying with her emotions, like *Mamm* said he would.

Susie went back to sit in the chair and tried to read the magazine. Her mother was right. She couldn't keep moping around forever. But she wasn't sure what else to do. Maybe she would go back to her quilting circle, but only after they finished the wall hanging. She had already told them she was too busy to do the project, and she didn't want them to ask any questions. That would also give her time to get her emotional feet under her. *I hope.*

A knock sounded on the front door. She wondered if *Mamm* was expecting anyone. When she got up and opened the door, she was stunned to see Ida Mae, Malinda, Norma, and Velda standing there, their black bonnets dotted with white snow.

"Hello, Susannah," Ida Mae said, her black purse hanging over her elbow. Her usual friendly expression was surprisingly stern.

"We're here to talk to you," Norma added, looking just as grim.

"And your *mutter*," Malinda said, lifting her chin.

"Both of you together." Velda crossed her arms over her chest, her black purse, identical to Ida Mae's, slapping against her stomach.

Susie frowned. They all seemed upset. "*Mamm*'s headed to the grocery store—"

"We saw her outside." Ida Mae's expression softened. "She's in the kitchen now, waiting on us."

Susie took a step back. She didn't like the idea of being ambushed, even by well-meaning friends. "I don't feel like talking right now."

The women bustled through the door into the living room. "Sorry," Malinda said. "You don't have a choice."

"We're not leaving until we all hash this out," Norma said.

"Right." Velda nodded once.

"Hash what out?"

Ida Mae touched her arm. "You and your mother have a problem, and we're here to help both of you solve it."

———◆———

"You're going to sand that chest down to twigs."

Alex looked up as Stan hobbled into the workshop. He stopped in front of the hope chest Alex was working on, the last project from the long list of back orders that needed to be completed. "Sorry," Alex mumbled, easing up on the sanding. Stan was right. He'd almost over-sanded the lid, nearly wasting a prime piece of cedarwood.

"Eh, it happens." He looked directly at Alex. "Especially when you don't have your mind on your work."

Alex looked at his work boots, which were covered in sawdust. He couldn't argue with the man. Work had been the last thing on his mind.

Stan brushed off the excess dust from the lid. "Looks like this is ready for staining. How about I give you a hand?"

"How about you don't?" Alex half grinned to let Stan know he wasn't being rude. While the man had almost miraculous healing ability, something he chalked up to drinking a quart of milk a day, he wasn't quite ready to get back to even light duty. But that would be happening soon enough, probably in little more than a week. Then Alex's time here would be up, and he could return to Middlefield.

"It was worth a try." Stan went to sit on an old office chair on the opposite side of the wall. For the past three weeks, he'd sat in this chair and supervised Alex and David's work. Mostly Alex's since David was still able to help out only three nights a week. Alex had learned a lot during the time he was here, but he knew there was more he could learn.

Stan leaned his cane against the barn. For two months he'd been unable to use crutches because of his injured wrists, and the family had rented a wheelchair to help him get around. After lots of physical therapy, he was now able to walk with a cane and his wrists were completely healed. "I'll be getting back to work soon enough. Then you'll be free to *geh* back home."

"About that." Alex set the sanding block on the worktable. "I wondered if you'd given any thought to *mei* suggestion about getting an assistant."

"I have."

"And?"

"I think it's a *gut* idea. Probably something I should have done a while ago."

Alex nodded. "I'd like to apply for the job."

Stan's brow arched. "You?"

He leaned against the chest. "You know *mei* work. You know I'm responsible. You've taught me everything I know too. I'd be the perfect assistant."

"That you would." Stan stroked his bearded chin. "The answer is *nee*."

"What?"

"We didn't ask you to help us so we could lure you away from Middlefield, Alex. Carrie and I both know how important your hometown is to you."

It used to be. No, that wasn't accurate. His family and friends were still important to him, and he could still visit them if he lived in Millersburg.

"Besides, I thought you were eager to see your *maedel* again," Stan added.

Pain squeezed his chest. "Not anymore."

"Ah. I thought something had happened," Stan said. "You've been moody for months now."

"Sorry." He'd thought he'd hidden his emotions better than that.

"We didn't want to pry or anything, though."

"I appreciate that. So will you reconsider hiring me?"

Stan nodded. "On one condition, though."

"What's that?"

"You have to tell me you don't have any feelings for Susannah anymore."

Alex froze. He wanted to say those exact words to Stan more than anything. But they would be a lie. Susannah might not care for him anymore—and he had no idea what changed—but that didn't mean he didn't still have feelings for her and would for a long time.

Stan nodded. "I've got *mei* answer. I just wanted to make sure you were really wanting the job and not trying to avoid going back home to work things out."

"Her last letter to me was final. I don't think there's anything to work out."

"So you're going to give up on her that easily?" Stan shook his head. "I pegged you for a better man than that."

"She's the one who rejected me." Alex gripped the edge of the worktable, remembering the ache in his heart when he'd read her last letter.

"Then you must have done something wrong."

"If I did, she didn't tell me." Resentment filled him. He'd never thought Susannah would be fickle, but that's exactly how she turned out to be.

"Hmm." Stan rubbed his chin again. "Let's see if I have this straight. You two are writing each other, everything is *gut* for a while—you're even excited to introduce her to us—and then . . . poof! She tells you to stop writing."

"She didn't want me to call her either."

"But you still care about her."

He paused. "*Ya*. I do. But she doesn't care about me, so what am I supposed to do?"

"For one, you can find out the reason why. Are you sure you have *nee* idea?"

"I'm sure—" Wait. He suddenly remembered the last time he saw her, when her mother had come into the kitchen. He'd been in such a hurry to leave that he hadn't paid much attention to her reaction, but now he recalled catching a glimpse of her expression . . . and she hadn't been happy. Could her mother be keeping them apart? But why?

"I tell you what," Stan said, getting up from the chair. "You *geh* back to Middlefield and try to work things out with Susannah. If you can't, then I'll be happy to hire you on. And before you get to thinking that I'm a softy or something, this is more about having an employee who can 100 percent pay attention to the job, not have half his mind in another town. Got it?"

"Understood."

After Stan left, Alex worked on staining the cedar chest, making sure to keep his attention on the task and not on Susannah. But when he shut down the shop for the night, he knew what he had to do. He had to go home before it was too late. He would see Susannah again and find out what was truly going on, something he should have done in the first place, but he'd been too hurt to do so. And too prideful. *No man wants to be rejected.*

And if she didn't want to be with him? He'd find a way to move on . . . somehow.

EIGHT

Susie looked at her mother, who was sitting on the opposite end of the kitchen table. On the other sides of the square table sat the rest of the quilting circle. But no one was saying anything. Once everyone had sat down, they all seemed reluctant to talk.

Malinda huffed. "We won't get anything accomplished if we just sit here."

"Agreed," Ida Mae said.

"You all should mind your own business." *Mamm* kept her gaze on the table, not looking at any of the women.

"Also agreed." Ida Mae, who was sitting closest to *Mamm*, touched her arm lightly. "But we wouldn't be here if we didn't care."

"Everything is fine." *Mamm* shrugged off Ida Mae's arm.

"*Nee*, it's not." Velda held up her hands. "We know how much you love quilting, Susie, but you stopped coming to our group."

"I'm busy," she mumbled, unable to look at them.

"But you love flowers," Malinda said. "We chose the Daliah pattern just for you."

Susie glanced up, filled with guilt.

"You two don't sit together at church anymore." Norma lifted her hands. "Do you think we haven't noticed?"

Susie looked at the four women. Even Malinda, who usually had a cool demeanor, was out of sorts. *They really do care about me and* Mamm.

"Rebecca, you've been so distant with us." Ida Mae touched her *mamm*'s hand. "Let us help you."

Because her mother would never agree to talk, Susie piped up. "She doesn't want me to see Alex Lehman."

All four women looked surprised. "You and Alex Lehman?" Norma said.

"I had *nee* idea," Malinda added.

Ida Mae clasped her hands together. "I think you two would make a sweet couple."

"*Nee!*" Mamm slammed her palms on the table. "They won't."

For some reason Susie found her voice. "You don't even know him, Mamm."

"I know his type. I was married to his type."

"But you even agreed Alex isn't like *Daed*—"

"That was before he left you."

This time Susie couldn't keep herself from rolling her eyes in frustration. "To help his friend."

"That's exactly what your *vatter* said!"

Silence engulfed the room. Susie was stunned. Mamm had never discussed the details of *Daed* leaving, so this was news to her. "He did?"

"*Ya*." *Mamm* sat back in the chair, her lower lip quivering. "Marvin said one of his friends in New York needed farm help. That he'd be gone only a few weeks."

"He never came back," Susie whispered.

"*Nee*, he didn't. And I found out later it was all a lie. He never went to New York. He left the church and went to California." Tears formed in her eyes. "You have *nee* idea how much that hurt. I can't bear the idea of you going through such pain. What if you and Alex had gotten married and had *kinner*, and he decided he didn't want the responsibility anymore? Raising *kinner* by yourself is so hard . . ." She burst into tears.

"Oh, Rebecca." Ida Mae took her hand. "Why did you keep all this bottled up for so long? We could have helped you through it."

"You have," *Mamm* said. "You've always been there for me. But there were times I didn't want to bother any of you. You had your own families and responsibilities. *Nee* one wants to listen to someone's personal problems."

"You're wrong about that." Velda took a napkin from the holder in the middle of the table and dabbed at the corner of her eye. "We're here to share one another's burdens."

"*Mamm*." Susie got up and ran to her, putting her arms around her shoulders. Her mother was always so stoic. So strong. Susie had no idea she was holding in so much. "I'm so sorry."

"I love you, Susie. I want what's best for you." *Mamm* looked up at her. "Please understand that."

"I do." She looked at Malinda, Ida Mae, Norma, and Velda. She saw the concern and care in their eyes. That gave her courage to speak what was on her heart. "Alex isn't *Daed*."

"But what if he is?"

"Then I'll have to deal with that, won't I? Just like any other problem that comes up. When I need help, God will be there . . . and I know you will too."

"Don't forget about us." Malinda sniffed, although this time her eyes were filled with tears. "We'll be here for you too."

"For both of you." Ida Mae nodded.

Susie looked at *Mamm*, who was crying freely now. "Can you forgive me, Susie?"

She threw her arms around her mother, her tears joining the rest of the ladies' weeping. "*Ya*," she said, even though she wasn't sure she needed to forgive her mother for loving her so much. "I love you."

The quilt circle stayed for the rest of the afternoon. Susie was quiet, as was her way. But she observed her *mamm* and the women interacting together and could see how much her mother was enjoying the time she spent with her friends. Time she'd had to give up because she had to work so hard.

Ida Mae was the last one to leave. As she picked up her purse off the kitchen counter, she said, "You need to quilt with us again, Rebecca."

Mamm shook her head. "I'm so busy with *mei* work at Jane's."

"I can help you," Susie said. "With both of us sewing, that will free you up to quilt with us."

Mamm looked at her, then nodded. "I'll talk to Jane."

"*Gut.*" Ida Mae gave them each a hug. "We've missed you," she said to *Mamm*. "Now our circle will be complete again."

After Ida Mae left, it was nearly suppertime. "How about we have something quick and easy for supper," *Mamm* suggested, her eyes still swollen from crying earlier.

Susie nodded. While today with their quilting circle friends had been cathartic, they were both exhausted. "How about sandwiches and some of that potato salad left over from the other day?"

"Sounds wonderful. I'll slice the bread."

They didn't say much for most of the meal, but as Susie took the last bite of her bologna and cheddar cheese sandwich, *Mamm* asked, "Do you really think Alex will come back home?"

She stared at her almost empty plate. She had believed in Alex for so long, but now she wasn't as sure as she had been. "I hope so." That was all she could say.

"This is *mei* fault." *Mamm* fiddled with the crust on the corner of her sandwich. "I was wrong for keeping you two apart. I see that now. I'll write to him and explain everything—"

"*Nee,*" Susie said quickly. Even though she and her mother had finally come to an understanding, the last thing she wanted was for *Mamm* to get further involved. This was her relationship—or at least it had been. "I'll write him."

Mamm nodded, and they finished the rest of their meal. Susie got up to clear the table.

"What about visiting him?" *Mamm* asked.

Susie blinked. "Are you serious?"

"If you still care for him after all this time, then you should tell him in person."

Her mother was actually telling her to go see Alex. *Today is the day for miracles.* Not wanting *Mamm* to change her mind, she said, "I'll leave in the morning. I'll call him tonight and let him know."

"Or," *Mamm* said, giving her a small smile, "you could surprise him."

She could hardly believe this was her mother speaking. Then again, *Mamm* had changed this afternoon. The lines of tension that always seemed to be on her face were gone, and a rare sparkle was in her eyes after spending time with her friends. *Thank you, quilting circle.* It was amazing how a group of supportive friends were able to get through to *Mamm* when Susie never could.

"I'll surprise him," Susie said, her heart filling with excitement. Then she took her mother's hand. "I'll be okay," she added. "No matter what happens."

Mamm nodded and squeezed her hand. "I know you will."

NINE

The driver pulled the bus to a stop in front of the bus station in Ashtabula. Alex blew out a breath. He was home . . . again. But this time he didn't feel nervous anticipation. He just felt plain nervous about seeing Susannah. For his own sanity he had to find out why she had suddenly cut off their budding relationship without any explanation. He also had to prepare himself if she told him what he didn't want to hear. Either way, he would get to the truth.

He waited until all the other passengers got off the bus, then he grabbed his backpack from under the seat in front of him. He got off the bus, slung his pack over his shoulder, and started for the parking lot.

"Alex!"

His heart stopped. He knew that voice. *Susannah.* His heart shot back into a fast-paced rhythm. Oh, how he'd missed her. When he turned, he saw her hurrying toward him, a suitcase in her hand and excitement on her face.

She stopped a few feet in front of him, her pretty eyes wide and expectant. "What are you doing here?"

Showered with shame, he realized how close he'd come to not returning and fulfilling his promise to her. Even if she did reject him, he had always been a man of his word. That shouldn't change because he didn't get what he wanted. Thank God Stan had brought him to his senses. "I came back to you, Susannah."

She dropped her luggage and threw her arms around him, then nestled her face in his neck. "I knew you would," she murmured. "I knew you would."

Stunned, his thoughts were hazy as he returned her hug. Then he tightened his embrace. They were making a display, but he didn't care. How many times had he dreamed of holding her in his arms? Nothing compared to the real thing. Did this mean . . . ?

"I can't believe this," she said, giggling, her hands moving to his shoulders. "I was going to see you, and you were already on your way home. What a coincidence."

More like providence. Again. He smiled, but it faded a little. "I thought you didn't want to see me anymore."

She moved away from him and grabbed her suitcase. "I have a lot of explaining to do. If we hurry, we might be able to catch Max. He just dropped me off and there's a lot of traffic in front of the station. He might still be here."

They raced to the front of the station. Sure enough, Max's red four-door was still stuck in the drop-off zone.

"Max!" Susannah waved her hand. "Don't leave!"

He watched as she ran over to Max's car and tapped on his window. He'd never seen Susannah like this before.

Confident. A little bold, even. Definitely sure of herself. He grinned. *I like it.*

———•◆•———

Susie slid next to Alex in the back seat of the taxi. A bold move, for her at least. But she didn't think about being shy right now. All she could think about was that Alex had come back. And that she had to fix what she had messed up.

Max, who had been taxiing the Amish for many years, could be trusted not to eavesdrop, or at least not to discuss what he heard during his trips, so Susie felt free to explain everything to Alex. She told him about *Mamm* not wanting her to see him, how she was afraid Susie would be hurt, and how Susie had never wanted to stop writing to him. Finally she said that her *mamm* encouraged her to visit him and tell him what happened. "I'm sorry," she said, looking him directly in the eye, pleading with him to forgive her.

He took her hand. "It's all right," he said, nodding. "I can see you had a tough decision to make."

She held on tight to his large, work-roughened hand. "I made the wrong decision."

"*Nee.* You did the right thing. You honored your mother. Honoring our parents is what we're supposed to do."

"Even when they're wrong?"

"It's understandable why she thought that, though. I'm just glad you worked through everything."

"Thanks to the quilting circle," she said. "They are true friends."

"Got one of those of *mei* own." Alex told her about Stan,

and how he encouraged him to find out why Susie had stopped writing to him.

Disappointment filled her. "So that's the reason you came back? Because Stan told you to?"

"Stan just reminded me what a *dummkopf* I am sometimes." He entwined his fingers around hers. "I should have been more persistent."

She looked at their clasped hands. "You only did what I asked you to do."

"Hey, who am I dropping off first?" Max said. "Neither of you said."

Susie raised her hand. "Me—"

"Susannah—"

Max chuckled. "Got it. We'll be there in about five minutes."

She turned to Alex. "I need to let *Mamm* know I'm home."

"*Ya*. And I need to let *mei* parents know I'm back." He paused. "But I'd like to see you tonight, if that's okay."

"I'd like that." But there was a question she had been meaning to ask him for a long time, and she needed to know before Max dropped her off. "Why do you call me Susannah instead of Susie?"

His eyes locked with hers. "Susie's a *maed*'s name. You're not a girl anymore. Not to me."

Oh my. Susie—Susannah—could barely breathe, not with him looking at her the way he was now. Fortunately, Max turned into her driveway because she wasn't so sure she would have been able to stop herself from kissing Alex right there in the back seat. *So much for being shy.*

Max pulled the car to a stop but didn't turn off the engine. "I'll get your bag, Susie."

"*Danki.*"

As soon as Max was out of the car, Alex leaned toward her. "*Gut*, that gives me a second to do this." He pressed a soft kiss on her lips, then let *geh* of her hand. "See you tonight, Susannah."

When she got out of the car, she was floating on air.

EPILOGUE

FIVE MONTHS LATER

Susannah sat down on the bus seat and took off her scarf. The air was still chilly outside, but the heater kept the bus warm.

Alex slid into the seat next to her. "Going *mei* way?"

She grinned. "Always."

As the bus pulled out of the station, Susannah pulled a list out of her purse, pausing to touch Alex's red handkerchief she always carried with her. "Are you sure you don't mind going with me to Helping Hands? Everyone in the quilt circle asked me to pick up something for them, plus there are things I want to get for myself."

"I can't think of anything I'd rather do than spend a day at the quilt shop." At Susannah's arched eyebrow, he said, "Okay, there's a lot I'd rather do. But as long as I can spend time with you, it will be worth it." He reached for her hand.

She entwined her fingers with his, still feeling a little

thrill every time they held hands. They settled their clasped hands between the seats, out of view of anyone else. There were plenty of Amish travelers on the bus today, and while holding hands with her new husband wasn't a terrible thing, it was still a public display some would frown on.

Alex leaned his head back against the seat and closed his eyes. Business had picked up after the holidays and he and Roy had been working six days a week. Now that there was a lull, they were able to take a short vacation to visit Stan and Carrie. She was looking forward to meeting them, almost as much as she was about shopping with Alex in Berlin. There were plenty other shops and places to visit in Holmes County, and Alex was eager to show her around.

As he slept, she looked out the window and thought about how much had changed the past five months. That night when they had their first date, Alex came inside and talked to *Mamm*, answering all her questions and reassuring her he was in Middlefield to stay. A few days later, Ben had vouched for him, something Susannah had appreciated. "*Mamm* should have asked me about him," he'd said. "Then you both could have avoided the problem."

But Susannah knew everything had happened exactly the way it was supposed to. Or as her new husband always said, it was all providential.

From the time he had returned to Middlefield, they had seen each other as much as possible and before long, everyone suspected they would get married eventually. Even Julia had congratulated her and said that she was getting a "*gut mann*." She'd also said a bunch of other things, more than Susannah could, or needed to, remember. There was that one thing about her sister's foot, but at that point she had tuned Julia out.

Mamm had rejoined the quilting circle, and Thursday afternoons were filled with laughter, food, and of course, quilting. Susannah also helped out at Jane's when the seamstress had extra work. But now that she was married to Alex, she wouldn't be working for much longer. God willing, they both wanted to start a family right away.

She felt Alex squeeze her hand, and she turned and looked at him.

His eyes were open. "I love you," he whispered, squeezing her hand again.

"I love you too." She smiled. "Ready for a new adventure?"

"As long as you're with me . . . always."

ACKNOWLEDGMENTS

A big thank you to my editors Becky Monds and Karli Jackson for their help and expertise, and to Natasha Kern, who is always there when I need her.

DISCUSSION QUESTIONS

1. Susie enjoys the time she spends with the quilting group. What groups or organizations have you belonged to that you enjoy?
2. Frannie tells Alex, "I know the Lord says we're not to be anxious." What are some ways we can deal with our worry and anxiety?
3. Do you think Susie's *Mamm* did the right thing trying to spare Susie the same pain she felt when Marvin left? How could she have handled the situation differently?
4. Susie's *Mamm* told her, "Time heals all wounds." Is this statement true? Why or why not?
5. Alex and Susie both needed help from their friends in order to get their relationship back on track. Discuss a time when your friends helped you through a tough situation.

STITCHED TOGETHER

———◆———

SHELLEY SHEPARD GRAY

Live one day at a time and make it a masterpiece.

<small>AMISH PROVERB</small>

God places the lonely in families.

<small>PSALM 68:6</small>

ONE

"I think this quilt might be your best one yet," Rosie Raber's sister Bethany said as she carefully spread the pieced sections of fabric on the worktable. Running a finger along the center of one of the compass blocks, she added, "There are so many parts to this design. I think I'd go blind before I finished even two blocks."

Rosie chuckled. "You're always too modest. I'm sure you'd have no trouble making this quilt." Privately, though, Rosie wasn't sure if her statement rang exactly true. Her lovely sister was talented in many things, but Rosie's current project was a difficult one. She had made many, many quilts, but this one had certainly stretched her skills. Three months ago, when she'd been only halfway through the blocks, she'd felt like throwing up her hands in surrender. It had been that challenging.

Still examining the intricately pieced compass pattern, Bethany frowned. "I might be able to stitch this . . . but even if I did get up the nerve to try it, we both know it wouldn't look as gorgeous. You really have a gift, sister. I'm proud of you."

217

"*Danke*. However, if I ever do finish this thing, I'll know that I didn't make it alone. *Got* blessed me with a talent for sewing," Rosie replied. "I'm grateful for His generosity—especially when I can use my gifts for good."

Leaning back in one of the Sewing Shop's comfy bright-green chairs, her sister seemed to think about that for a spell. Since it was the end of the day and they were the only two people left in the shop, Rosie sipped her peppermint tea and relaxed.

All in all, it had been a good day. Just like every February, the streets in Pinecraft, Florida, were busy with tourists and snowbirds happy to spend the winter months in warm sunshine instead of the cold and snow. Though some of the other locals made no secret that they dreaded the arrival of the first wave of Pioneer Trail buses, Rosie always found the influx of newcomers exhilarating.

Of course, she didn't know any different. Rosie was one of the few in the Amish community who'd been born in the middle of Sarasota, Florida. And she rarely ventured farther from Pinecraft than her weekly sojourns to Siesta Key, the gorgeous white-sand beach just a thirty-minute ride on the SCAT—the Sarasota County Area Transit. The quick and inexpensive bus service had stops everywhere. There was even a stop right outside her shop.

After setting her own mug of hot tea down, Bethany said, "Rosie, tell me true. Do you think you might win this year?"

Rosie knew she was referring to the award given by the Mennonite and Amish community club just hours before the large quilt auction was held for the public. For almost two decades, one of the biggest churches in the area had held the auction to raise funds for their mission work in Haiti.

"I couldn't say."

"Come now. Don't you think you're being too modest? You've been spending most of this year working on your quilt. It must be special."

"I like my design, but I'm running behind this year. I'm starting to worry it won't get done. And don't forget—only the top ten quilts get put in the running for the prize."

And out of those ten, one of them was always chosen to be the Quilt of the Year. Though Rosie had sewn many quilts for the show, and her last four had been chosen to auction, none of them had ever received that highest honor.

Bethany placed her mug on the table. "Oh, come on, Rosie. It's just the two of us here," she half whispered. "I won't accuse you of bragging or anything either. What do you really think of your chances?"

"I think . . ." She looked around, just to be sure no one could overhear her. "I think I might have a really good chance this year. If I ever get it done." She felt her cheeks grow warm in embarrassment, both because she was being so prideful and because she couldn't figure out what was wrong with her. Usually, all she ever did was work on her quilts and dream of winning the biggest prize. However, this year, life seemed to be getting in the way.

"Oh, you'll get it done," Bethany declared. Her eyes lit up as she continued. "And won't it be so exciting when you do win? Why, from that point on, you could always say you've sewn a Quilt of the Year."

Allowing herself to imagine that, Rosie smiled. "I could."

But just as quickly she tamped the vision down. Not only was it not right to want to be the winner but there was a good chance the quilt might not turn out as she hoped. "Winning a prize doesn't really matter. I mean, we all do make the quilts for charity, you know."

"Oh, I know." Bethany's sarcastic tone relayed everything she wasn't saying. "So, have you seen the competition?"

"You know it's not a true contest," Rosie chided. It might be one thing to secretly imagine winning, but it was another to think of the other women's works as competition.

"It's close to one, though . . . right?" When Rosie nodded, Bethany grinned. "So, what are Allison and Mary Jo's quilts like?"

"I haven't seen their work, but I heard Allison is making hers in an abstract design out of remnants. Mary Jo, on the other hand, has designed a children's quilt with blocks and letters."

Bethany inhaled sharply. "Have you seen it? Mary Jo is mighty talented."

"I haven't seen it yet, but I heard it's eye-catching and unique. She's a very gifted quilter."

Her sister bit her lip before smiling. "I guess we'll see what happens."

"As long as we have buyers for all the quilts, the day will be a success. The money is for a good cause." Seeing that it was already after six o'clock, Rosie carefully folded the quilt and placed it on the coffee table. "Are you ready to go home?"

"Yep." Getting slowly to her feet, Bethany yawned. "I'm so tired all of the sudden. This pregnancy seems harder than the last one, which makes no sense. I'm only having one *boppli* this time. Not two."

"You told me the midwife says every pregnancy is different."

"Nan did say that, though I'm starting to think maybe my age has something to do with it."

"You're only thirty-two, Beth. I reckon you're more tired because of the girls."

"Probably so." Her sister's voice brightened as they gathered their belongings. "Maybe Joe will have started working on supper with the girls. What do you think the chance of that is?"

"Not too *gut*, I'm afraid," Rosie said. She led the way out of the shop and locked the door. The early evening was still rather warm. Their sweaters over their dresses were more than enough to guard against any chill. "Lydia and Becca are darling girls, but . . ." She let her voice drift off.

"Don't tiptoe around the truth, Rosie. We both know they're a handful."

Saying they were a handful was like saying the sand at Siesta Key was pleasant to walk on. Neither description did the actuality justice. "They are twin four-year-olds, Bethany. You know I love them." They also had a lot of energy and a penchant for destruction.

"I love them too." A small frown formed between Bethany's brows. "Perhaps they have gotten a little bit better. I mean, they were very naughty two-year-olds."

"And three-year-olds," Rosie teased.

Bethany brightened. "You're right. They were worse last year. Maybe they'll be even better behaved when the new baby comes." Looking down at her tummy, she frowned. "If I last that long."

Rosie chuckled. "You poor dear. You need to stay off your feet as much as you're able. I'd be happy to come over and cook supper for all of you tonight."

"*Danke*, but I don't want to take advantage of you any more than I already do. You cooked for us two nights ago."

"I didn't mind."

"I think we'll be okay on our own. You can go home and work on your quilt. I know you're anxious to do that."

Rosie smiled at her sister, though her heart wasn't exactly in full agreement with her expression. The truth was that she wasn't exactly looking forward to going home to her own quiet house or spending the whole evening piecing together a complicated pattern. For the first time, she was starting to doubt her motivation. After all, the quilts were supposed to keep people warm—that was what mattered at the end of the day. And yet she'd been so caught up in making the most intricate pattern she could that, truth be told, she wasn't enjoying it very much.

Struggling to shake off her sudden onslaught of doldrums, she smiled at a courting couple passing by on a bicycle built for two. "It will be good to sit down for a spell." That wasn't a lie.

"Don't forget, you said you would greet the Pioneer Trails bus tomorrow morning."

"I haven't forgotten." Though she was always happy to help Bethany and Joe, Rosie wasn't exactly excited about waiting with the throng of people for the bus from Ohio to arrive. She enjoyed the arrival of winter visitors, and the crowds always had a festive air. But everyone would be asking one another questions about who they were waiting to see. She'd have to admit she was only doing a favor for her older sister.

Then, too, there was her lack of enthusiasm about meeting the elusive Tim. All she knew about the man was that he was Joe's older brother and that he seemed to care more about his mission work than his own family.

But, of course, Bethany didn't need to know any of that. "I promise I will bring Tim to your house safe and sound."

"If he's hungry, take him out to get a pizza or to Yoder's for a real meal." When it took Rosie a minute to wrap her head around that, her sister looked at her plaintively. "Or . . . take him somewhere else. Wherever you want. Will you do that, please?"

"I will. I'll make sure he feels welcome." Instinctively, she knew Joe's mystery brother wasn't going to want a quick slice of pizza. No, she was probably going to have to stand in line with him at Yoder's and then share an hour-long lunch before walking him to his brother's house. The whole event was likely to take at least three hours, which wouldn't be a problem if she were visiting with someone she cared about. But since it was this stranger, Tim Christner, all she felt was annoyed. She bit back a sigh.

Bethany noticed. "We do appreciate your help. Joe didn't feel he could say no to the overtime wages."

Oh, why couldn't she just be kind? Hurrying to ease her sister's concern, Rosie said, "Of course Joe couldn't say no. You know I don't mind, dear. I'm always happy to help you."

"*Danke*. I promise, even though you've never met Tim, you won't find being with him a hardship."

That drew her up short. She didn't find being around goats to be a hardship either . . . but she didn't want to spend an afternoon with one. "What is Tim like?" she said in an effort to appear more accommodating. Joe's brother had been in Mexico on mission work when Bethany and Joe got married.

"He's easygoing and nice."

That told her nothing. "Anything else?"

"He's rather attractive."

Rosie mentally raised her eyebrows. Bethany wasn't usually one to comment on a person's looks. "Well, I'll look forward to meeting him."

Halting at the stop sign where they always parted, Bethany hugged her tight. "I love you, Rosie. Have a good evening."

"Love you back," she said before she turned left and Bethany turned right.

She kept her smile firmly in place for a full block. It wasn't until her small cottage came into sight that she allowed it to slip. Her little home was snug and pretty and had a nice outside patio and garden. She kept it immaculate and neat, with everything in its proper place. But as she unlocked her front door and stepped inside, all she could think about was how Bethany was being greeted by a loving husband, two adorable girls, and a long-haired dachshund named Prince. Rosie knew their house would be messy, supper would be likely late, and there might even be a fine layering of sand on the floor since the girls loved going to the beach at Siesta

Key and neither of their parents was very good at sweeping it up. But there would be love and laughter and hugs.

In contrast? Well, all she had were thoughts about what had almost been, a hamster named Butch, and utter, complete silence.

TWO

R osie?" an attractive, brown-eyed man wearing a long-sleeved blue shirt asked as he approached. "It is you, isn't it?"

So, it seemed her sister had been right. Her brother-in-law *was* very attractive. "Yes, I'm Rosie. Are you Tim?"

"I am." He grinned as he held out a palm. "May I shake your hand? I'd hug you, but I haven't showered since yesterday morning. I don't want to scare you off before we've had a chance to say hello."

Rosie smiled as she held out her own hand, though she was starting to think she probably wouldn't have noticed if he hadn't showered in three days. All that seemed to register in her brain was that Tim Christner shared his brother's smile and eyes but not much else. While Joe was rather ordinary looking and had a serious disposition, Tim appeared to be full of light. Everything about this man's expression and stance spoke of good nature and contentment. And then, of course, there were his broad shoulders, firm jaw, and lightly bronzed skin.

His palm and fingers were slightly rough, signaling that he wasn't the type of person who sat behind a desk all day. His grip was firm, too, almost like he considered her someone he wanted to know, not just his brother's wife's younger sister.

When their hands parted, she felt curiously let down, which was mighty silly. She needed to get ahold of herself and fast. He was merely a relative, not a long-lost beau. "So, um, let's go get your bag."

"No need. I've got it right here."

She noticed then that a rather complicated nylon duffel bag sat on the pavement next to him. It looked high tech and the opposite of Plain. "That's rather fancy."

He grinned as he easily lifted the bag and slipped his arms through its straps, like a backpack. "I reckon it is, but I've learned over time that ignoring fancy things can sometimes be a detriment when one is constantly moving around. This holds a lot, is easy to carry, and has lasted for four years so far."

And . . . now she was embarrassed. She'd sounded judgmental instead of merely interested. They hadn't even taken a step across the parking lot, and he was already having to defend himself. "I'm sorry. I have a habit of speaking my mind a bit too often."

He shrugged off her words. "No worries. I wasn't offended. Honestly, I'd rather you tell me what you're thinking instead of me always wondering. Say anything you'd like. I promise, I have thick skin."

"*Danke.*" Noticing the crowd around them had already started to disperse, she said, "Shall we go?"

"Of course." He took off his straw hat and brushed back his longish brown hair from his face before placing it on his head again. "You lead the way."

Tim really was an amiable and easygoing man. Smiling hesitantly at him, Rosie motioned a hand forward. "Let's head down this road. Here on Bahia Vista, there are some restaurants nearby, and then your brother's *haus* is just beyond."

"Sounds good."

As they started off, she noticed that he walked easily, as if he carried nothing more than a bag of cotton on his back. He was also looking around at everyone in interest.

"Everything is so bright here," he said. "I feel like I've stepped into the middle of a summertime picnic."

She couldn't help but giggle at the statement. "You're right. I've met people who come from up north and comment first thing on the blue skies, abundant flowers, and jaunty red and blue bicycles." Looking up at him as they stopped, she added, "First thing they do is head to the dollar store to buy a pair of sunglasses."

"I can see why. If one is used to gray and cloudy skies, the bright sun can be a bit of a shock. It's a blessing that I own a pair of sunglasses already. Where are yours?"

"In my purse."

"Is it not sunny enough for you to need them?"

"I guess I forgot about them." She didn't want to admit that she'd been wary about having them on when they first met. There were some church districts that regarded even the simplest of sunglasses as ornamental instead of necessary. Once again, Rosie realized that she'd been guilty of assuming what Tim was like based on the few things she knew about him. Now all her presuppositions seemed so silly.

"Speaking of sunglasses and such, how come you are so tan?" she asked before she realized she'd blurted the rude question out loud. "I thought you came here from Berlin, in Holmes County."

He laughed. "I did, but I'd only been in Ohio a couple of weeks. Before that, I was in Mexico and Buenos Aires for several months."

"Buenos Aires? Isn't that in South America?"

"It is. It's summer down there, you know."

"Why were you there? More mission work?"

Tim looked a bit taken aback by her tone, but after a second he shook his head. "Not at all. I went there on vacation."

"I see." Realizing how nosy she was being, she brightened her tone. "And now you are here." She was pleased for not adding "at last" to the end of her statement.

"*Jah.* I wish I could've come earlier, but it couldn't be helped. I can't wait to see the girls again. How are they?"

Again? She'd thought he'd never met them. "When did you see them last?"

"I saw them once in Berlin when they were barely two. I imagine they're a bit different now?"

"I'd say so." She grinned. "The girls are *gut.* Busy, as four-year-olds often are." They were also adorable and a handful. She couldn't wait until Tim got a good dose of their antics.

"I reckon so."

Just as he looked about to speak again, Rosie said, "Bethany asked me to make sure you ate something when you arrived. Your choices are either pizza by the slice or Yoder's. Which is your preference?"

"Which restaurant would you rather go to?"

"Either is fine with me. The pizza is good. Or if you'd rather, we could sit down at Yoder's, and you could have a proper meal. It's typical Amish fare, of course." Unable to help herself, she added, "They also have a wide variety of pies."

"I do love pie, but I think a slice of pizza will suit me fine."

"Are you sure?"

"I don't want to take up much more of your time. And besides, it's been a long time since I've had a good slice of pizza."

To her surprise, she felt slightly disappointed that he'd chosen the quickest option. "Pizza it is, then." She pointed down the road at the sign for Village Pizzas by Emma. "We can sit outside, if you'd like."

"I'd like." He smiled at her.

When she smiled back at him, she realized that had been a huge mistake. Tim Christner wasn't just a handsome man. There was something so compelling about him that she found she was having a hard time thinking about anything else.

"I'll go inside and order our slices. What would you care to have?"

"How about we switch places? You sit down with my duffel, and I'll go inside and order. That way I'll be able to look at the choices."

She couldn't think of a reason not to agree with that . . .

except for the fact that one had to pay when one ordered the food. "All right. Order me a slice of pepperoni and an iced tea."

"Anything else?"

She reached for her purse. "*Jah.* Wait one moment so I can give you some money."

Tim put up a hand, like he was batting her ten-dollar bill away. "You'll do no such thing, Rosie."

"But I'm happy to treat you. You're my guest."

"*Danke* for saying that, but I think we both know I'm your duty. Besides, I think I can handle paying for a couple of slices of pizza."

He turned and walked away before she could reply to that. Maybe it was just as well. It wasn't like she could say much about his observation anyway.

Instead, she pulled her sunglasses out of her purse, slipped them onto her nose, and attempted to catch her breath. Though it wasn't exactly her lungs that needed a break as much as it was her insides. Tim had taken her by surprise and made every coherent thought leave her brain. In its place sat something she'd thought she'd never feel again: interest.

It was mighty disconcerting.

Years ago, she'd felt that same initial attraction to another man. Levi had been so handsome and fun, and their interest in each other had soon led to deeper feelings. They'd been very much in love. On more than one occasion Levi had told Rosie he couldn't wait for the years to pass so he could save up enough money to formally propose marriage. She'd been a different girl in those days—hopeful about her future and anxious to follow Levi's lead no matter where he took her.

But then, in the span of seconds, both Levi and her dreams had left the earth, leaving only a fierce hole in her heart so jagged and tender that even now she hated to try to fill it back up.

But maybe the Lord was letting her know she'd been mistaken. Maybe it was time to imagine falling in love one day in the distant future. Maybe it was possible for her heart to finally heal again. If that was the case, then she would be grateful for Tim Christner's appearance in her life. It wasn't as though she expected anything with this man she'd barely met. But in the span of just a few minutes, he'd opened her eyes to . . . possibilities. He was a good reminder to keep looking forward instead of mourning the past.

Yes, she decided, Tim was going to be a good friend to her. He would remind her about hope and blessings. All that was surely the only reason she was looking forward to the opportunity to spend time with him again.

THREE

The stars were out, his brother was telling a good story, he had showered and was wearing clean clothes, and for the first time in ages Tim felt completely relaxed. He was content.

Warm too. After experiencing so much cold and snow in Ohio for the last couple of weeks, being able to sit outside around a firepit in February in only a light jacket was a true blessing. During his whole time in Ohio, he'd felt like he would never warm up.

But it was more than just the warm weather that made him feel so comfortable. It was also the feeling that he'd finally come home. That had been a surprise.

Actually, so far, everything about this trip to see his brother and his family had been full of surprises. Though he already loved them, he hadn't expected to feel tears in his eyes the moment he'd spied Lydia and Becca. He hadn't expected to feel like he and Joe had been apart for only a couple of weeks instead of years. And he really hadn't expected to feel such an instant connection to the woman who'd met him at the bus. Was it just happiness he was feeling . . . or was this sudden sense of belonging something else entirely?

"You're awfully quiet, Tim," Bethany said from her spot next to Joe on the other side of the fire. "Are you exhausted? If so, don't feel like you have to sit here with us. You're welcome to go up to bed if you'd like."

True concern shone in his sister-in-law's eyes, making him feel like a heel. He'd hosted enough guests at the mission to know that a brand-new, unhappy visitor could be stressful. "I'm sorry I've been so quiet. I guess my mind was drifting. I am tired, but I'm not quite ready for bed." He sat up straighter. "I'll try to be a little more engaged."

"You don't have to do anything you don't want to do," Joe said. "You're here to relax, not put on a show."

"I realize that. *Danke.*"

"Those bus rides always wear me out," Bethany added. "It's a long journey from Berlin to here."

"It was long but not bad. There was a good group on board. The conversation was lively, and the rest time was blissfully quiet."

Joe grinned. "That is something to be pleased about. There's nothing worse than being seated next to a chatty couple who prefers not to sleep."

"Indeed."

"I reckon you're used to traveling too," Bethany murmured. "You've been to so many interesting places."

Though it was dark, he could see the interest in her eyes from the fire's flickering glow. "I am used to it, though the trip to Mexico is much different, *jah*? Flying on a plane is much quicker than a sixteen-hour bus ride." Tim kept his voice light, but he couldn't help but reflect just how different those trips were in comparison to visiting his brother's family.

Mission trips were enjoyable but always filled with a sense of urgency—like the Lord was giving him only a short amount of time to make a difference. In addition, he was always reminded of the families' needs that he was serving. That made his own weariness seem inconsequential.

"I have to say that you didn't look all that exhausted when you walked into the *haus* this afternoon," Joe said lightly. "I noticed you laughing with Rosie."

"She was good to get to know. Bethany, I would've never guessed you two were sisters. You don't look much alike."

"We get that a lot. Though we both have hazel eyes, her blonde hair is far lighter than mine."

Rosie's hair had looked like spun silk. "Are you two close?"

"We are, though some people find it hard to believe since we're so very different—and not just in looks."

"She's your younger sister, right?"

"*Jah*. We're two of six siblings, and both in the middle. My parents used to say we were the most even-keeled of them all."

"You are both even-tempered, but different for sure," Joe said. "While my Bethany is as calm as a secluded bay, Rosie is more like a deep, strong current. Steady but hard to either ignore or move around."

Bethany smiled at Joe. "That's a good way of putting it. My sister is friendly and loving but hates to stray off course."

"Does she have a beau?" Of course, the moment he asked that question, Tim wished he could take it back.

Just as he'd feared, his brother sat up straighter. "Why? Are you interested in Rosie?"

Was he? "Even if I was, it wouldn't be advisable, would it? I mean, I'm only here in Florida for a short amount of time." And even though he hadn't accepted a new contract yet, there was a good chance he wouldn't even be in the United States for long. That, of course, would make any long-distance relationship almost impossible to sustain.

"I don't know if it is advisable or not. That's for you to say, not I," Joe replied. He leaned back. "That said, to answer your question, Rosie doesn't have a beau."

"Any reason why not?"

"Well, she did have a steady beau about five or six years ago," Bethany explained. "Levi was a good match for her. He was fun and spontaneous where she is steady. He also loved her very much. We all thought—Rosie especially—that they were going to get married." She cleared her throat. "Oh, but she was so happy in those days. Giddy as could be! But then . . . Levi died."

"Died?"

"It was a boating accident," Joe explained.

Bethany nodded. "We were all devastated."

Tim couldn't help but gape. "I had no idea. What a shock that must have been for her."

She nodded sadly. "It was a terrible shock for all of us. Levi was a good swimmer and an experienced sailor too. He was out in a storm and, from what the Coast Guard said, lost control when the winds got near hurricane force."

"That's all very tragic."

"It was," Joe said. "Rosie not only had to deal with Levi's loss but with the fact that his death could've been prevented—if he'd only heeded the warnings."

"Of course, the Lord is always in charge, yes?" Bethany murmured. "There had to be a reason He wanted Levi with him. I'm sure one day we'll all know why too."

"That had to be hard for Rosie," Tim said before wishing he could have offered something a bit more meaningful. His statement sounded so trite.

"Rosie was mighty grief-stricken. For months, it felt like all the light had left her eyes. She was truly a shadow of her former self." Staring into the fire, Bethany added, "We were all worried about her. But then, one day, she started feeling better. She started making plans for the future again, which is when she started her business and sewing so much." Smiling, she finished her thought. "Now my sister has one of the most successful sewing shops in the area. People come from all over Florida to see her store and take her quilting classes."

"Some even travel down to Pinecraft from up north to take her classes," Joe added. "She's extremely talented."

"She quilts? Well, that's a nice hobby."

"It's more than a hobby," Joe said. "Rosie designs and makes intricate works of art. Each one of her pieces sells for thousands of dollars."

"But what she's really known for is her annual quilt for the auction for the Mennonite church," Bethany added. "All the best quilters in the area make an entry, and then the best of the best are judged and eventually auctioned. All the money goes toward the mission work."

"It sounds like the Lord is working through her in amazing ways."

"I guess He is. I know Rosie is my sister, but there are few women I know who are as impressive," Bethany said.

Tim was beginning to think that as well. His first impression of her had been that she was very pretty. Then he'd found himself charmed by her sense of humor. But now? After hearing about her tragic history and the fact that she'd developed such a successful business? Well, he was even more intrigued. "I'll look forward to getting to know Rosie better."

"I'm sure you will enjoy her friendship," Bethany said with a smile before it faded. "But, Tim? Please try to remember that underneath her drive and determination is a woman who works too hard, gives up a lot of herself, and still is nursing a broken heart."

"I'll remember." He smiled at his sister-in-law through the dim light but couldn't deny that she'd given him a lot to think about.

An hour later, he finally called it a night and went to his room in the attic. Joe and Bethany had finished out the space into a homey arrangement that was both comfortable and private. After taking a long shower, he lay on the bed and tried to think of nothing but his blessings and how glad he was to have this time with his family.

But he was unable to stop thinking about Rosie. He realized that his first impression of her had been sadly lacking. She wasn't just a woman driven toward making her business a success. She was more than simply Bethany's younger sister who had lived alone for most of her life. Her life had been filled with its own tragedy and disappointments.

Rosie was also more than a beautiful woman with light-blonde hair and unusual hazel eyes. She was complex, interesting, and had captured his attention in ways no other woman ever had before.

He wasn't sure what that meant, but he was anxious to find out.

FOUR

Rosie was spending the day at home in her sewing room. Everything was silent save for the whirl of her treadle sewing machine and occasional twirl of Butch on his hamster wheel. Both sounds were familiar and comforting—and welcome.

Of late, she'd been putting in more and more hours at her shop. That had felt like a blessing at first. But she was starting to realize she'd used her store as yet another reason not to make her contest-entry quilt a priority.

Last night, she'd been so confused about her feelings for Tim she'd forced herself to concentrate on the quilt. It was now time to either focus and get it done or make peace with the fact that she wasn't going to have an entry for the show.

It was a relatively easy decision. She was going to concentrate on winning the award. That, at least, was something she could depend upon.

Now that she had refocused, she'd put a new plan into motion. Today, Fran and Violet were both working so she could spend the entire day on her quilt. She was finishing the backing and tracing the quilting pattern onto it. Tomorrow, she would begin to quilt in earnest.

It was going to be a tight finish, but she couldn't regret the pieced pattern or the quilting design she'd chosen for the show. In order to win, one had to push oneself, and that was what she was doing. All she had to do was hope and pray that nothing unexpected happened in the next two weeks.

Though . . . that did seem a bit hard to imagine. It had been her experience that the Lord often had a way of making sure something unexpected did happen.

Smoothing a hand over the fabric, she murmured, "What do you think, Butchy? Do you think I'll really be able to finish this quilt without anything unexpected happening or me getting sick?"

Butch directed a long, slow stare her way before continuing to nibble the carrot she'd put in his cage that morning.

"I don't blame ya, Butch. I get sick every February, don't I? Too many busy days, I suppose." She shrugged. "But that's all right. Work is a blessing. I'm so very thankful to have a job that I love."

Though she might have gotten sick every year for a very different reason. She might have kept herself busy so she wouldn't be tempted to think about all the things she could've been doing if she'd still had Levi.

Levi!

Even now, his name made her insides clench with pain.

After all these years, why was she suddenly thinking about him all the time? It wasn't healthy. Not healthy at all.

For months after his death, Rosie had almost felt as if she had died too. Nothing had interested her, and she'd spent the majority of her days either in her room alone or out walking. Remembering back to the combined restlessness and grief she'd struggled with, Rosie figured she must have walked miles all around Sarasota and on Siesta Key those first few months.

Being around any of her family had hurt—for a while she'd even been unable to cope with her parents, because all their presence did was remind her of how they'd been blessed with decades of marriage while she hadn't had even one day of marriage to Levi.

Eventually she'd come out of her fog. Still later, she'd almost been her old self around others. Quilting and sewing had saved her. She'd thrown herself into her new life as a seamstress and had sewn clothes for friends and family, then started taking orders, all while making quilts in her spare time.

When people began asking for lessons right around the time old Mr. Hanson decided to close his shop, she'd decided to open her own store. Her parents had helped fund it with her promise to pay them back as soon as she could.

And she did. She'd repaid them within three years and then had gone forward. She'd created a successful business and garnered a good reputation too. All were things to be proud about.

But now she wondered if she'd spent all her energies on work instead of focusing on her personal life.

"Or lack of one," she said to Butch.

When her tiny black hamster wiggled his nose at her, she

smiled. "Your company counts for sure, Butch. However, I am sorry to say you are a poor substitute for a man."

Butch responded by turning his back to her while he chewed on his carrot.

She'd just returned her focus to the quilt when two raps sounded at her door before it opened. "Rosie, please tell me you're home."

Only her sister would let herself into her house without asking if it was okay to barge right in. "Of course I am."

"Aunt Rosie!" Becca called out just before launching herself into Rosie's arms.

She'd barely gotten the quilt out of the way before the little girl clambered into her lap. "Umph. Well, isn't this a nice surprise."

"Uh-huh." Becca pressed her hands to Rosie's cheeks. "*Mamm* and me were out for some time together."

"Just the two of you?" she asked as Becca climbed back off her lap and scampered to her mother's side. Noticing that Becca had a chocolate ice-cream stain on her cheek, Rosie quickly turned to set the quilt farther out of the girl's reach.

"Lydia is with *Daed* and Uncle Tim. They're at the hardware store."

"Oh?" Joe was a lot of things, but he wasn't especially handy with undertaking and finishing little house projects. "What is he getting?"

Bethany flopped down on the chair next to her. "For some reason, Joe and Tim decided to build some shelves in the laundry room."

"Really?"

"I know. I felt the same way." Bethany shrugged. "But I guess Tim has gotten good at building stuff while in Mexico. He offered to help Joe fix up some things."

"That is kind of him."

Bethany nodded, but she didn't especially look all that pleased. "I do think it's nice of him. I could use more shelves too."

"But . . ."

"But I don't know, Rosie. I am not all that excited about the idea of Joe starting more projects right now. We've got a lot going on."

"*Jah*, I suppose you do."

Becca pulled on Rosie's dark-purple dress. "Aunt Rosie, may I play with Butch?"

Realizing that Bethany would probably like to share some things without little ears listening, Rosie nodded. "Of course. You can take him to his Habitrail in the living room if you'd like."

"Let's go, Butch," the four-year-old said as she reached in and took hold of the unsuspecting hamster.

"Gently, now," Rosie murmured. "Butch is much smaller than you. I don't want you to accidentally hurt him."

"I won't hurt him. I love Butch."

After Becca left the room, Rosie looked at her sister with more concern. "Is there something else that's the matter?"

"No. It's just normal end-of-second-trimester crud. I'm sick every morning and want a nap every afternoon. And the girls!" She lowered her voice. "Every morning they wake up with more energy than I can recall ever having. Sometimes, all I want to do is sit, but if I don't keep them busy, the girls find something to do . . . which usually involves destruction."

"Oh, dear." Rosie completely agreed. Her nieces were adorable, but they were also full of bad ideas.

Bethany pursed her lips. "I'm afraid Tim is going to start all kinds of projects with Joe and then fly away to his next mission trip."

"Which will leave you with a batch of unfinished projects."

"*Jah.*" She paused, then added. "That's selfish of me. Ain't so?"

"I don't think so. You can only do so much in a day. Sister, you should speak to Joe about that."

"I would, but he wants to spend time with Tim, and it's not like they're going to sit on the couch all day and talk. And it's not that I don't want Joe and Tim to have a good time together. I just . . ." She stopped. Looking sheepish, she added, "I have a feeling that I'm not making a bit of sense."

"I think you are. You want Tim to have a good time with your husband but not tear up the house or create more work for you after he leaves."

"Exactly." She smiled hesitantly. "That's why I came over here."

So, this wasn't a quick little social visit. Rosie was suddenly wary. "I'm sorry, I'm not following."

"I'd like you to spend some time with Tim."

"What?"

"Please, Rosie? If you spend some time with Tim every day, then Joe will be able to help me with the girls. Or, at the very least, help me clean up after them."

Rosie had the quilt to finish. And her shop. And . . . and she wasn't sure how she felt being around Tim. In just a few hours he'd made her feel things she'd thought were gone forever, made her think about a different future. A future she'd started to believe would never be possible.

Not that there was anything wrong with that, of course. But she didn't want to let herself fall into the idea that possible future might include Tim himself. After all, he wasn't going to be around for long.

Rosie took a breath, ready to say no. But then she caught sight of the strain in Bethany's eyes. Her sister was just about at the end of her rope. She needed Rosie.

There was really only one thing to say. "Fine."

"Are you sure?"

Nee. No, she was not. "Of course I am."

"*Danke!*" Now that Bethany had gotten her way she looked slightly guilty. "I know I'm kind of heaping this on you, but I didn't think I would be so exhausted all the time."

She knew Bethany was talking about her pregnancy. "Of course you didn't."

"I'm just so tired." Her sister sniffed. "And I seem to be more emotional too."

"Don't worry about it, Beth. I'll think of something to do with Tim."

"Oh, you won't have to think too hard, Rosie. Just take him out and about! Tim wants to play tourist."

"All right . . ."

Sounding way too eager for Rosie to take her brother-in-law around the area, Bethany added, "Tim wants to go to

Siesta Key and explore Sarasota and go to the markets and maybe even take the SCAT all around the city."

Rosie privately thought all of those things sounded like a whole lot more than just an hour or two every day. "Hmm," she said.

Bethany's pleased smile faded. "'Hmm'?"

"Aunt Rosie!"

Worried, Rosie jumped to her feet just as Becca ran into the room. "What is it?"

"Well . . ."

"Yes?"

"Well, you see . . ."

"Spit it out, child."

Little Becca took a deep breath. "Aunt Rosie, I've lost Butch!"

Bethany hurried to her daughter's side. "Becca, what happened?"

I was trying to get Butchy to play in the tunnel I made him out of pillows, but I guess he didn't want to go. He jumped out of my hand and headed to the kitchen."

Rosie groaned. "What? Oh, Becca."

"I bet he's sitting on your rag rug or something," Bethany said as she led the way to Rosie's small galley-style kitchen.

"I doubt it." Walking in, she quickly scanned the area. "Butch?" she called out hesitantly.

But of course there was no rustle of tiny feet. Butch was a hamster, not a dog. Of course he wasn't going to come when she called. "I wish you would have been more careful with him, Becca. You should have put him in his Habitrail."

"I thought he wanted to play on the couch."

"He was eating his carrot when you came over. He likely didn't want to play at all."

Becca's eyes widened in surprise. "You seem really upset, Aunt Rosie."

"That's because I am." She got down on her knees to look under things, hoping to see a twitchy nose and shiny fur.

"But it was an accident." Tears filled the four-year-old's eyes.

Bethany curved an arm around her daughter's body. "Rosie, Becca didn't mean to lose Butch."

"I know, but I'm still worried about him."

"The men will help," her sister announced as the door opened again and Joe, Tim, and Lydia entered the room.

There was only one reason Tim had come by, and it wasn't to search for missing hamsters. Obviously, Bethany had already made these plans and informed her husband of the fact. Aggravated to be manipulated, Rosie shot her sister a dark look before getting up to greet the newcomers. "I'm glad you all are here," she said. "We've got a problem."

Tim strode to her side. "Are you missing something?" He scanned the floor. "Did you drop a straight pin or something?"

"*Nee*, I'm afraid I'm missing a hamster."

Lydia gasped. "Butch is lost?"

"I don't know if he's lost as much as decided that he wanted to explore."

"Becca decided to play Habitrail with him—using pillows instead of the real thing," Bethany explained.

Joe rubbed his eyes with one hand. "Oh, Bec."

"I said I was sorry!"

"I hope he doesn't die," Lydia said. "'Cause then it will be all your fault, Becca."

And . . . there went the tears again.

"Girls!" Bethany called out. "Be nice."

Before they could argue more, Tim cleared his throat. "Well, everyone, let's spread out and start looking for the rascal before he starts causing damage."

While Lydia went with her father and Becca and Bethany began lifting pillows off the couch, Tim stepped closer to Rosie. "Want to tell me what damage a tiny hamster could do?"

"He's chewed holes in clothes, a rug, and my couch."

"And you kept him after that?"

"He's not perfect, Tim. I realize that."

"I told her to take him outside and let the little devil fend for himself," Joe said.

Turning to her brother-in-law, she glared. "Which would've been heartless, Joe. Butch is a good hamster."

"Except when he's not," Bethany added.

"This . . . this, uh, adventure Butch is on is not his fault." It was only because Tim was there that she refrained from adding anything else. She wouldn't want him to think she was a shrew.

"I hope he's not cold and hungry," Lydia said as she crawled around on her hands and knees.

"He's only gone missing for a few minutes, dear," Bethany answered. "Even Butch couldn't be hungry yet."

On they looked. Under the couch, on the coffee table, and even inside her small bookshelf next to the back door.

But not once did they hear the hamster's squeaking or catch a glimpse of a wiggling tail.

After thirty minutes had passed, Bethany sat down on a chair. "I'm exhausted."

Joe walked over to his wife's side. "Maybe it's time you lie down."

"I am sleepy. Lying down would be heavenly." Then she had the grace to look worried. "But I would hate to leave Rosie with this mess."

It was a mess too. All the books from her bookshelf were scattered on the floor. So were three throw pillows, one of the couch cushions, and a worn quilt that was her favorite to curl up under on cool evenings.

"But what about Butch?" Lydia called out. "He's probably scared and lonely. Or dead."

"I reckon if he was feeling scared or lonely, Butch would've come out to join us," Joe said.

"But maybe he can't," Lydia said. "Maybe he hurt his paw and he's limping and can hardly walk. Or he's dead."

Becca started crying. "You shouldn't say that."

"Why not? It's probably true and all your fault. You're a hamster killer!"

"Girls, you two stop now," Bethany said.

Ignoring her mother, Becca started crying even harder. "That's not fair. I was only trying to help Aunt Rosie."

"You weren't helping. You were hurting Butch. Or killing him."

"Now, girls, you shouldn't fight," Rosie said, just as she noticed Bethany rest her head against the back of the chair and moan softly. Rosie looked down at her feet to stop herself from rolling her eyes. Bethany's daughters might be full of drama and emotions, but Rosie knew they'd learned from the master. Even when Bethany was small, she'd been an expert at producing instant tears.

"Oh, Beth. Come on, now, let's get you home," Joe said. "You don't mind, do you, Rosie?"

"Of course not. Please, take your family home."

"Except for Tim, right?" Bethany roused herself enough to ask.

"Of course." Turning to him, she tried to summon a somewhat welcoming expression. "Tim, if you don't mind, I'd be grateful for your help."

From the glint in his eyes, it was obvious he wasn't fooled for a second about what was happening. "*Danke*. I'm happy to stay."

That seemed to be all Joe and Bethany needed in order to usher everyone else out of the house. The last to leave was a teary Becca who hugged Rosie's waist tightly. "I'm sorry I lost Butch."

"Don't worry, dear. He'll turn up."

"Will you forgive me?"

She gentled her voice. "Of course, child. I love you no matter what. I know losing Butchy was an accident. Don't worry. He'll show up soon."

"Promise?"

"Of course, Becca, dear. Now, off you go. I'll see you later."

After waving at Lydia and Becca, she stood on her side of the screen door until they were out of sight. Then she turned back around and caught Tim's eye. "I would say that I'm sorry you got dropped off here like a wayward child, but it is a whole lot quieter here. If our situations were reversed, I would be longing for a break."

"I wasn't quite longing, but I do appreciate the quiet."

"I bet."

Tim's arms were folded over his chest, and he looked amused by the whole situation, something she couldn't help but be relieved by. Not every out-of-town guest would be taking what had just happened with such ease. "I was about to start putting your books on the bookshelves, but I thought you might like them organized in a certain way."

"I do. I alphabetize them by author. But how about before we start cleaning we take a break. Would you like some cranberry cookies or lemonade?"

"May I say yes to both?"

She found herself laughing as she led the way into the kitchen. "Of course. I was going to have both myself. Let's sit down and revel in the calm."

FIVE

Tim was torn between feeling like another problem for Rosie and being delighted to have a break from his brother's house. While it was good to see Joe, Bethany was as sweet as ever, and the girls were fascinating, living with them was like being stuck in the middle of a town fair. There was a constant stream of noise and activity.

In contrast, Rosie's house felt like an oasis. Sure, it might currently be a cluttered, girlish oasis with a hamster on the loose, but all in all, it gave him the sense of peace he'd been craving the last few months.

To top it off, Rosie made wonderful-*gut* cookies. Realizing that the three he'd put on his napkin were long gone, he stopped himself just in time from grabbing yet another from the plate in the center of the table.

She noticed. "Please, help yourself to another. Or better yet, a couple more."

"Are you sure?"

"Of course. I usually only eat a few and then take the rest over to a neighbor's *haus* or to Bethany's girls." After a brief pause, she added, "I won't be delivering any cookies to them today."

He chuckled before realizing there was a good chance she preferred that to being stuck with him. "Thank you for not minding me being here. I promise I'll try to stay out of your way."

Her eyes widened as a fierce blush covered her cheeks. "I'm sorry. I didn't mean that the way it sounded. I'm glad for your company. I was referring to my sister's girls."

"Ah."

"I'm not really upset about Butch getting let out. It's more, well, everything Bethany did. She can sometimes try my patience." She brightened. "In any case, how about we take a walk, and I'll show you some sights around Pinecraft?"

He loved how she was trying so hard to put his needs in front of her own, but in this case it wasn't necessary. "How about we clean up your living room and look for a wily hamster instead?"

"You wouldn't mind?"

"Of course not." After swallowing the last of his fifth cookie, he said, "I would never leave you with this mess."

"I'll accept your offer, then. *Danke*."

"Of course." He stood up and deposited his glass in the sink. "I'll go start alphabetizing books." He was glad to catch sight of a smile before he walked back into the living room.

After scanning the area in case Butch had come out of hiding, he sat down on the ground and began sorting the titles by authors. A few minutes later, Rosie joined him in the room, placing pillows and cushions back where they belonged. They worked in companionable silence for a while. When things were looking a little less like a tornado had struck, he decided to learn a little bit more about her.

"How did you become a hamster owner, Rosie?"

"I didn't set out to own one, but for some reason, hamsters seem to suit me."

Amused, he paused his task. "Really? How so?"

"I like having a pet, but I don't want their fur to get all over my sewing projects. And since I have my sewing shop and often help out Bethany and Joe with the girls, I didn't want to have a pet that would be sad if I wasn't home all the time. Hamsters don't seem to mind being alone much at all."

"I guess not, since Butch has wandered off on his own," he joked.

"I suppose it serves me right. If I did more with him besides give him carrots and food and clean his cage, he might be more inclined to stay nearby."

"Or perhaps if a little girl hadn't decided to build her own hamster playpen . . ."

She giggled. "*Jah*, that too."

Glad to see her smile, he added, "I don't have a lot of experience with hamsters, so I couldn't tell you how they usually act. I'm guessing, though, that the little guy was given an opportunity he couldn't ignore."

"You are probably right. Anyway, like I said when the others were here, Butch might destroy some things, but he'll turn up eventually."

"That's a refreshing attitude."

"It's not as selfless as you might think." Pointing to the quilt she'd been working on, she added, "There's only one thing in the house that I would be really upset about if Butch ruined it: my quilt for the benefit auction."

"The auction is for an orphanage in Haiti, yes?"

"It is. The money raised will help the *kinner* in many ways."

"Indeed it will." Carefully gathering more books, Tim placed them in neat piles. "This quilt is a lovely testament to your generosity."

Her eyes widened as she sat down next to him on the floor. Then she took a deep breath. "Tim, I wish I could say that was true, but unfortunately I'm not quite that generous."

"Oh?"

"*Jah*. You see . . . I've been working on this quilt for far more prideful reasons." Still averting her face, she mumbled, "I'm hoping the quilt will be named Quilt of the Year."

"Having a prize-winning Quilt of the Year sounds pretty special, Rosie. What an accolade."

"Oh, it is. There are so many gifted quilters and some truly amazing designs. I know it is a prideful thing, but I would be so happy to finally have one of my quilts attain that title."

He really did think she was being too hard on herself. Even people with the noblest of intentions found joy in their hard work being acknowledged. "There's nothing wrong with wanting your hard work to be recognized. I know I've felt pleased when folks at the mission's home office call to tell me they think I'm doing a good job."

"This is different, though. I'm not doing mission work. Just sewing."

"I don't think it's quite that cut and dried, Rosie." When

he saw she was about to argue, he said, "How about we agree to agree on something else?"

"Such as?"

He grinned. "Such as that we both hope we'll locate your wayward hamster before he nibbles your quilt?"

"I can agree to that," Rosie replied with a laugh. "Not only am I worried about the little guy, I really don't want him to adopt my quilt as his new home."

After neatly gathering the first pile of books by authors at the beginning of the alphabet and beginning to place them on a shelf, she said, "So, tell me about your mission work. What are your days like?"

"Busy."

She glanced at him. When he didn't add anything more, she grinned. "That's it?"

"It sums it up the best." Tim smiled to take the sting out of his terse reply but didn't add anything more. Work was the last thing he wanted to talk about at the moment. It had been so long since he'd spent time alone with a woman he wasn't working with at the mission. No, that wasn't it. It had been so long since he'd felt such interest in a woman. Years. He'd much rather talk about other things than work.

"Now I understand," she teased. "You're going to make me ask you a hundred questions."

"*Nee*! Please, no." The last thing he wanted was to inadvertently share something embarrassing about himself.

A look of surprise crossed her face. "Have I offended you in some way?"

"It's not that. It's . . . Well, to be honest, right now I am grateful not to be working. I'm afraid if I start talking about everything, I'll start worrying about how things are going in my absence." And how he hadn't made a lot of space in his life for anything but mission work.

"Of course. I think that way about my shop. Um, not that our two jobs have many similarities."

"You might be right about that, but I believe we have some other things in common."

"Oh?"

He noticed she'd stilled and was listening intently. Choosing his words with care, he continued. "Oh, *jah*. We are both close to our siblings . . . and I believe we have both experienced some pain over the last few years."

Rosie looked away. "I'm not sure what you mean."

"Well, like you, I've lost someone I loved."

"Who have you lost?"

"Bridget. She was my girl for years. We flirted when we were teenagers and always paired up whenever our group of friends got together." He swallowed. "I started courting her in earnest about six months before I went to Mexico for the first time."

"What happened?"

Meeting her gaze, he said, "Two days before I planned to propose, she broke up with me."

Her eyes widened. "That's awful."

"I was shocked, though I guess I shouldn't have been." He paused, then forced himself to relay the rest of his story. "Looking back, I've realized that while Bridget was pleased I was one of the youngest men to have been selected to be a missionary, she wasn't too happy about the thought of eventually being one too."

"She broke up with you because she didn't want to go to Mexico?"

"*Nee*, she broke up with me because she didn't love me enough to leave all her friends and family. My dream wasn't hers." He took a deep breath. "I know my breakup isn't close to what you've been through, but I wanted you to know that I do have a small understanding about how it feels to lose a person I'd planned to spend a lifetime with." Taking a chance, he said, "Joe told me about Levi."

Her eyes widened as she visibly regained her composure. "Wow, you don't mess around with tough subjects, do you?"

"Sorry. I usually have a bit more tact."

"Is there tact when it comes to discussing someone's dead boyfriend?"

"I apologize. I shouldn't have brought him up." Noticing that she was still holding herself stiffly, he added, "We can talk about something else if you'd like."

She sighed. "There's no need for that. It is I who should apologize. I have a talent for acting as if Levi's death bothers me none but then being as prickly as a porcupine whenever his name is brought up." Putting down the pair of books she'd been clutching, she said, "If Joe and Bethany told you about Levi, then you know his death was sudden."

He nodded.

"His passing was really hard, as I guess you can imagine."

"Anyone would've been shaken by it, Rosie."

"I was. But I've been starting to realize that though several years have passed, I didn't do as good a job of dealing with his death as I could have," she said quietly.

"Don't be so hard on yourself. I don't believe there is a right way of dealing with death."

"Spoken like a true missionary. I'm sure you have a lot of experience counseling people."

"I developed a talent for listening, but I've always believed that prayer helped more than anything."

"Perhaps."

Her answer was filled with both doubt and a quiet acceptance, like whatever he was saying was nothing less than she expected.

"I'm guessing a lot of people have given you advice about grieving over the years."

"They have. I've heard everything from 'Time heals' to criticism about how I've reacted since." She smiled slightly. "But at least now I've realized that I'm going to be okay and that it's all right to still live."

"I can't imagine Levi would've wanted anything different."

"I don't think he would. He was a good man. But he was young, as was I. I've changed a lot since he died, and to be honest, sometimes I wonder if he'd lived and we'd married, would I have ever wished for something different?"

"Sometimes people say the Lord isn't in charge, but your words confirm that that is so, don't you think?"

She blinked. "Do you believe that?"

"I believe that your success in sewing and quilting can't be a mistake. Especially since Bethany told me there are a great many women who have benefited from your classes."

"I . . . I don't know what to say."

Rosie looked flustered by his comment, which he thought was very cute. Tim was just about to tease her when he realized she had tears in her eyes. "I've hurt you." Boy, he was really messing things up! "Please, for—"

"*Nee*, Tim. You—Well, you have just given me something no one else has. Acceptance."

When the tears started running down her face, he pulled her into his arms before thinking better of it. And when Rosie leaned against him, seeming to take in his comfort like a dry sponge, he held her closer.

It might not have been proper, but it felt right. Righter than anything he could remember in recent years.

SIX

She'd just fallen into Bethany's brother-in-law's arms and cried like a baby. Worse, it had felt like she belonged there, which was not good for her to assume or think. Tim had been trying to comfort her because he was a missionary, and he was a genuinely compassionate person.

He also hadn't had much of a choice in the matter.

Getting to her feet, Rosie nervously refolded a piece of scrap fabric. "I don't know what came over me. I'm better now." She smiled. "A lot better." Smoothing a nonexistent wrinkle from her dress, she forced herself to sound bright and cheery. "Hey, I promised to show you around Pinecraft. Would you like to go for a walk? I could show you the sights."

"Rosie—"

"Or, I have an idea!" She knew she was babbling like a brook but couldn't seem to stop herself. "If you'd like, we could even stop for lunch at Yoder's. Have you been there yet?"

Tim said nothing for a few seconds. Then he stood up. "I haven't. If you'd like to get out of here, I'm game."

She'd never heard that expression before, but it certainly

seemed to suit the situation. "*Gut*," she said eagerly. "I'll go wash up and then we can go."

He didn't move. "What about Butch?"

"I'm going to leave both his Habitrail and cage open and put some carrots and a cracker in each. Those are some of his favorite treats. He'll find them soon enough."

"You're not worried about him damaging anything?"

She was more eager to give them some space than to continue searching for a wayward rodent. "There's not a lot I can do at this time. He's not going to come when I call."

Looking relieved, he chuckled. "*Nee*, I guess not."

She hurried to the bathroom and closed the door behind her. Then she leaned her head against it and breathed deep. She needed to get a grip on herself. First and foremost, she needed to stop babbling like a besotted fool. Then she needed to firmly put some distance between Tim and her heart. She absolutely could not start thinking about him as anything more than a temporary friend or a long-lost relative. If she allowed herself to start dreaming about Tim Christner in other ways, all she'd get was a broken heart. Soon he would be gone, and she would be left in Pinecraft. That wasn't a bad thing either. She needed to concentrate on how blessed she was.

Yes. That was what was important. Her blessings.

Quickly, she splashed water on her face, took off her *kapp*, and smoothed her hair. Then, after repositioning the *kapp* on her head, she checked her appearance. Thankfully, her eyes weren't swollen and red. Instead, they appeared rather bright.

Finally collected, she walked down the short hallway and then almost felt like crying again. Not only had Tim organized her sewing notions but he had even washed and dried the two plates she'd left in the sink.

"Is everything better?" he asked when he caught sight of her.

"I'm not sure if you're referring to myself or the room," she joked.

His eyes lit up. "Maybe a bit of both."

"In that case, *jah* to both. But Tim, you didn't have to wash the dishes too."

"It was no trouble. I happen to have a lot of experience cleaning up messes."

She believed him. Tim really was acting like picking up clutter and organizing it was no trouble at all. "I'm starting to get the feeling that missionary work is more demanding that I'd first realized."

He laughed as they walked out her front door. "When I first started, that same thought crossed my mind almost every night."

"I'm sure it was a lot to get used to."

"It was, but it wasn't too much for me to handle. After all, it wasn't like I had anything else to worry about."

She noticed that while his quip might have been true, there was something else in his tone. Regret, maybe? Though she was curious about his work, Rosie had the feeling it was time to lighten their conversation.

After locking her door and leading him down the short sidewalk, she decided to play tour guide. "I'll have you know that this is one of the main streets here in Pinecraft," she began as they turned right. "If you walk on it enough, you'll get the chance to meet people from all over the country."

"That's what Joe appears to like about it. Among other things, that is."

"Joe seemed to enjoy Florida from the minute he arrived. I talk to a lot of visitors, and most only want to vacation here or only come in the winters. The hot, humid summers can be brutal."

Helping her move to the side so a mother pushing a buggy could pass, he said, "I suppose you meet a fair amount of visitors in your shop too."

"I do. Years ago, when I started, I tried to keep track of everyone and remember something special about their states or communities."

"But no longer?"

"*Nee.* I soon discovered that everyone is basically the same, no matter where they hail from."

"I've come to the same conclusion in my job as well. One of my favorite things to see is the changes some of our newest missionaries experience while working with us."

Fascinated, she glanced his way. "How so?"

"Some arrive so full of themselves and their grand plans to 'fix' everyone they've been asked to serve. But what they soon discover is that we're all pretty much the same—and that they are being helped as much as the people they've come to assist."

"You do so much good," she said as they walked to join the long line of people waiting to go inside Yoder's.

Again, Tim didn't seem as enthused as she thought he might be. "I try, but then I think we all try." Looking curiously at the folks in line, he said, "Tell me about this line."

"This line is a common sight. Yoder's has wonderful-*gut*

food—and it's a good spot to visit with people and chat while one is waiting."

"I see."

Rosie was just about to tell him a couple of stories about chance meetings in line when her employee Fran ran up to them.

"I'm so glad I found you, Rosie!" she announced in a rush. "After I couldn't find you at home, I ran into someone who saw you both walking toward Yoder's."

"Is everything all right?" Tim asked.

Fran shook her head. "Joe just rang the store, looking for you." Reaching out for Rosie's hand, Fran added, "Bethany tripped on one of the girls' toys and fell and hit her head."

Rosie gripped the woman's fingers like a lifeline. "What?"

"She was unconscious for a time. Joe was going to take her to the hospital, but then she came to."

"Where is she now?"

"Joe took her to urgent care." After gathering herself together, she added, "Bethany started having contractions, Rosie."

Dropping her hand, Rosie tried to wrap her head around what she was hearing. "But . . . but that canna happen. Bethany's baby isn't due for several months."

"I heard she went as a precaution."

Fran was practically speaking in circles. Bethany was having contractions but was only sitting at urgent care? "What does all of this mean? Is she going to be all right? Was the baby hurt? Did anyone contact the midwife?"

"I don't know. No one has heard anything yet."

"Which urgent care?" Tim asked when it looked as if Fran was about to start talking a mile a minute yet again.

After Fran named the intersection, Rosie attempted to pull herself together. "I need to go to Bethany right away, Tim."

"Of course you do." Pressing a hand on the small of her back, he led her toward the sidewalk. "Don't worry, I'll go with you."

Fran shook her head. "I'm sorry, Rosie, but you're needed at Bethany and Joe's. Their neighbor Martha is watching the girls, but she doesn't want to be there much longer, and I fear the girls don't want her much either. Can you come help?"

"Of course." Rosie was disappointed not to be able to see her sister, but she was just going to have to hope and pray that Joe and the Lord were making sure Bethany had the help she needed. Looking up into Tim's eyes, she said, "I guess our plans have changed."

Reaching for her hand, he nodded. "Yes, it seems *God* has other plans for us today."

SEVEN

As Tim walked beside Rosie toward his brother's house, he couldn't help but reflect on how the Lord always, always worked with a plan in mind. During his travels from Mexico to Berlin to finally Pinecraft, he'd spent many a moment wondering why God had led him on this journey to Florida. It wasn't that he didn't want to see Joe and his family but rather that he'd been confused as to why he'd felt so compelled to see them right then and there.

It had been slightly maddening, given that he'd only been back in Ohio for a few weeks. He'd been spending time with his parents and at the mission home office. The director had been happy to see him in person and had even hinted that Tim could take over some of the director's responsibilities for a while.

But instead of being thrilled, all he'd been able to do was share that he needed to go to Florida instead.

That response wasn't usual for him, and it had caught the director off guard, but Tim hadn't felt like he had a choice.

Now, as they crossed an intersection and he even had to take Rosie's arm so she wouldn't knock into a small toddler, Tim realized the Lord had needed him to be here. Not just for Joe and Bethany and the twins but for Rosie too.

She needed someone to look out for her while she looked out for everyone else, and he knew without a doubt he was glad to be that person.

Walking another block, Tim noticed that Rosie seemed to retreat more and more into herself with every step. "Rosie, you need to think positive. If Bethany was in danger, they would've taken her to the hospital."

"I know."

He tried again. "The Lord is with her too. He'll watch over her. As will Joe." He had absolute faith in both.

"I know."

Seeing she still didn't look relieved, he said, "What's on your mind?"

"Nothing."

"Are you sure about that?"

She sighed. "As much as I love my nieces, I sometimes wish I wasn't always their babysitter." She covered her mouth with her hand. "Oh, please, forget I said that. I'm glad I can help them."

He understood how she felt. "There's nothing wrong with wishing you weren't always needed."

"It's not that. I mean, not really. I guess I would just rather be at Bethany's side." Looking crushed, she blurted, "That's selfish, I know. Please don't tell Joe I said anything."

"Of course I won't."

When they walked in the door at Bethany's house, both

girls were sitting in little chairs and looking very sad. As they didn't rush over to greet either him or Rosie, Tim said, "What's going on?"

"We've been naughty. We're not supposed to get up for ten minutes," Becca whispered. "But I think it's been a lot longer than that."

"What did you two do?" Rosie asked as she knelt in front of them.

Lydia's bottom lip trembled. "Miss Martha said we were crying about *Mamm* too much."

Before his eyes, Rosie went from being slightly irritated by her childcare duties to a formidable aunt. Getting to her feet, she put both hands on her hips. "Where is Miss Martha now?" she asked.

"In the kitchen," Lydia answered.

"I see."

Deciding to step in before the situation got worse, Tim rested a hand on her arm. "How about I go speak with her, Rosie?"

She must have seen something in his expression, because after a slight pause, she nodded. "That might be for the best."

As he walked into the kitchen, he heard Rosie tell the girls to get up out of their chairs and give her a hug.

Martha was at the sink scrubbing dishes with so much force Tim feared one might break. "Rosie and I are here now, Martha. *Danke* for helping with the girls."

"You are welcome, though they really are quite the handful. Their parents need to be far firmer with them."

Since their parents were his brother and sister-in-law, he

wasn't exactly of the same opinion. "I think they are doing a fine job."

"Hmph." Leaving the pan in the sink, she pulled on a black sweater and picked up her handbag. "I need to go home now."

"Of course." He walked to the kitchen door and opened it. "*Danke* again."

"Tell Bethany not to ask for my help tomorrow. I'm busy," she warned as she walked out the door.

After he closed it, Tim rested his forehead on the wood and fought back a smile. Maybe the woman's comments shouldn't have struck him as amusing, but his mission work had helped him to look at the light in most situations. While it was a blessing that she'd come right over, Martha was definitely not a ray of sunshine. It was no wonder Joe had sent Fran to find him and Rosie.

Rosie was sitting on the floor with the girls and teaching them some kind of complicated-looking clapping game when he returned. Both Becca and Lydia were smiling.

"Now you girls look like my favorite nieces," he said.

"I'm happy 'cause Aunt Rosie is here," Becca said.

Lydia nodded. "Me too."

"Me three," he said as Rosie stood up to face him.

"Is Martha still here?"

"*Nee*. She um, had to get on her way."

"I see."

Since the twins were playing the clapping game and ignoring them, Tim leaned closer to Rosie. "Is everyone okay?"

"Oh, yes. We talked about the benefits of listening better

to Martha, prayed for their *mamm* and the babe, and then decided to keep busy."

"They certainly seem happier now."

Looking down at the girls, Rosie smiled. "They do, indeed."

"Wouldja like to learn a clapping game, Uncle Tim?" Lydia asked.

"Though that does look like fun, I think I'll be of some use and make supper."

Becca's eyes widened. "What are ya gonna make, Uncle Tim?"

Remembering the charcoal grill outside, he grinned at them. "What any man in a pinch makes. I'm gonna grill hamburgers."

The giggles that followed him back to the kitchen made him smile.

Please, God, let Bethany be all right. And please, God, help me be a comfort instead of another source of stress for my family.

EIGHT

Though two days had passed since Bethany's close call, Rosie was still giving thanks. After careful observation, the doctor at the clinic had declared Bethany did not have a concussion and that her babe was still doing well. He and the midwife, however, did ask Bethany to take it easy for the next couple of weeks. She'd been sent home with firm instructions to do less and rest more.

After the fiasco with Miss Martha, Tim and Rosie decided to help out with the girls as much as they could. In order to stay sane, they'd devised a loose schedule of sorts. Tim would help Bethany and the girls around the house in the mornings and Rosie would take over in the afternoons.

The girls were darling and truly wanted to be pleasant and helpful. That was the good news.

The bad news was that the deadline for Rosie to enter her quilt into the contest was fast approaching. In addition, her employee Violet had gotten the flu just as a whole busload of quilting enthusiasts from southern Ohio arrived in Pinecraft. They were pleasant women but had no problem relaying that they'd come to Pinecraft specifically to visit her store and take classes in the days leading up to the big show.

Next thing Rosie knew, she was working at the shop in the morning, helping with the twins in the afternoons, and then returning to the shop to teach classes to her eager students.

To make matters worse, Butch now seemed to be enjoying his newfound freedom and was running amuck around the house. Just last night, he'd broken into a bag of cereal and left a trail of crumbs across the entire kitchen floor for her to find in the morning.

That was bad enough, but Rosie had found hamster droppings on the floor, too, which was very aggravating. She'd had to mop the whole floor again, just in case the girls decided to sit there when they came over to play.

All that meant she had very little time to finish the quilt. After attaching the batting and pinning the back together, Rosie reluctantly admitted to herself that she wasn't going to be able to hand quilt the intricate design she'd envisioned. Therefore, she spent every spare moment the next day applying a new, far simpler pattern. The overall appearance would be serviceable and pretty, but it gave her no artistic joy. But although she could practically feel her chances of producing a Quilt of the Year slip through her fingertips, she'd come to terms with that. Bethany's fall and Tim's arrival had reminded her there were other things besides awards to focus on.

Even though Fran wasn't happy with her, Rosie had told her she was taking the day off from the shop. The quilters from Ohio were sightseeing, and no classes were scheduled.

Though chances were slim that she could win any award, Rosie definitely still wanted to finish her piece on time. Even if her quilt wasn't the best in the show, she could still make sure it was good enough to be selected for auction.

She was dwelling on that idea when Tim came by with Joe and the girls late that afternoon.

Tim's tan looked darker, thanks to the days he'd spent outside with his brother and the girls. He was smiling when he caught sight of her. "Working away, I see."

"I am." At least, she'd been trying to. With a look of longing, she put her project to one side yet again. Then, summoning a smile, she got to her feet. "How is everyone today?"

"Good enough," Joe said. "Bethany is feeling better."

"I'm so glad. That is a blessing, isn't it?"

"It truly is."

"Hiya, Aunt Rosie," Becca said as she trotted forward with her father on her heels. "We brought you something."

Leaning down, Rosie gave her a quick hug. "Really? What could it be?"

"It's ice cream!" Lydia said. "Your favorite too. It's chocolate-chocolate chip."

The ice cream had oozed down Lydia's hand. "And you so thoughtfully put it in a cone."

Becca nodded. "Uh-huh. Even though the person at the shop said a cup would be better, we told him to give ya a cone, because we know that's your favorite."

"It is. *Danke.*" After exchanging a glance with both men—because honestly, what had they been thinking?—Rosie hurried over to her kitchen sink, tore off a paper towel, and wrapped it around the cone. Deciding the best place to finish the melting treat was right where she was, Rosie hovered over the sink while she took a big bite.

As much of a mess as the ice cream was, though, she couldn't deny it was delicious. "It's been too long since I've treated myself to a cone. Thank you all."

Becca grinned as she hopped up and down. "You liked it!"

"I did. Very much." Holding out a hand, she motioned for the girls to come closer. "Now, let's get you two cleaned up."

"Just a second, Aunt Rosie," Lydia said. "I want to see your quilt."

Her quilt. In the few seconds it took for Lydia's comment to register, Rosie remembered the little girl's hands. She turned quickly. "Lydia, don't touch—"

But the warning came too late. Lydia was holding up the quilt with both sticky, chocolate-covered hands.

Only then did Tim and Joe seem to remember they were still on twin duty too.

"Lydia, drop that quilt!" Joe called out.

She released it immediately. Down it went onto the floor . . . where Becca promptly picked it up with both hands. "Here ya go, Aunt Rosie."

Seeing that Becca's hands were also a mess—with something that looked suspiciously like rainbow sherbet—Rosie snatched the quilt from her hands . . . and then promptly lost her temper.

"I need all of you to leave!"

Joe grinned. "Are you serious?"

She nodded. "I love you all, but I wasn't supposed to have the girls here for another hour. Why did you come so early?"

Lydia's bottom lip trembled. "So you could have some ice cream."

Ignoring the child, Rosie walked over to Joe and Tim. "Listen, I love the girls, and I love spending time with them. But, Joe, don't you see that I'm trying to get this quilt done?"

"Don't you think you're getting a little excited, Rosie?" he responded. "I mean, it's just a quilt."

That was the last straw. Walking to the door, she opened it. "You're right. It is *just a quilt*. But it is also important to me. And . . . and you all practically ruined it within five minutes of showing up."

Tim had been watching this exchange with a worried expression. Now he held up his hands. "You're right. Listen, we'll go. And don't worry about watching the girls tomorrow. I'll do it."

Though her conscience encouraged her to back down, the selfish part of her spoke before she thought better of it. "*Danke.* Now, good-bye, everyone."

"I'm really sorry, Aunt Rosie," Lydia said.

Seeing the child had tears in her eyes, she knelt down and gave her a hug, pulling in Becca at the same time. "I'm sorry too," she whispered. "I shouldn't have gotten so irritated."

But then, before she lost her nerve, she stood again. "I'll see all of you in two days."

Without a word, all four of them walked out.

With a sinking heart, Rosie smoothed the quilt over the work surface and inspected the damage. As she feared, smudges of pink, orange, and brown ice cream dotted both sides. It was going to take her several hours to carefully clean the stains.

With a sigh, she dampened a cloth with warm water and got to work and tried not to think about how disappointed she was about Joe's comment . . . or her response to it.

But as the time passed, it seemed she could think of nothing else.

NINE

Feeling terrible about the way she'd treated Joe, Tim, and the girls, Rosie showed up at their house early the next morning. Bethany, wearing a loose, light-gray dress that made her look slightly washed out, opened the door when Rosie knocked.

"I didn't expect to see you here," Bethany said. "I thought you had a very important quilt to finish."

The comment stung, mostly because she deserved it. "About that . . . Well, I came to apologize. May I come in?"

"Of course, but I have to tell ya, I'm not all that happy with you right now. I had two crying girls, a grumpy husband, and a worried houseguest to deal with last night. It wasn't easy."

"No, I suppose it wasn't."

"If you didn't want to spend time with everyone, you should have just told us that."

Realizing she wasn't going to be allowed any farther inside until Bethany said her piece, Rosie folded her hands behind her back. "It wasn't exactly like that, Beth, and I think you know it too. I love Becca and Lydia, but I also have a business to run and other things I like to do with my time."

"I know that."

"I'm sorry, but sometimes I feel that you forget." She sighed. "I'm far from perfect, Beth. There's a part of me that hates being alone with my thoughts, so I constantly give myself a lot to do. Then, as soon as I have a lot to do, I get overwhelmed. None of that is your fault."

Compassion shone in her sister's eyes. "I could also be more understanding." She lowered her voice. "After we got the girls to bed, Joe told me what happened. I don't blame you for feeling annoyed." She rolled her eyes. "I guess you could say that I'm feeling a little overwhelmed right now too."

Glad that they'd talked things out, Rosie hugged her sister. When they parted, she looked Bethany over. "Now, how are you feeling?"

"Beyond tired, I'm *gut*. I feel mostly like my regular self again."

"Don't forget that you're still supposed to rest," Rosie warned.

"I haven't forgotten." Finally smiling brightly, Bethany said, "Come on back. I'm sure the girls are anxious to make sure they're still your favorite nieces."

"They are, and it doesn't even matter that they're my only nieces." Impulsively, Rosie linked her arm through her sister's. "Please tell me you have some *kaffi* brewed."

"I just brewed another pot," Tim said from where he sat at the dining-room table. "Would you like a cup?"

"I sure would, but don't get up. I can get it." Catching

sight of Lydia's pensive face, Rosie cleared her throat. "But first, I want to apologize to all of you for my snippy attitude yesterday."

"You're allowed to be human," Joe teased. "All is forgiven. I'm sorry for bringing two little girls with dirty hands into your house. I should have thought about that drippy ice cream before letting them run loose near your worktable. If anyone had brought a drippy ice-cream cone near house plans I was working on, I would have gotten upset too."

"No worries. I got the stains cleaned. You can hardly tell they were there."

Bethany raised an eyebrow. "'Hardly'?"

Since there was nothing to be done about it, Rosie shook off her sister's look. "It's nothing to worry about."

"Does that mean you still love us, Aunt Rosie?" Lydia asked.

"It does. Will you forgive me for being grumpy?"

When their little heads nodded in unison, her heart melted. No, the girls weren't perfect, but neither was she. Hurrying to where they sat, she kissed each on their brow. "Now, what does everyone have planned for today?"

"We're going to all stay around here and do some cleaning," Bethany said.

"How can I help?"

"By going back home and working on your quilt," her sister said. "You've done enough."

"I appreciate that, but I can do something."

"I know," Tim said as he brought her a bright-yellow mug filled with coffee. "Take me to Siesta Key."

In spite of all her best intentions to be helpful, her heart gave a little leap. She would like nothing better than to spend a few hours at the beach. "Are you sure that's okay?" She looked at Bethany and Joe.

"It's more than okay," Joe said as he walked to her side and squeezed her shoulder. "I spoke to my boss and said I was going to need to take a couple of days off. Your words yesterday reminded me that my girls are worth more than overtime pay. And both of you deserve to have a day at the beach."

"So, what do you say, Rosie?" Tim asked. "Are you ready to play hooky for a spell?"

"I am. I'll first need to go home, but I could be ready in an hour. Could you come to my *haus* then? There's a SCAT stop near me."

"I'll see you then."

She quickly finished her coffee. Then, after a quick chat with the twins, she was on her way back home, already feeling light at heart.

———•·———

Four hours later, Rosie sat on a striped beach towel with the hem of her dress pulled up to her knees. The rays of sun felt warm on her skin, while Tim's attempts to play volleyball with some teenaged boys lifted her mood even more.

After a truly remarkable serve over the net, Tim seemed to be all over that volleyball court. While the boys eight and ten years younger hardly moved as they bumped and spiked the ball back and forth, Tim continued to scramble. Even more fun to see was the way all the other guys didn't seem to mind. They chatted with him, joked, and even gave him high fives whenever they scored a point.

She also couldn't help but notice that he looked back her way several times. Whenever their eyes met, he smiled. And she felt slightly breathless. Something was happening between them that seemed to get stronger with each hour that passed. Rosie now realized that it wasn't just their siblings or their love for their nieces that connected them, it was their personalities. They both took on too much and had trouble saying no. They also found humor in unlikely places . . . and had learned to keep going even when they were hurting or tired.

Just as important, there seemed to be a spark between them. She couldn't help but let her gaze linger on his smile a little longer than needed. Or, if she was being honest, she wasn't immune to the way he looked playing volleyball with his shirt half unbuttoned and his pant legs rolled up to his midcalves.

When the game finished at long last, she giggled as Tim shook hands with everyone around him—both the boys he'd been playing with and the men and boys on the opposing team.

"Are you laughing at my antics?" he teased as he strode closer.

"Maybe," she allowed.

"Did I look that silly?"

"Not at all," she said as he plopped down on the towel next to her. "I was just thinking that it's charming how easily you seem to make friends."

"It's a by-product of my job," Tim replied with a shrug.

"I like talking to people. Always have. Now, because of my mission work, I've had experience talking to people from all walks of life. I enjoy it."

"Well, I enjoyed watching you relax and have fun."

"Every time I glanced this way, it looked as if you were having a good time yourself."

Smiling up at him, she nodded. "I love many things about living in Florida, but I love going to the beach the most. And out of all the wonderful beaches nearby, my most favorite is Siesta Key."

"I can see why. I've never seen sand so fine and soft. It's like sugar."

"People come from all over to experience the beaches here. I'm glad I got the opportunity to bring you here."

"Me too." Leaning back on his hands, he said, "What should we do now?"

"There's a little beach shack that serves the best po-boys. It opens in about an hour or so. Would you like to stay on the beach until then? We could get something to eat and then head back."

"I would like that."

The way Tim answered, together with the intent look in his eyes, made Rosie wonder if he was referring to something more than just beach time and po-boys.

Quickly reminding herself that he would soon be leaving, which meant they didn't have a future together, she got to her feet. "Since we've got some time, let's go walk on the beach for a spell."

Jumping up to stand by her side, he grinned. "Rosie Raber, I thought you'd never ask."

TEN

Two days had passed since he'd spent the day at Siesta Key with Rosie, but it was already feeling like it had been a whole month. Ever since then, he'd been helping Joe and Bethany around their house. At first, Joe had tried to persuade him to do some sightseeing on his own, but Tim had shaken his head. As far as he was concerned, it was a privilege to help his brother when he was in need. He certainly hadn't done enough of that in the past.

Now, though, he was at Rosie's house with the girls. Rosie had knocked on their door early that morning to ask if he could fill in for two hours while she taught a private lesson for one of her out-of-town clients. They'd decided it would be best if he went to her house instead of taking the girls back and forth.

However, he was starting to regret that decision. From the moment he'd arrived and Rosie had left, the twins had transformed into tiny terrors. Truly, his pretty little blonde nieces could cause destruction in the blink of an eye.

Especially right that moment. They were staring up at him with big blue eyes and almost innocent expressions.

It was difficult, but he folded his arms over his chest and tried to sound very stern. "All right, you two. It's time to tell me the truth. Which one of you accidentally got marker on your Aunt Rosie's coffee table?" He was definitely using the word *accidentally* in a loose way too. After living with them for over a week, he realized that neither of the girls did much on accident.

"I didn't do it," Becca blurted.

"Me neither," Lydia said with a little foot stomp.

"Well, I didn't do it. I was too busy cleaning spilled hot chocolate from the couch."

"Aunt Rosie never lets us sip drinks on the sofa, Uncle Tim."

"Lydia, you should have told me that before I gave them to you." As she attempted to glare even though her bottom lip was sticking out, he added, "Or better yet, you should have sat down at the table. You two are big girls now."

"I know, but I still make mistakes sometimes."

Tim couldn't argue with that. "I suppose we all do."

"Does that mean we can stand up now?" Becca asked. "I'm tired of being in time-out."

"You've only sat there for two minutes."

She squirmed like she had ants in her pants. "Ain't that long enough?"

Just as he was about to explain to them the simple concept of *time-out*, Butch, the missing hamster, ran across the floor toward them.

His little furry body coming out of nowhere was enough to make a grown man jump. Which was what he did.

And that, of course, made the girls jump . . . which was no big surprise, given that they were already screaming at the top of their lungs. Next thing Tim knew, they were out of their chairs and on the move.

"Butch!"

Butch froze, stared at the little hands reaching out for him, and then turned the other way . . . right toward Rosie's small reading table.

After that, everything felt as if it were happening in slow motion. Lydia squealed and rushed toward the hamster. So did Becca. And then he—fool that he was—trotted into the fray. "Wait, girls!"

His attempt at an inside voice was a terrible failure, though, because, one, neither of them cared about his attempt to lead by example, and two, even if they might have cared, they couldn't hear him because they were continuing to scream Butch's name at the top of their lungs.

"Becca! Lydia! Inside voices!" he yelled.

One of them turned to stare at him, just as Butch—obviously dazed and confused—switched directions and ran toward Lydia's bare foot. Butch's change in direction made the girls jump, knock into the table, and tip it over.

Unfortunately, it had a candle on it, so he dove to save the house from fire. The good news was that he did catch the candle—even though he belatedly realized it was battery operated. The bad news was that there was also a lamp that crashed to the floor and broke. And that two little girls realized there were broken lamp pieces on the ground about two seconds too late.

Next thing Tim knew, both children were crying, their feet were bleeding, and he'd tossed the nearest blanket he could find onto the floor so they didn't hurt their feet any further.

And that was the exact moment Rosie walked in the door.

"Hiya, everyone. I'm sorry I ran late, but it couldn't be helped. You see—" She stopped and gaped at the scene.

"Aunt Rosie, I'm hurt!" Lydia called out.

"Me too," Becca said. "I'm bleeding bad."

"There's blood?" Her face turned pale.

"They just have cut feet," he said as he knelt on the floor in front of them.

"'Cut feet'?" she repeated as she tossed her purse to the floor. Before Tim could try again to explain the situation, Rosie had hurried over to the girls and knelt down beside him on the blanket. "What happened here?"

"The lamp broke when your table knocked over," Becca said as she stuck a foot out for Rosie to inspect.

Pulling a couple of tissues from a pocket in her dress, Rosie dabbed Becca's foot before turning to Lydia. "Any reason the table suddenly knocked over?"

"Uh-huh," Lydia said. "See, that happened when Uncle Tim tried to save the candle from burning your house down." She wrinkled her nose. "Is my foot better now?"

"*Jah.* You hold the tissue on it for a spell. You do the same, Becca." While both girls silently and obediently did as she bid, Rosie looked back at Tim. "I'm guessing you saved the candle?"

He had a feeling she was being sarcastic. "I did."

"So you saved the *haus* from burning."

"I did." Deciding to move on from his heroics—or lack of them—he added quickly, "Um, you see, it all started with Butch."

"Surely you're not going to blame this . . . this *awful* mess on a tiny hamster?"

"It might not have been all Butch's fault, but he had a lot to do with it," Tim retorted. "You see, he came out from practically nowhere and scared us all."

"*You* were scared of a tiny pet."

Well, now he was feeling rather stupid. "Uh, 'scared' might not be the best descriptor. It was more like 'startled.' I was startled. He came running toward us."

Lydia nodded. "He was super speedy, Aunt Rosie."

After kissing each girl on the forehead, Rosie got to her feet. "Well, now, let's get you girls fixed up. We'll go to the bathtub and wash . . ." Her voice drifted off.

Having just picked up Becca, Tim paused. "What's wrong, Rosie?"

She was looking down at the floor in dismay. "This is my quilt," she whispered.

All of them looked down. There, sure enough, lay Rosie's quilt entry. He'd used it as their impromptu floor covering.

And it was now covered on one side with dots of blood and dirt from little-girl bare feet and ground-in glass on the other.

The realization was so awful, for once not even a four-year-old twin said a word.

ELEVEN

Tim felt terrible for Rosie. He really did. He also felt terrible for himself. He'd always considered himself to be a fairly competent person. He'd managed an entire staff in more than one country. He'd also coordinated jobs for dozens of volunteers from the time he was seventeen. All that meant he'd begun to feel like there were very few activities involving childcare that he couldn't handle.

He'd been wrong.

This experience had just taught him that he might be a lot of things, but a capable babysitter was not one of them. "What can I do to help?" he asked after giving Rosie a full minute to process that he'd just ruined her quilt.

She slowly turned to him. "Not a thing." She sounded a bit dazed.

"Are you sure? Perhaps if we shake out the quilt, it won't be so bad."

She pursed her lips. After a few more seconds passed, she spoke again. "We need to take care of the girls."

"*Jah*. Of course."

He followed her to the bathroom, where she gently deposited Lydia on the thick bath mat on the floor.

"Do not move," she warned the little girl.

"I won't, Aunt Rosie," Lydia whispered.

Tim placed Becca on the toilet-seat lid while Rosie ran the bathwater. When about six inches of warm water had filled the tub, he and Rosie helped Becca and Lydia sit on the side of the tub and soak their feet.

"This feels *gut*," Becca said.

"I imagine so," Rosie murmured. "Now, let me see your feet, child."

It was a tight fit with all of them in the small bathroom. It was also obvious that Rosie didn't need him there. She was quietly washing the twins' feet and inspecting cuts. Tim reckoned he could be of more use to her if he returned to the living room and began cleaning. But he couldn't let himself do that. He needed to be near her. She honestly looked so sad, he wished he could do anything at all to make things better.

But he couldn't change the past—that was impossible.

"How are their feet?"

Still smiling down at the girls, she said, "No glass seems to be stuck in the cuts. They don't seem to be bleeding anymore either. All we need to do is put on a couple of Band-Aids, and then they'll be as good as new. Right, girls?"

"*Jah!*" they chorused.

"I'm ready to get up now," Lydia said.

"Where are the bandages?" he asked. "I'll go get them."

"In a basket under the kitchen sink," Rosie responded as she released the drain on the tub.

"I'll be right back."

Rosie didn't answer, but Tim wasn't sure if that was by choice or if she simply hadn't heard. In any case, by the time he returned with a box of pink Band-Aids with cartoon figures printed on them, Rosie had already dried their feet.

He knelt on the floor by Rosie's side and helped apply three bandages to each foot. There was really no need for quite so many, but the girls looked delighted, and Rosie seemed to need to bring smiles to their faces. Ironically, their grins seemed to make him feel even worse. He wished he could make Rosie's world brighter with just a few strategically placed bandages.

After Becca and Lydia took a few trial steps and announced they were fine, Rosie set them up in her spare bedroom with some wood-carved farm animals and cheese crackers. Only after leaving them contentedly playing did her relaxed expression crack. When she returned to the living room, Rosie gazed at the quilt that lay abandoned on the floor and sighed. "I guess it's time to face the music, ain't so?"

"*Nee*, it's time for you to relax. You went straight from working at your shop to wading through chaos here. I'll pick up the quilt and inspect it for damage." He sat down on the couch, gently flipped the quilt over, and started removing shards.

"Careful, now."

"Don't worry. My fingers are tough. I'm not going to get a nick and cause more havoc."

Sitting down next to him, she rested a hand on his

arm. "Tim, do you really think that this quilt is all I care about?"

"Of course not." But he did think that she'd put a ton of time, effort, and care into it. There was nothing wrong with that either. Spying another sizable shard, he carefully pulled it loose from two stitches and added it to his small pile of broken pieces on the table. "I don't know what I was thinking. I should have looked more carefully at what I grabbed to cover the glass."

"*Nee.* Your first concern was with the girls. That's what mattered." She reached out and stopped him from fussing with the quilt. "I know I've seemed upset, and I have been. But with myself, not you."

"You did nothing wrong, Rosie."

She smiled softly. "Oh, yes, I did. I left the quilt out in the open. I should have put it away so nothing could touch it while I was gone. But more important, I stopped listening to all of the Lord's signs. Instead of postponing my dream of winning the prize for another year, I held tightly to it. Even when I started running out of time. And when Violet got sick. And when Bethany needed to rest."

"And when I came?"

She nodded. "My attempt to ignore the way I felt about you has been the worst transgression of all." Meeting his gaze, she said, "You see, from the moment we met in the parking lot by the buses, I knew there was something special about you. I wanted to get to know you better."

"I felt the same way."

"I know, Tim. I could tell that I wasn't the only person who felt our relationship was something to cherish." She looked down at her hands. "But instead of valuing it, I kept thinking only about producing a quilt to be proud of."

He wasn't sure if Rosie had been as selfish as she seemed to think. But it didn't even matter. "How about we both stop blaming ourselves for accidents and start looking forward?"

"Could we even have a future together? You're going to leave on another mission trip soon, aren't you?"

"I'm not sure."

Her eyebrows rose. "Really?"

"See, while you have been soul-searching about quilts of the year, I've been doing some reflecting on my job. It might be time to do something closer to home." He grinned. "Besides, Joe and Bethany might need me in the future. Becca and Lydia are such a handful now. What are they going to do when the new babe arrives?"

She winced playfully. "You're exactly right. You must stay here, if only to help me!"

Just as Tim leaned forward to kiss her on the cheek and offer to take her out to supper soon, the front door opened. He got to his feet. "Hiya, Joe . . . and Bethany."

"Hiya," Joe responded. "Sorry if we were interrupting anything."

"Nothing too important." Rosie carefully put the quilt to one side.

Looking around the room, Bethany said, "Um, where are my *kinner*?"

"They're in the spare bedroom," Rosie replied. "I'll go with you to fetch them."

When they were alone, Joe studied Tim, the messy floor,

the broken lamp, and what looked like a trail of hamster droppings. His eyebrows rose. "What's been going on?"

"Everything," Tim said with complete honesty. "Absolutely everything."

TWELVE

After everything went so wrong, Rosie cleaned up the quilt as best she could and hastily finished it over the next few days. She'd been determined to get it done—not to glorify herself but for the charity. Realizing she had her priorities straight at last had lifted her spirits. While the quilt wasn't exactly a work of art, it wasn't shoddily constructed or stitched either. It would keep someone warm, and that was what mattered.

She was wearing a smile when she approached Emily Troyer, the woman in charge of the quilt portion of the benefit.

"Ah, Rosie, just in the nick of time," the older woman called out as she approached. "I was almost starting to think you wouldn't have a quilt to contribute this year." Emily winked, showing that her comment was all in jest.

"You know I wouldn't let that happen," Rosie said. "I love being a part of the quilt show, especially since it is for such a good cause."

"Indeed." Emily reached for Rosie's entry. "I must confess, ever since I heard rumors about the pattern you chose,

I have been waiting with bated breath to see this." Almost like she was a carnival barker, she lifted up the corner of the quilt. "May I?"

At least thirty women surrounded them. Some were volunteers for the church, others were entrants like she was. However, the two closest were fellow members of the steering committee with Emily. It was likely her imagination, but Rosie had the distinct feeling half the room had stopped to peer at her quilt.

In the past—okay, maybe only two weeks ago—Rosie would've stood tall and proud. But now? Well, the emphasis all seemed so silly. A beautiful quilt was a work of art, indeed. But it couldn't compare to the other things in life that were far more important. Orphans in Haiti, for instance.

But still, she stood to one side while Emily ordered the women around to make sure the table was spotless and then carefully unfolded the fabric.

Rosie could tell the moment her quilt didn't meet Emily's expectations. The woman's dark-brown eyes fastened on the stitching on the back of the quilt and immediately took in the rather simplistic design. Soon after, she obviously caught sight of several inches of uneven stitches along the bottom corner. And then her eyes widened at the distinct line of tiny paw prints in the center. Butch had struck again.

"Are you sure you didn't make a mistake when you left your *haus*?" Emily asked.

Rosie had no idea what she was talking about. "I'm sorry?"

Emily cleared her throat. "I thought perhaps you mistakenly brought an older quilt for the sale."

"*Nee*, I'm sure this is the quilt I was working on last night."

"I see." Looking at all of the women around the table, Emily said, "Ladies, let's flip."

Emily and the two others standing nearby carefully turned over the quilt and then simply stared.

It did, indeed, have the intricate compass pattern Rosie had chosen. The colors that she'd pieced together did coordinate nicely. The fabrics chosen were varied and interesting. There were no discount-store remnant pieces on display. But the overall effect?

Well, it was not a spectacular quilt. Not even close. It was, however, free of bloodstains, which was a plus.

Rosie bit her lip to keep from chuckling at how far her lofty goals had fallen.

A few of the other contestants gazed at the quilt in shock, followed by expressions that could only be described as pleased. When Mary Jo met her gaze, Rosie smiled back.

"Rosie, dear, later this evening the committee will vote on which quilts will be auctioned off."

"I understand."

"I hope so." Standing up straight, Emily pointed to one of her minions. "Please fold up Rosie's . . . entry and put it in a safe place, Katie." Then she turned to Emily and displayed an especially fake smile. "Thank you for contributing to the show. Your efforts will help a great many people in need."

"*Danke* for once again leading this project," Rosie replied. "It's not an easy task, I know."

"It's a labor of love, for sure and for certain."

Rosie nodded solemnly before turning and walking out

the door. Only when she was half a block down the sidewalk did she smile, then grin, then burst into laughter. What an experience that had been! She realized now that it had also been something else. A wake-up call.

For too many years, she'd slaved over each quilt. She'd worried over each slightly crooked seam, uneven stitch, and color choice. At times, she'd even found herself catering to Emily when they'd seen each other around town. Why, once she'd even insisted Emily and her party be seated ahead of her and Bethany and the girls because she thought that maybe her small gesture might give her a better chance of winning.

Those memories embarrassed her now. They also afforded her some real insight into how much pressure she'd put on herself. And for what?

To win the approval of Emily and her cohorts?

To feel the looks of envy from the other contestants?

Only to herself could she answer yes. Yes, she really had wanted all of those things.

Instead of going straight home, she decided to stop by the shop. It was usually a slow day there, but she could finally give Fran and Violet a break and work the rest of the day.

As expected, Fran, was half dusting, half looking out the window when Rosie entered.

"May I help—Rosie!"

"Hiya, Fran. How are things?"

"Slow today."

"They always are on quilt-show days."

"Always." Clearing her throat, Fran said, "I didn't expect to see you here. Is something wrong? Do you need an item for the show?"

"Not at all. I decided to give you and Violet the rest of the day off."

Fran's eyes lit up before she tamped her excitement down. "I don't understand. This is your big day."

"In some years it surely was. But today?" She shrugged. "Not so much." When she saw that Fran seemed ready to ask a dozen questions, Rosie made a shooing motion with her hands. "It's a lovely afternoon, dear. Go enjoy it. If you could stop by Violet's room on your way home and tell her the news, I would appreciate it."

"*Jah*. I can do that." Still looking a bit stunned, her employee murmured, "Well . . . um . . . *danke*."

"Of course. Now, is there anything happening with the shop that I need to be aware of?"

"*Nee*. It's been one of those long, quiet mornings."

"*Gut*. I'll look forward to relaxing a bit, then."

Fran chuckled as she took off her apron, picked up her tote bag from the cubby under the front counter, and walked out the door.

When she was alone, Rosie studied the area with a critical eye. It was definitely time to do some cleaning and organizing.

While she did all of that, she was going to do some praying too. She had much to be grateful for, and it was time to give thanks.

THIRTEEN

The morning after the quilt show, Bethany told Tim and Joe all about Rosie's entry while they sipped coffee. Not only had it not been chosen for the auction round, it had been sold for one of the lowest prices in the whole show. That wasn't news to Tim, though.

Joe rolled his eyes. "I think it's a real shame that these women put on the show for the sake of charity but still gossip about one another's projects. It ain't right."

"I don't think you're being completely fair," Bethany admonished him. "It's human nature to want to do a good job. You would be mighty disappointed if your construction business got several poor reviews."

"You're right, I would, but this ain't the same thing. Rosie's job isn't all about quilting." When Bethany raised her eyebrows, he looked sheepish. "All right, fine. I reckon it is."

Tim decided it was time to enter the conversation. "So, how is Rosie handling it? I knocked on her door yesterday afternoon, but she didn't answer."

"She didn't answer when we knocked on her door either," Joe said. Lowering his voice, he added, "Of course, I assumed she was afraid I had the girls with me."

"Perhaps she was taking a nap," Bethany offered. "I'm sure she's exhausted."

Tim wasn't so sure it was about physical fatigue. During their conversations together, he'd gotten the feeling Rosie was struggling with other issues—still being single while her sister was expecting her third child, the fact that she still mourned Levi, and maybe even her goals for the future.

And then there'd been their conversation at Siesta Key and most especially their talk after the quilt debacle. They'd been honest with each other about their feelings.

Which had led him to his own round of soul-searching. He'd been so sure that his plans included going back to Ohio and eventually another country. However, in recent days he'd changed his mind. He'd decided he was definitely going to speak with his boss about staying stateside for a few years. He could even see the advantages of remaining in Pinecraft. After all, their organization depended on both Mennonite and Amish volunteers from all over the country. There were few better places in the country to speak with prospective volunteers than in Pinecraft.

"I think I'm going to pay a call on Rosie this morning," he said.

Joe nodded. "That's a good idea."

"You two seemed to have gotten close," Bethany said in an airy tone, just like that thought had suddenly occurred to her.

He chuckled. "I think it's obvious that we've gotten more than close."

After exchanging a quick glance with her husband, Bethany stepped closer. "What are you saying, Tim?"

"Nothing else to you," he teased. "At least not yet." When he noticed Joe and Bethany exchange knowing looks, Tim decided it was time to get on his way. There was only one person he wanted to see at the moment—and she wasn't in this house. "I'll be back later," he said as he rinsed out his coffee cup.

"You're going over there now?" Bethany asked. "It's barely eight o'clock."

"I am and I know," he said as he walked out the door. He grinned when the last thing he heard was Bethany's grumble of annoyance.

———◆———

She'd made a fruit salad for Butch. Yesterday afternoon, after working in the shop until close, Rosie had hopped on the SCAT and ridden over to the largest pet store in Sarasota. She'd gotten Butch there a year or so ago, and had found them to be knowledgeable and patient with her many questions. Yesterday, she'd spoken with a young man named Will who had listened to her patiently explain her dilemma with the wayward hamster. After informing her that getting a friend for Butch was not going to make him come out of hiding, he sold her a bag of hamster treats. "If this doesn't work, give him some fruit," he added.

She'd been shocked. "Really? I thought hamsters only liked vegetables."

"They like those fine, but every hamster I've known loves apples, oranges, and bananas." He winked. "If these treats don't do it, I think you should make him a fruit salad."

She'd laughed, but late last night, after the hamster had ignored the treats, she'd decided to go the fruit-salad route. This morning, she'd visited the farmers market at Yoder's and bought some delicious-looking apples and bananas. Then, because the strawberries looked so perfect, she'd bought a pint of them too. If nothing else, at least she would have a treat for herself.

She'd just arranged the fruit on a plate when there came a knock at the door. "Come in," she called, fully expecting it to be Joe and the girls. When she realized it was Tim, she felt herself flush with happiness. "Hiya, Tim."

His expression seemed to match hers. "Hey. I'm glad you're here."

"Why wouldn't I be?"

"I stopped by yesterday, but no one answered. Joe stopped by too. We were starting to worry about you."

"Really? Why?"

"Well, you know . . . the quilt show."

She grinned at him. "Believe it or not, I didn't even think about it this morning." Truth be told, now that the show was over, she felt as if a load had been lifted off her shoulders.

He walked closer. "Really?"

She pointed to the plate of fruit. "I've been a little pre-occupied with something else."

"Eating strawberries?"

"*Nee*, silly. Finally convincing Butch to come out of hid-ing." As Tim plucked a tiny cube of apple from the plate and popped it into his mouth, she told him about her trip to the pet store the evening before.

"And let me guess, your hamster don't care for fancy treats?"

"Not at all. But I haven't given up. After all, this is a Floridian hamster. He's got to love fruit, right?"

"Right." He picked up the plate. "Where do you want it?"

She pointed to his crate in the corner of the living room. "There. I'm not sure what will happen, but I'm going to give it a try."

"I have a good feeling about this," he teased.

"Me too."

After Tim deposited the plate in the open crate, he sat down on the couch beside her. "Rosie, I didn't just come over here to check on you. I wanted to talk to you about something too."

Her heart sank. Was he about to leave? Folding her hands tightly in her lap, she attempted to look encouraging. "All right."

"Even though I came here to connect with my brother and his family, as each day passes, I realize that you are the person I can't stop thinking about."

"You know I've been thinking about you a lot too."

"I've been all around the world and met a lot of interesting people, but no one has inspired me like you have." He took a deep breath. "No, what I mean to say is that I'm falling in love with you."

His words were so sweet, she felt tears prick her eyes, though she firmly held them at bay. "But what about your job?"

"I've been thinking about it and have come to the

conclusion that it is just that—a job. I mean, yes, I do good works, and I care about the people I've been serving, but it's time I concentrated on myself too." Running his hands down her arms, he lowered his voice. "Rosie, I've always believed that the Lord called me to serve Him through mission work. But now I've realized something just as important: He also wants me to find love and happiness. I think He brought me here to you."

His words were so meaningful, so tender, she felt chill bumps rise on her arms. "If He brought you here to me, I think He helped me open my eyes and see how much better my life has become with you in it, even in a few short weeks."

Tim closed his eyes briefly before leaning closer and wrapping his hands around her waist. "That's all I needed to hear. Rosie, I'm going to do my best to stay here."

"Are you sure?" Tim's words were everything she'd hoped to hear him say, but she was still afraid to dream. "But what about your mission work?"

"If the Lord can bring me to you, I'm pretty sure He'll help me find other ways to serve Him here in Florida too. I have some ideas I'm going to talk with my boss about."

"I . . . Tim, that's wonderful news." Even though she probably would have left Pinecraft to be by his side if he asked her to, Rosie knew she would have had a difficult time. She liked living in Pinecraft, and she adored living near Bethany and her family.

He smiled. "Are you saying that you like my decision?"

"I'm saying that I'd like that very much," she answered as she rested her palms on his chest. Raising her chin, she spied a new tenderness in his eyes.

Just as he lowered his head to kiss her at long last, Rosie caught sight of something out of the corner of her eye.

"Butch!" she yelled.

"You see him?" Tim turned to where she was looking and then began to laugh.

Butch was standing on his hind legs in the center of the plate. In between his front paws sat a large chunk of strawberry. The rest was evidently in his cheeks.

Unable to help herself, Rosie pulled out of Tim's embrace and went to kneel by the little hamster. "Sir, I see that you've at long last decided to come out of hiding."

Butch responded by stuffing the rest of the ripe red fruit into his mouth. He didn't even tense when she picked him up and ran a finger along his side.

Before Butch decided to run off again, Rosie returned him to the crate and closed the door. The hamster picked up a banana slice and began to nibble.

"Looks like you figured out how to get a hamster out of hiding, Rosie," Tim said as he wrapped his arms around her middle. "All you have to do is give him fruit."

"And not give up," she added. "Even when something is unexpected and not quite perfect, I've learned to not give up. Not with hamsters or quilts . . . or, perhaps, life."

Tim leaned down and gently kissed her cheek. "I reckon you're right. As long as there's hope, something can be stitched together and given new life. Even love."

Turning toward him, Rosie raised her head to receive his kiss. Tim brushed his lips lightly against hers, then pulled her closer and kissed her again.

Rosie held on, enjoying their closeness. Yes, they had

indeed found love. Love and humor and happiness. It wasn't something she would ever for take for granted again. Instead, she was determined to hold on to this moment for as long as possible. Hold on to it tightly . . . and never let it go.

ACKNOWLEDGMENTS

I've been so delighted for the opportunity to write a novella alongside Amy Clipston and Kathy Fuller. We've been friends a long time, and I always welcome the opportunity to collaborate with them.

Many thanks go to the team at HarperCollins Christian Publishing, line editor Leslie Peterson, and my first reader, Lynne Stroup. It's been a pleasure to work with you all.

DISCUSSION QUESTIONS

1. This story takes place in one of my favorite Amish communities to visit: Pinecraft, Florida. Have you ever been to Pinecraft or to any other Amish community? What did you think of that experience?

2. I loved how proud Rosie was of her hometown. What are some things about your town that you enjoy sharing with visitors?

3. Many New Order Amish travel for missionary work. Have you ever been on a mission trip? Where might you like to serve?

4. Rosie's quilt-making skills have become both a blessing and a curse for her. What do you think will happen at next year's quilt auction?

5. Like Rosie, I think everyone has become overwhelmed by their commitments from time to time. What have you found helpful to do when you're inundated with obligations?

6. I especially liked the Amish proverb I found for this story: "Live one day at a time, and make it a masterpiece." How do you think that's possible to do?

ABOUT THE AUTHORS

Amy Clipston

Photo by Dan Davis Photography

Amy Clipston is the award-winning and bestselling author of the Kauffman Amish Bakery, Hearts of Lancaster Grand Hotel, Amish Heirloom, Amish Homestead, and Amish Marketplace series. Her novels have hit multiple bestseller lists, including CBD, CBA, and ECPA. Amy holds a degree in communication from Virginia Wesleyan University and works full-time for the City of Charlotte, NC. Amy lives in North Carolina with her husband, two sons, and five spoiled-rotten cats.

Visit her online at AmyClipston.com
Facebook: @AmyClipstonBooks
Twitter: @AmyClipston
Instagram: @amy_clipston
Bookbub: @AmyClipston

Kathleen Fuller

With over a million copies sold, Kathleen Fuller is the author of several bestselling novels, including the Hearts of Middlefield novels, the Middlefield Family novels, the Amish of Birch Creek series, and the Amish Letters series as well as a middle-grade Amish series, the Mysteries of Middlefield.

Visit her online at KathleenFuller.com
Facebook: @WriterKathleenFuller
Twitter: @TheKatJam
Instagram: @kf_booksandhooks

Shelley Shepard Gray

Photo by: The New Studio

S helley Shepard Gray is a *New York Times* and *USA TODAY* bestselling author, a finalist for the American Christian Fiction Writers prestigious Carol Award, and a two-time HOLT Medallion winner. She lives in southern Ohio, where she writes full-time, bakes too much, and can often be found walking her dachshunds on her town's bike trail.

Website: ShelleyShepardGray.com
Facebook: @ShelleyShepardGray
Twitter: @ShelleySGray